ALSO BY THE AUTHOR

The Pulpit is Vacant
Death of a Chameleon
A Christmas Corpse
Courting Murder
Walk on The Dark Side

KT-162-543

This is the book my husband, Ivor, was going to help me with as we wanted to incorporate everything we loved about this beautiful island, Penang and our favourite hotel, originally The Rasa Sayang and now The Rasa Sayang Resort and Spa. We met so many lovely staff and guests at this hotel and its sister hotel, The Golden Sands.

Sadly, Ivor died in Penang after a short illness, in October 2013 .

I know that every time I return, his spirit returns to his second home to share yet another holiday with me.

It was Ivor who chose the name of the murdered guest!

CHAPTER I

Summer in Glasgow, the Glasgow Fair to be exact and the weather was as it usually was, wet and grey with not even a hairline crack of blue sky to be seen. Despondent faces were in evidence. People scurrying to the shops, some optimistically with shorts and tee-shirts on under their waterproofs; others wearing their winter wardrobe still, not trusting the fact that July was officially summertime. Then there were the lucky ones, diving out for last minute purchases prior to making the journey to train or bus station or airport to get away from it all.

Fiona Macdonald watched them from her eyrie in the top flat of a Shawlands' tenement. She was one of the fortunate few, leaving in a few minutes for a holiday in the Far East. She was going away with her lover, Charles Davenport and his young daughter Pippa.

She and Charles worked together in a Southside police station, he as DCI and her as DS. No one there knew of their ever - deepening relationship though one of the PCs there, Frank Selby, was forever hopeful that his likening them to Bonnie Prince Charlie and Flora Macdonald would become a reality. They had not told anyone that they were holidaying together this summer but Charles knew that Solomon Fairchild, his assistant chief constable, would have guessed, as he always did know what was going on in his station, unlike the chief constable Grant Knox who treated his staff with a modicum of disdain laced with rudeness at times.

The station had been very quiet recently, a murder hunt having been successfully brought to its conclusion and Penny Price, his likeable, chatterbox PC having been silenced somewhat by being suspended for unprofessional conduct in the course of the case. Salma Din, another member of what Charles liked to call his 'team' had been subdued lately too following the sudden death of her mother.

Fiona looked at her watch. The taxi, booked for 10.30, had not yet arrived and it was 10.45. Always a stickler for time-keeping, this made her fume. She peered to the right, up the street towards Grantley Gardens, locally known as the more posh street. Ah, here it was, the familiar black cab, crawling down the street towards her close. She grabbed her handbag and hauled her heavy case out onto the landing. She was halfway down the stairs when the taxi-driver hooted his horn impatiently, three times. Drat the man! He was late and now he was shifting the blame onto her. She opened the main door to the close and went out into the rain. The taxi driver sat impassive as she opened the door and heaved her case in after her.

"To the airport. I have to be there for 11.30" she informed him.

A grunt was all she heard in reply.

The taxi came for Charles and Pippa at 10.30. They were meeting Fiona at Glasgow Airport at 11.30. They had two large suitcases and a carry-on bag each as, not knowing what the weather would be like, they had tried to cater for every eventuality. Charles had wondered about taking some ties and a dressy jacket and in the end had packed both. Pippa was proudly carrying her new white handbag, a large one and her first adult bag, bought for her by Fiona.

The taxi driver helped Pippa with her case, getting soaked in doing so but he was a cheerful young man and did not seem to mind. Pippa talked non-stop and the young man encouraged her, asking questions about where they were going and for how long. Their voices and the swish of the windscreen wipers made a background noise for Charles's thoughts. He was so hoping that the three of them would get along well on this holiday.

They were held up on the motorway just before the turn-off to the airport but they were in plenty of time and soon they were pulling up at the 'drop-off' point. Charles paid the driver and tipped him well. They crossed the road and Charles pointed out the trolleys to his daughter and she fetched him one. Charles had been to Manchester Airport in the last year and he had had to pay for the trolley but money was not needed here.

There was no sign of Fiona and he decided to wait for her before joining the queue as they wanted seats together.

"Dad look at the red carpet. Who's that for?" Pippa asked.

"It says First Class and Business Class, pet. That's for people who pay a lot more for their seats and get more leg room and special lounges to sit in."

The queue they were to join was getting longer and Charles looked round anxiously for Fiona. It was not like her to be late and they had agreed to meet at 11.30 am. It was now 11.40.

Then she was with them, apologising and telling them that the taxi driver had arrived late to collect her. They joined the queue, Pippa having collected another trolley for Fiona. The queue moved slowly but at last it was their turn. Charles had all three passports and asked for a set of three seats which they got. He hauled all three heavy suitcases onto the conveyor belt.

"Did you pack your own suitcases?" they were asked, to which they replied that they had.

Pippa took both trolleys back to where she had got them then they made their way upstairs to an area where they could have coffee and juice. Time passed slowly. Pippa got restless so Charles took her to John Smith's to look for another book to add to her holiday collection.

"All passengers for flight number EK 001 should proceed to the departure gate."

At last, the announcement they had been waiting for and they gathered up their carry-on bags and made their way to the gate. There was a long queue and they envied the people who went down another corridor without having to wait. These were, Charles explained to his daughter, the lucky First Class and Business Class passengers who had had the red carpet.

At last it was their turn to show their boarding passes and be welcomed on board. Their seats were quite near the back of the plane and they had to wait quite a few times while people in earlier seats put their baggage in the overhead lockers. Then they reached their seats, 45A, B and C. Charles found space for their bags and their jackets, then they sat down with Pippa in the middle and Fiona at the window, Charles opting for the aisle seat as it might give his long legs some extra room.

They watched other passengers seating themselves then eventually everyone was seated and the plane began to taxi towards the take-off runway. The engines began to rev up noisily and seeing Pippa look a bit apprehensive, Fiona took her hand. The plane seemed to hurtle down the runway for an eternity and it seemed unlikely that this huge metal bird would fly but fly she did and Fiona let go of Pippa's hand.

This being their first long-haul flight, the journey passed quite quickly with firstly drinks then a meal being served. Pippa watched two films but Charles did his Guardian crossword, having bought the paper at the airport and Fiona read a book she had already begun at home. She had just finished 'Jane Eyre' before their last case ended and was now deep in another Bronte novel, this time a reread of 'Wuthering Heights'. She had also brought two Anne Perry books. She had just discovered this writer of Victorian crime novels

The only fly, or rather large beetle, in the ointment was a man seated across the aisle from Charles. He was very fat, almost bald and had obviously been drinking before he came on board and had continued to drink, summoning the stewards at regular intervals and ordering whiskies and brandies. Emirates' policy was to provide free drinks and this was obviously encouraging him. Charles hoped that, like some drunks, he would fall asleep but no, he remained loudly awake and tried to engage Charles in conversation. Charles pointedly kept his eyes on his newspaper crossword.

"Service is dreadful. I usually fly first class and I will certainly never fly cattle class again," he informed anyone within listening distance. Eventually Charles had had enough and he called one of the stewards and asked her if she would bring the man a strong, black coffee.

"I'm not drinking that disgusting stuff. Bring me another brandy!" demanded the man loudly when it was placed in front of him. His wife on his right hand side looked embarrassed but made no effort to persuade him. She had, Davenport noticed, a yellowing bruise under one eye and he wondered if the man was abusive towards her.

"You're having no more alcoholic drinks, Mr Grant, on this flight and if you persist in your unruly behaviour, I'll recommend that you are not allowed on your next flight."

This seemed to jolt the man out of his truculent mood and shortly afterwards he fell asleep and began to snore.

Pippa giggled.

"He looks like a hippopotamus, Dad," she said to Charles.

"And sounds like one," he added.

It hardly seemed possible that they had flown for over six hours but soon they were landing at

Dubai International Airport where they spent about three hours. Pippa and Fiona toured the shops and marvelled at the modern airport with its large mural of galloping horses. Fiona thought that the up-market airport was at odds with the serried ranks of poorly-dressed people sleeping on the floors in the walkways. Charles was content to stay with the bags and watch the people moving around him. He loved trying to guess relationships, much to his daughter's disgust. She said he was just nosy.

When Pippa and Fiona returned, Fiona had bought Pippa two postcards of Dubai, one to keep for her proposed collection of places visited and one for Hazel who was to have one from everywhere.

"Bit of a cheat," said her father. "You haven't actually been in Dubai, just the airport."

It was not long till their flight to Kuala Lumpur was called. This time they felt like experts as they boarded and found their seats which were further forward this time and on the other side, being 37 G, H and I. Fiona offered to let Pippa have the window seat and Pippa thanked her and accepted. This time the announcements were made first in a language foreign to them, followed by what was presumably the same information in English. It was announced that, among them, the cabin crew spoke twelve languages. These were read out.

As the flight took off, Pippa scanned the films available to her and soon was engrossed in her chosen film, "The Lion, the Witch and the Wardrobe."

Fiona and Charles read for a while then started chatting.

"Do you think we were right not to tell the others we were going off together?" said Fiona. "They must think it funny that we both took the same three weeks off," she added.

"I explained to Salma that Mr Fairchild had allowed it as it was a quiet time usually. I said I was taking Pippa to Malaysia. I didn't mention where you were going and she never asked. Did any of them ask you where you were off to?"

"No. Penny would probably have asked under normal circumstances but having been suspended and brought back so recently, she was very subdued and, unlike her, not inquisitive. I think the other two were so busy being protective of her, that they weren't thinking of anything else. No doubt they'll have had some thoughts by the time we get back but then Penny will be on her holiday break and Frank will be about to set off too. Salma is never nosy; just keeps her thoughts to herself."

"How would you feel about them knowing?" Charles asked.

"About the holiday or about us?"

"Both."

"Well I think if they find out about the holiday, they'll guess that we're more than just friends. It's inevitable that they'll find out. The thing is should we both stay at the same station?"

"I know, that's what's been bothering me. I don't want to move again but then neither do you I suppose."

"Not really but we work too close together for it to work if we decide to live together, don't you think?"

"Yes. Never mind, let's just enjoy this holiday and not think about it," said Charles smiling.

"Agreed."

Their conversation was stopped as Pippa's film had finished and she wanted her light put out to let her sleep. They all nodded off, waking at various times and falling asleep again. They had all brought neck pillows. Charles had put his watch forward the seven hours which was the difference in time between Glasgow and Penang and he saw that it was about midday now and they would soon be arriving in Kuala Lumpur, called KL by most people..

The airport at KL was awe-inspiring, brand new and spacious. They went on a driverless train to take them from their arrival terminal to their departure one. This only took a few minutes and they passed another train going in the opposite direction. Pippa bought another two postcards of

KL with pictures of the Twin Towers. The flight to Penang took just over an hour. This time they flew with MAS, Malaysian Airways on a much smaller plane, arriving in Penang Airport with its large sign reading 'Salamat Datang' - Welcome'. They were weary but excited and could hardly believe the heat, even inside the airport. There was a man standing with a placard bearing the names, Davenport and Macdonald and they went with him to a minibus. They were the only passengers and the hotel had sent cold towels and water for each of them.

Pippa fell asleep, resting her head on her father's shoulder. Charles and Fiona were too excited to sleep though dog-tired. They were surprised and a bit disappointed to see factories and built-up areas at first but as they neared the hotel area, called Batu Feringgi, the scenery became more beautiful and they even saw some small monkeys on the telegraph wires. A sad note crept in when the taxi man pointed out Miami Beach, a small cove, where a number of local people and fishermen had lost their lives in the Boxing Day tsunami a few years ago. Then the taxi was pulling up in front of their hotel, the Rasa Sayang Resort and Spa and a red-uniformed doorman with his name, Sugu, on his tunic, welcomed them.

"Welcome to paradise, Mr Davenport, Miss Davenport and Miss Macdonald."

Pippa giggled at being called Miss Davenport and Charles and Fiona smiled at him as he led them inside the cool lounge and told them that a cold drink would be brought to them before they were shown to their room.

A lovely young girl, also in red, a long red and gold dress with matching jacket, brought them a refreshing drink then another girl came to escort them to their room. If anything, she was even more beautiful than the first girl and so slim, Fiona noted with envy.

"My name is Jill," she told them. "Jill Wong," she added.

She took them along a corridor which passed a well-appointed gymnasium and a young man in a red polo shirt and white shorts welcomed them. Round a corner and into another corridor, carpeted this time, a turn to the left and finally in the last corridor they came to their room 2246. The girl inserted the card which opened the door and stood back to let them enter.

It was a fantastic room and on first sight of it Charles was glad that they had decided on the premier room to make their holiday even more special. Jill opened the balcony window on one side of the room and took them out to show them the massive marble bath in the centre of the balcony.

"You give us a call and we run it for you," she said. "There's a bath menu on the desk."

"A menu!" exclaimed Fiona, wondering what concoctions would be put in the baths.

The balcony had a day bed on one side and a table and two chairs on the other. Going back inside, they were in the day area with settee and chairs. An area led off with closets and drawers and from that two doors led into the huge bathroom and shower area.

"Look dad, two alligators!" exclaimed Pippa as she touched the two iron figures which formed the door handles of the closets.

"I think they're lizards," said her father.

The other side of the large room contained three single beds.

"Can I have the one at the window?" asked Pippa.

"Of course you can. I'll be the meat in the sandwich and have the middle one," said her Dad.

"A rose between two thorns," laughed Fiona.

A ring at the door told them that their luggage had arrived and Charles gave Sugu and Jill five ringgits each, hoping that what was about one pound was an acceptable amount. Both smiled delightedly and wished them all a good night's sleep.

"If you want a meal, the Spice Market is open all night. You'll see everywhere signposted or you can telephone for room service if you'd rather," said their young guide as she was leaving.

"Room service, Dad. Can we, please?" asked Pippa, delightedly.

"Fiona?" asked Charles.

"It would be fun, wouldn't it, though I'm not very hungry with all the food on the planes. Will we get unpacked first though?"

Charles's face fell.

"I tell you what. Why don't you and Pippa go to the... what was it... the Spice Market and eat there while I unpack for all of us then we can have room service another night?"

"Yes, Dad, let's," said Pippa.

The two of them left, arriving back about an hour later to find everything packed away and Fiona in her white, hotel, towelling dressing gown. They were tired but eager to tell her about the variety of food in The Spice Market. They had had a la carte, not being hungry enough for the buffet meal.

"I just had soup and crème caramel," said Pippa, "and Dad had a club sandwich."

"I've read all the bumph, folks and do you know we get free afternoon tea between three and four and canapés and free drinks between six and seven."

"What's can -a- pes?" asked Pippa, yawning hugely.

"It's lots of wee savouries," explained Fiona.

Pippa was almost asleep standing up so they suggested that she get ready first.

"Remember pet that there's seven hours' difference between home and here so you might not sleep very well as 2am is only 7pm and 8am will be 3 in the afternoon here. You'll probably be wide awake during the night and tired during the day for a wee while till you get used to it."

Pippa was asleep almost as soon as her fair head hit the pillow. Fiona clambered into her bed and was able to raise a sleepy, "Goodnight," as Charles came back from his shower.

There was a violent thunderstorm while they slept but none of them heard it.

CHAPTER 2

There was a chink of bright light shining through the long, heavy curtains when Charles opened his eyes the next morning. He yawned and turned over, then picked up the clock which lit up when he lifted it. It was 9.25!

"Hey sleepyheads, wake up."

There were groans from either side of him.

"If we're not ready soon, we'll miss breakfast. They stop serving in the Grill Room at 10.30."

That appeared to shake them awake and then there was a scramble for the bathroom, Charles and Pippa reaching the door together, with Fiona, who never had to share a bathroom with anyone at home, a poor third. Charles, knowing that Pippa never took long, let her go first.

"You go next, Fiona," he said. "It's a pity my daughter's here or we could have showered together," he added softly.

He blew her a kiss.

"Then we'd probably have missed breakfast altogether," she laughed.

They were climbing the stairs to the Feringgi Grill just before 10.15am and Charles apologised to the waitress who brought them the menu.

"We expect our guests to be late the first morning. No worries," she said smiling. They read her name....Jasleena.

Charles ordered what he called 'a heart attack on a plate', a full English breakfast. Fiona had seen the buffet spread out and said she would just help herself to all the lovely fruits and some cereal. Pippa gleefully ordered pancakes and syrup.

"I've never had that for breakfast before," she announced. A smiling young Asian man brought them a pot of English Breakfast tea and a pot of coffee for Fiona and asked if they would want toast and if so did they want brown or white bread. He was tall and thin and his name was Istvan.

The room was emptying fast and by the time they had finished, there was no one else left eating. Charles was wearing his swim shorts with a polo shirt so he said he would go down to the nearest pool and wait for them there. Fiona and Pippa went back to put on their swimwear and fill the large bag that Fiona had brought in her case, with sun tan lotion, books and three towels and sunglasses.

They walked round to the lobby they had sat in last night for their refreshing drink and asked the way to the pool.

"I'm sorry but your daughter won't be able to swim in the Rasa pool. It's for people over sixteen," said the young receptionist. "The other pool is over by the Garden Wing."

Fiona thanked her and they moved on down some steps flanked by beautiful flowers in varying shades of red and purple and into the lovely gardens. They found the first pool and Fiona went round it to where Charles was sitting to tell him that Pippa could not swim there. It was obvious that older people sat here for peace and quiet. Charles got up.

"We brought towels and they provide them here," he said as they walked through the gardens.

"I wish we'd known that," said Fiona. "There would have been more room in the cases."

They passed a kind of hut, open on all four sides, containing books and they stopped to have a look at what was on offer. A small, smiling man greeted them and told them it was a mini library made up of books left by guests who had finished with them.

"My name is Tony," he told them. "Is this your first time here?"

They said it was and he told them to choose three loungers and he would come along and put towels on the mattresses which looked very clean and fresh and were striped in brown and cream.

"Once I know where you like to sit, I'll have your loungers ready for you every morning," he promised them.

They walked a short distance and came upon a poolside bar and behind that was the other pool, really three pools with one small one for young children. They chose three loungers away from the largest pool, with a view of the sea.

"What sea is that, Dad?" asked Pippa.

"The Malacca Straits," he answered. "One of the busiest waterways in the world, I believe," he added. He pointed out what was almost a line of varying sizes of ships along the horizon and a myriad of small fishing boats, nearer to land.

Tony came over with their brown towels, two for each of them and spread them out on their loungers for them. He had seen them gazing out to sea and told them that the largest ship on the horizon was a ship which held a casino.

"I'll bring you some water," he said and walked away.

"Will it be safe to drink the water?" Fiona asked Charles.

"I don't know but I wouldn't like to offend him so just take it but don't drink it till we find out."

The girls took off their outer clothes and made for the pool. Pippa was a good swimmer and was about to dive in when her dad pointed out the sign saying, 'No Diving'. The water was warm and the temperature must have been in the 30s so after their swim and a seat in the jacuzzi part of the pool, they dried off and then went to the pool bar for a drink, Charles opting for beer and Pippa and Fiona for a yellow concoction called a mocktail, with pineapple and mango in it. Charles asked about the water and was told that the hotel had its own filtration system and that the water was perfectly safe to drink.

They swam again then lazed under the shade of a huge tree nearby. It was laden with scarlet flowers and some had fallen and lay scattered on the grass. Tony brought them more water. They asked him about the tree and he said it was known locally as the flame tree. He told them that the hotel had six gardeners and pointing to a nearby bush, said the flowers were hibiscus. These ones were a soft, delicate peach shade with a darker orange in the centre but further over they could see yellow and red varieties of the same flower.

No one was hungry for lunch so they settled for ice creams at the Pool bar, Pippa enjoying the chocolate sauce she had asked for. They sat and read before swimming again. Charles ventured to the beach but the sand was too hot for his feet and he spotted a notice warning about possible jellyfish which was a pity as Fiona had told him that she loved swimming in the sea.

Around 3pm, a smiling young girl brought round skewers of tropical fruit, pineapple, water melon and kiwi, for all the guests in the gardens and about half an hour after that a young boy brought them small, frozen towels, rolled up like sausages.

"I could get used to this," sighed Fiona contentedly.

Soon after this, Pippa went back to the pool. Charles followed her and sat on an unoccupied lounger to watch her swim, trying not to draw her attention to himself as she would be annoyed at being treated like a child. He saw her talk to another youngster about her own age, coming out of the pool and sitting on the edge to chat. He went back to Fiona.

"This is going to be difficult. I want to keep an eye on her but she'll be angry with me if she thinks I'm watching her," he said.

"Is she still in the water?" asked Fiona.

"No, she's talking to another girl and they're both sitting on the edge of the pool right now but they'll soon be back in."

Pippa solved the problem, coming to them shortly afterwards to say that the girl was called Nancy and that her parents were sitting right at the poolside and would they mind if she stayed with them for a wee while. Charles went to see them and they said they would keep an eye on both girls, so he decided to go upstairs to their room to get cool. Fiona said she would stay a while longer and wait till Pippa was ready to go back to the room. This arrangement seemed to meet with that young lady's approval. Fiona went across to Nancy's parents after a while to ask if they minded keeping an eye on Pippa while the two girls were together and found out that they were also from Scotland, from Dundee, and they too were staying in the Rasa Wing.

"If the two of them make friends maybe we could take turns in watching them and the other couple could have a swim in the adults' pool," said Nancy's mother, introducing herself as Hope White and her husband as Rory. Not wanting to make them curious, Fiona merely told them that she was Fiona and that Pippa's father was Charles and that that seemed a good idea.

Pippa came over to Fiona at about 4.30, telling her excitedly that Nancy had been to a snake temple and that she and her dad played putting in a hotel competition most mornings at 11 and could she go too. It looked as if their young charge was making a friend and getting settled in quickly.

Gathering up their things, they took the towels across to Tony who told them just to leave them where they were the next time and he would collect them. When they reached the room, Charles was sound asleep on his bed so they tiptoed about, getting their clothes out for the evening, then

Pippa lay in the shade on the balcony, on the day bed and Fiona sat at the table and read her book.

They had to wake him at about 5.30 so that they could go down to the lounge for their free drinks at 6pm. By this time they were both dressed and ready, Fiona a bit sore from where her shoulders had caught the sun. Charles got ready quickly and they walked to the lounge where they found a table at the window. There was a young man and two Malaysian girls serving and they brought Fiona white wine and Charles a whisky, apologising that it was only Chevas Regal and asking if that was that OK

"Ok? I can't afford that at home," said Charles.

Pippa asked for another mocktail, this time a blue concoction which she said was terrific. They had decided to stay in the hotel to eat tonight and having seen the menu at the Pool Bar, had chosen this venue, so after another drink, they made their way to it in the darkening evening.

There was the sound of insects in the night sky and the smell of food mingled with the heady scent of flowers.

Sunny Tan gave them menus.

"Are there any mosquitoes?" asked Fiona.

"Yes but not the malarial kind," he told them. "Don't worry if you get bitten."

They all chose fish and chips for their meal and thoroughly enjoyed it though Fiona could not finish hers. They went back up to the lounge for coffees and another cold drink for Pippa then, yawning hugely, they made off for their room at about 9 pm and were all, even Charles, sound asleep by about 10.

CHAPTER 3

Alan P Grant was holding forth from his seat at the Rasa Wing pool.

"I'm extremely fit for my age. Always have a swim before breakfast at home. I had a swimming pool built in the garden two years ago, heated of course and with a roof which can be extended over it when necessary. I swim ten lengths summer and winter. These people who have arthritis are just namby pambies. It's a case of mind over matter. I have no intention of having such a thing, as I'm always telling Jean. Amn't I, my dear?"

"Yes, Alan...Alan, dear," answered his tiny, fragile-looking wife.

One woman tried to slink away but he called her back.

"What's your name dear? Don't go yet. We're just getting to know each other."

"My name's Sylvia, Sylvia Bennett."

"Who is Sylvia?" Alan Grant boomed out in a very flat rendition of the song of that name. He chortled with laughter at this witticism not noticing the woman's resigned expression at the joke she had heard countless times.

"You must introduce us to your husband, my dear and you too, love. What's your name?"

This to the other woman he had accosted some time ago as they were walking past him to reach their loungers.

"I'm Lorna Jamieson. We really must get back to our loungers Mr Grant..."

"Alan, my dear, call me Alan. Now we'll meet you and your husbands in the lounge for afternoon tea. 3pm on the dot eh?"

"Alan, maybe the ladies have other plans," said Jean Grant timidly.

"Rubbish. What other plans? Afternoon tea is free so nobody's going to miss it are they?" he guffawed loudly. "Time we went up to our room to get freshened up. We're in a suite, did I tell you?"

"You did Mr...Alan," said Sylvia Bennett, pulling her friend along towards their loungers.

"Who is that awful whale of a man, Syl?" asked Jack Bennett.

"Alan Grant. He owns an engineering firm in East Kilbride, near Glasgow. Don't worry you'll find out all about him when we meet them for afternoon tea."

"What?"

"There was no way we could get out of it short of being plain rude. Do it today and tomorrow we'll sit somewhere else. The grounds are huge, thank goodness."

"We? Did Lorna get her and Mike roped in too?"

"I told you there was no saying no to him."

Three o'clock saw the three couples seated round a large table in the lounge. The women introduced their husbands to the Grants. Obviously loving the audience, Alan waxed lyrical about his job, telling them about how he had risen from the shop floor to being managing director.

"I'm still a working class man at heart," he began, stopping to demand a bottle of champagne from one of the young waitresses.

"Put it on my bill, lass. Now where was I?"

"You were telling us about your working class habits," said Jack Bennett, sarcastically. Jean Grant squirmed but her husband carried on, unaware that he had been put down.

Alan went on to tell them about his family, "A son and daughter of whom I'm mighty proud," and his large house in Thorntonhall, "Did I tell you about our new swimming pool?"

"You did!!" chorused Sylvia and Lorna.

Undaunted, Alan told them again about his heated swimming pool.

"And Mrs Grant, Jean is it?" Mike smiled at her. "Do you enjoy swimming?"

"Her. She can't swim a stroke. She spends all her time listening to her infernal classical rubbish or reading highbrow books. Give me rock and roll in the background," her husband got back into the conversation, not allowing his wife a chance to reply.

Jack looked round for the arrival of the afternoon tea. The look on his face said it all. Mike winked at his friend then he said in a pseudo-respectful tone:

"Do tell us what you like reading, Sir."

"Oh, a good Jackie Collins. Something with some sex in it. The only sex my wife knows is the kind they bring coal in in Bearsden. Sex - sacks. Get it?"

The four laughed politely. Jean's face was pink.

"Where has that tea got to?" demanded her husband. "Really, I've just arrived but already I've got things to write to Shangri-la's head office in Hong Kong about. I thought Shangri-la claimed that their hotels were the best in the world."

He grinned suddenly and leaned forward, his double chins quivering.

"What to do is write a nasty letter when you get home itemising the things you didn't like about the hotel and you'll get freebies the next time you come. I did that with the Tanjung Aru in Borneo, didn't I dear, and we were given a week's free stay the following year."

Jean Grant got to her feet. She looked like a gazelle about to leap away from a predatory lion.

"I'm so sorry everyone. I feel a bit faint. If you'll excuse me..."

She almost ran from the lounge.

"Woman's got no stamina. Always feeling faint, or got a headache, especially if I mention the sex word. Surprising that I've got two children!"

He laughed coarsely. The waiter brought their tea and eatables at that moment. There was no champagne.

"Where's the champagne, boy?"

"Sorry, Mr Grant. I couldn't manage everything at once. I'll get it now," the boy bowed himself away, returning with a bottle of Moet Chandon on a silver tray with six glasses.

He poured five glasses and enquired about Mrs Grant.

"She's gone, silly bitch. Never mind, we'll drink hers," said Alan Grant.

"Now folks, drink up and don't worry about the expense. I'll be complaining about the slow service so will probably get the champers free."

He did not seem to notice the cool atmosphere. He took a quick breath then continued.

"I just decided at the last minute to come away on holiday. We couldn't get seats in business and there was no first class on the Glasgow to Dubai leg. I won't travel with Emirates again. Damn stewardess wouldn't serve me drink after a couple of hours. She said I'd had enough."

The four trapped holidaymakers drank quickly and left, saying that they had a trip planned for four o'clock.

"Trip? I'll come too," said Alan.

"I don't think so, Mr Grant," said Mike. "We're going on bikes and I don't think they'll have one that'll hold you."

Round the corner and out of sight of Grant, Lorna told her husband off.

"That was very rude, Mike and we're not going on bikes."

"I know. We're not going anywhere but I had to get us away from that awful man. I do hope he's not here for long. We must avoid him now at all costs. He's the type to always go to the up market spot like the Rasa Wing pool so we can lounge in the grounds from now on and either use the other pool or just go in to swim and go out again."

"If he goes back to today's spot, in the little garden area, as I'm sure he will and woe betide anyone who pinches his lounger, then he'll not be able to see who's in the pool." added his wife.

In her room, her suite, on the second floor, Jean Grant wiped tears from her eyes and wished she had the bravery to stand up to her husband, the way her two children had, the children she seldom saw since they had grown up and left home. As she looked round at the opulence of the suite, she wished she could be in a boarding house in Scotland somewhere with a man she loved and a family who cared.

CHAPTER 4

"The snake temple, Dad, please!" said Pippa, almost as soon as her eyes were open the next morning. They had got up quietly so as not to wake her and had been sitting on the balcony reading bits of the free newspaper which was hung on their door handle every morning. Called, 'The Straits Times', it was full of photographs of important people and even had a section full of revision for schoolchildren to do while they were on holiday. Charles had just found a crossword and they had decided to do one clue each during the day.

"Maybe we could ask for two copies of the paper and then we could have a competition," suggested Fiona.

"Good idea but you can do the asking. They'll think we're mad wanting two papers."

"I'm sure they've been asked for weirder things," laughed Fiona.

When a tousle-headed Pippa opened the balcony door to make her request, they were just beginning to feel hungry so they chased her into the bathroom to get washed and dressed.

"How do you feel about a snake temple, love?" Charles asked Fiona while they waited.

"We...ll. I'm scared of snakes. I don't even like seeing a picture of one but I can quite understand Pippa wanting to see this temple as it sounds really unusual so I'll come along quite happily as long as the snakes aren't free to roam about."

Over breakfast, poached eggs on toast with grilled tomato for Charles, cinnamon toast with marscapone cheese and mango for Fiona and pancakes with syrup again for Pippa, they tried to find out more about the snakes.

"Pippa, did your new friend, Nancy..."

"Her full name's Elizabeth, Dad. Did you know that Nancy is short for Elizabeth?"

"Yes. It can also be short for Agnes. Now pet, about these snakes that they saw in the temple. Were they in cages?"

"Oh no, they were up on the altars. They're sleepy snakes, Dad. They don't harm anyone."

Fiona shuddered.

"Right. We'll go but you'll have to excuse Fiona from coming inside. She hates snakes," Charles told his young daughter who was very sympathetic, having a dread of spiders.

Breakfast over, they went to the reception desk to ask a beautiful young woman called Anissa how they could get to the Snake Temple.

"Well, Sir. It's part of the round-the-island trip if you want to wait till Thursday."

Charles looked down at Pippa.

"Well, do you want to do that?"

"What else is on the itinerary for Thursday's trip?" asked Fiona.

"The Batik factory, the Butterfly Farm, the Kek Lok See Temple and the Fruit Farm," offered the young woman.

Pippa's face had fallen.

"Does it take all day?" asked Charles.

"Nearly. It leaves at 10 am and gets back here at about 4pm and lunch is included between the Temple and the Fruit Farm."

"I think that's too long for Pippa," said Fiona, earning herself a grateful look from that young lady.

"How else can we get to see the Snake Temple?" asked Charles.

"Well you can hire a car and drive yourself but I don't recommend that as the drivers, especially those on motor bikes, are quite scary to new visitors." laughed the girl. "We call them temporary residents because so many are killed on the roads every year. I would suggest taking a taxi. I'll get you someone friendly. He used to work here before the hotel was renovated."

It did not take them long to decide that this was the best policy and Anissa got out her mobile phone and, after speaking into it for a few minutes, informed them that Gopal would be at the front door in ten minutes.

They hurried to their room which had been cleaned and tidied and the beds made, and Fiona packed their beach bag with three bottles of the free water supplied for each room, sun tan lotion and their sunglasses. Charles had a bright blue sunhat which amused his daughter.

"You look funny in that, Dad," she said as they walked back to the front door of the hotel.

"Thanks for that," he replied. "My hair's not as thick as yours and Fiona's and I don't want my head burned, so you'll just have to put up with it."

Gopal's taxi was blue and white and the back seat had a decorated cover on it, a colourful affair which intrigued Pippa as the black cabs in Glasgow were so dull in comparison. Charles got into the front seat and as the taxi drove off, he commented on Gopal's stickers two of which were the saltire of Scotland and the yellow flag with the red lion from England.

"I have many friends from the UK," Gopal informed him. "They brought me the flags. I still need one from Ireland."

He pointed out things of interest on the way to the Snake Temple which was almost back at the airport. Pippa was most excited by the little monkeys on the telephone wires and Gopal told her she could see them close up at the Botanic Gardens which they could visit in conjunction with a trip up Penang Hill on a very steep funicular. He pointed out the huge mosque on a road which they were interested to see was called Scotland Road.

Charles and Fiona were amazed when Gopal told them he would wait for them at the Snake Temple and would charge them nothing extra for the wait.

"Take as long as you like," he said cheerfully.

They walked up steps surrounded on both sides by stalls full of colourful items for sale and Fiona said she would be perfectly happy to browse there while they went inside. She was amazed at the cheapness of the beautiful blouses she bought but remembered to barter as she had been told to, feeling guilty at not accepting the first price which was so reasonable.

Once inside the temple, it took Charles and Pippa a little while to get used to the gloom but once they could see, they made their way to the altar and sure enough there were thin, little, green snakes on it, some writhing about between and over the candlesticks, others motionless. Charles used his digital camera and felt quite brave until someone said, "Oh look. There's some on the floor!"

Pippa looked down and said excitedly, "Look Dad, there's a bigger one right at your foot. Take a picture, quickly before it slithers away."

Wishing he was outside with Fiona, but not wanting to show fear in front of his young daughter, Charles did as he was told and was relieved to see the snake make off after its photo shoot. They made their way back to the door and Charles felt himself relax only to be confronted by a man with a large snake wrapped round his neck, offering to let Pippa have it wrapped round her to have her photograph taken.

"Oh please, Dad, can I?" asked Pippa.

Somehow, this snake out in the sunlight was less scary, though much larger, so Charles paid for the snake photograph and asked the man about the ones inside the temple.

"They're pit vipers," he was told. "The temple was built over a nest of them and the incense drugs them. They haven't ever bitten anyone," he informed them.

Pippa had spotted Fiona and was calling to her to come and see the big snake but Charles was amused to see that Fiona appeared to have gone deaf and was looking in the opposite direction.

Photograph taken, the snake was unwrapped from round Pippa's neck and the man, having been paid, promised to have the photograph delivered to their hotel that same evening. Gopal was waiting, as promised, and on the drive home he described the other attractions of Penang to them, saying that they would all find the Kek Lok See Temple interesting with its variety of styles of architecture for the adults and the myriad of shops and the turtle pool for Pippa. They arranged with him to come for them in two days' time, right after breakfast so that it would be cooler for the trip and take them to this temple.

"Maybe next week you could take us to the Botanic Gardens to let Pippa see the monkeys and we could also take the funicular up Penang Hill," Charles told the friendly young man. He said he would be delighted to take them and that all the receptionists had his phone number.

Tired and hot, with three empty bottles of water, they walked into the lovely cool of the hotel lounge and sat down to have iced drinks.

"What's 'thank-you', in your language?" Pippa asked the Chinese waiter who had told them his name was Leong Ping.

"Terima kasih," he told her and Pippa tried it out.

"I'll give you a new word each time I see you," the man said.

Pippa was delighted. She skipped along the corridor to their room in front of the two adults and had used her keycard which Fiona had given her in the lounge and was struggling into her bikini by the time they had, more sedately, reached the room.

"Can I go to the pool now, Dad?" she said impatiently.

"Ok but don't go in unless Mr and Mrs White are there. Promise me?"

"I promise," she said hurriedly and was out of the door in a flash, forgetting to take her keycard which Fiona put into her beach bag along with her own card, sun lotion and both her book and Pippa's.

"Are you coming down for a swim, Charles? Or do you want some time up here to recover?"

"Would you mind going down before me? I'd love some time to just sit inside in the cool."

By the time Fiona reached the pool, Pippa was in the pool with Nancy and another young girl who looked Chinese. She found Mr and Mrs White, told them about their trip and offered to look after Nancy the next day for them if they wanted to go anywhere on their own. They were delighted, saying that they would like to see the Batik Factory which was something their daughter would be bored with. Fiona arranged to be at the same spot by the pool next morning at 10 am, then she found an empty lounger, got her towels and lay down in the shade of their favourite large tree to read her book. She was soon engrossed in it. Charles found her still reading when he came down in about an hour. She put the book away and the two of them went for a swim, keeping well away from Pippa whom he knew from experience did not like to be seen with him when she was with young friends.

It was nearly 5pm when they called to her that it was time to go upstairs. She came happily, shouting cheerio to Nancy and the other young girl whose name she told them was Mai Lee.

That night they ate in the Spice Market where the choice was superb and catered for all tastes and for all nationalities. Pippa was ravenous and helped herself to soup, followed by chicken with rice and vegetables. Fiona, not so hungry, went a la carte and had spaghetti Bolognese followed by ice cream and chocolate sauce and Charles had two slices or roast beef from the carvery section, with potatoes and salad. He enjoyed it so much, he went back for a second helping. Pippa was in seventh heaven when she went for dessert and found herself faced with a vast variety including chocolate fountains of white and brown chocolate and masses of bowls of things to add to her bowl of ice cream. Charles found a tureen of hot bread and butter pudding which was one of his favourites.

Fiona and he had coffee in the Rasa Lounge. Pippa spotted Nancy and went over to talk to her, coming back in about half an hour to tell them that they had missed free afternoon tea with sandwiches, scones and cakes. Nancy and her parents usually came up for that at 3pm but had decided to do without it today so that they would have an appetite for dinner in the evening

"We'll have it tomorrow. Don't worry," said Fiona, adding that she and Charles would be in charge of both girls the next day.

By now it was almost 9.30 and Fiona could see Pippa's eyes getting heavy, so she nudged Charles and he got up.

"Do you want to stay for a whisky?" she asked him. "I'll go along to the room with Pippa if you like."

"What an angel you are," said Charles. "A whisky would just round off the day, nicely."

He was sitting nursing his glass and thinking what a great time they were having when Mr Grant came into the lounge by himself. He spotted Charles and made a beeline for him.

"Good evening. Mind if I join you for a nightcap?"

"Certainly, Sir but I'll be going to my room when I've finished this drink. I'm still a bit jetlagged."

Charles managed to keep his feelings of dismay from showing on his face.

The waiter hurried over. Grant demanded, rather than asked for, a large brandy. The waiter scurried away and returned very quickly with the drink.

"I hope you've warmed the glass, man."

He touched the glass.

"No you haven't. When I first came here, the young girls would kneel down and light a burner and gently warm the glass. Wore dresses with slits right up to their armpits. Good old days."

As he was speaking, another member of staff came up to them.

"Mr Grant, how lovely to see you again."

"And you are?" enquired Grant with a show of disinterest which was blatantly rude.

"Jega, front of house manager. Anything I can do for you or Mrs Grant, please let me know."

As Grant turned from the man, Charles wondered why it was that complaining people always seemed to get all the attention.

He listened to a monologue of all the places Grant had holidayed in and all the freebies he had managed to get - upgrades, free meals - then rose to his feet and said he had to get to bed.

Both of his women were in bed when he got to the room. Pippa was asleep in the comparative darkness of her side of the room and Fiona was reading. He kissed his sleeping daughter gently and Fiona with more feeling. She smiled up at him.

"The photograph was under the door."

"What photograph?"

"The one of Pippa with the snake round her neck."

Charles crossed the room to look at the picture.

"Maybe on Friday, if the Whites take Pippa in charge, we can spend some time together, love," he said softly and her smile widened.

CHAPTER 5

Charles woke with a start. It was still dark but outside a tropical storm was unfolding or rather bursting open. A loud rumble of thunder followed immediately by a white lightning streak, told him that the storm was overhead and he went to the window and opened the curtain a fraction. As the lightning flashed he could see the gardens beneath him. They were awash with water. Glad that they were not on the top floor, he returned to bed, surprised that neither of his womenfolk had wakened. Pippa, brave about most things for her age, was terrified of lightning and he was glad that she was still asleep. He lay awake as the storm moved off, the peals of thunder becoming muted in the distance and the lightning fading as it went on to dazzle elsewhere.

In spite of being awake in the wee small hours, Charles was first to wake in the morning and he lay quietly for a time before getting up, showering and shaving then waking Fiona.

"Wake up, sleepyhead. Do you always sleep through storms?"

She opened her eyes sleepily and he kissed her gently, keeping an eye on Pippa.

"Storm? What storm?"

"The one you missed, you and Pippa. I was glad she missed it. She hates lightning."

"I don't mind storms. Is it bad weather today then?"

She sat up on one elbow and he sat down on her bed and again keeping an eye out for his daughter kissed her again, though more deeply this time.

"I wish I didn't have to wait till tomorrow, Miss Macdonald," he said huskily.

"Behave yourself. I asked about the weather, Mr Davenport."

"Why are you calling him Mr Davenport?" asked a sleepy voice from the third bed.

"Just a joke, Pippa. I call him that when he's being annoying."

"The weather is glorious. Pippa you missed a storm in the night, you and Fiona, but it's a beautiful day and the sky's a cloudless blue. Come on, Fiona, up you get and get washed before Pippa beats you to the bathroom."

Fiona did as he told her and Pippa lay back down.

"Don't go back to sleep. We promised to look after Nancy today and we're meeting them all after breakfast, in the Rasa Wing lounge. At ten o'clock and it's now almost nine."

"What are we going to do today, Dad?"

"I think the pool, this morning, then maybe we could hire bikes and cycle along Batu Feringgi. I was told that there's a restaurant there called, "The End of the World" and we could have lunch there for a change. I hope that Nancy can cycle."

"She's got a bike at home, Dad. She told me about it when I was talking about me and Hazel going on our bikes."

"Good. That's the plan then. The butterfly farm is along that way too so maybe after lunch we could go there. Has Nancy been, do you know?"

"Don't know. She's never mentioned it."

"You've probably been talking her ears off and she hasn't had a chance to say much." Charles laughed and ruffled his daughter's sleep-mussed hair. She pushed him away, saying indignantly that she had not been doing all the talking.

At that moment Fiona came out of the bathroom, wrapped in a big, white towel and Pippa scrambled out of bed and raced for the bathroom.

"Come here, darling," Charles said softly and Fiona walked over to where he sat on his daughter's bed. He pulled apart her towel and touched her breasts gently, flicking her nipples till they stood erect. She squirmed with pleasure and his right hand moved downward and felt the wetness there between her legs.

"Mm. Wet. Nice. Feel me please."

She leant forward and felt for him and felt him grow hard under his shorts. She unzipped them and put her hand inside then knelt to kiss him and give him little light licks. He groaned and took her hand away, kissing it and zipping his shorts back up.

"Woman, what are you trying to do to me?"

"The same as you were trying to do to me, man," she smiled.

"I'd better take a walk on the balcony and cool off or I'll not be able to come down for breakfast without the whole world seeing what you do to me. It's OK for you, madam."

Charles opened the balcony doors and went outside, leaving Fiona to get dressed in pale blue shorts and white top. She had hardly finished when Pippa returned and when she was dressed, they summoned Charles and they went off to breakfast.

At ten o'clock they met the Whites making for the pool where they had arranged to meet. They were perfectly amenable for Nancy to go cycling as long as she wore a helmet. Charles told them that he would not let anyone cycle without one. Nancy had not been to the butterfly farm as her mother was scared of butterflies and would not go in there so they were pleased that their daughter would not miss out on this treat.

Just as the Whites were about to leave, they heard an angry voice and round the corner came the man they had encountered on the plane to Dubai. They had seen him in the distance once or twice but not on the plane to KL and Fiona had presumed that he and his wife had gone on to Singapore and come to Penang from there. Charles had not told her about last night's encounter in the lounge. Right now Alan Grant was very angry and the whole world was to know about it.

"Bloody Wogs! Don't know how to run things. If I want a lounger and go down early to get it, I expect it to be there when I go back, empty, not with some foreigner lying on it!"

"Alan, dear. There's a notice saying that if you leave your lounger for over an hour, they can remove your towel."

The voice which replied was timid and apologetic.

"Don't give me that drivel. I'm an important guest. I'm in a suite in the expensive part of the hotel and I don't expect to be treated in this way."

This conversation had taken them up to reception and a smiling young woman asked him what was wrong.

"Get that bloody foreigner off my lounger. Pronto."

The man was almost purple in the face and in Charles's opinion he was a candidate for a heart attack or a stroke. Seeing his face, Fiona drew him aside.

"Charles, it's not your problem. Come on. Let's get down to the Garden Wing pool. At least we'll be away from him there."

Grimacing, for he had been about to jump in and help the young girl out with this obstreperous guest, Charles let himself be led away.

They spent the morning swimming and sunbathing. Charles had fun with the two girls, diving between their legs and coming up with first one then the other on his shoulders. Nancy had a beach ball and the four of them spent some time throwing it back and forward, trying to splash each other. Charles bought them all an ice cream from the Pool Bar and they ate them quickly before the hot sun melted them.

Then it was time for their cycle ride. Fiona had inquired at the gym and had reserved four cycles for twelve o'clock. They set off, Charles in the lead, with the two girls following him and a rather wobbly Fiona coming at the back. Their colourful helmets bobbed along, blue for Charles, pink for Pippa, yellow for Nancy who had claimed that was her favourite colour and green for Fiona who said it suited her as she was the rookie, having not cycled since she was in her teens. It was hot work. They passed lots of hotels on their right: the sister hotel, the Golden Sands and one they had heard about, the Park Royal where they had been told there was an upmarket restaurant called Tiffins which they were determined to try one night. There was The Lone Pine which sat back from the road so they could not see its facade. Along this route the stalls were set up in the evenings, they had been told and Fiona had decided that she would take Pippa one evening if Charles did not want to shop. There was a stretch without hotels and they saw on their left some kampongs, basic little houses on stilts which some locals still preferred to the new flats which were springing up on the road from Georgetown. Their taxi driver, Gopal, had told them this, informing them that he lived in a kampong, along with his wife and two children.

They reached the road end at a roundabout where one sign pointed to a dam and the butterfly farm and the other to the restaurant they were looking for. They were tired and hot when they clambered off their bikes, Fiona knowing that she was going to be stiff the next day, if not this evening.

The restaurant was basic in its decor and furniture, having red plastic seats round Formica-topped tables. The only other piece of furniture was a massive fish tank full of weird-looking fish, a couple of them very large. Pippa and Nancy immediately went to have a look while Charles and Fiona perused the menu.

"The waiter who told us to come here, said we should order lots of dishes and share them," Fiona reminded Charles.

This was what they did. They ordered butterball prawns, squid, soft-shelled crabs and chicken and tried them all. Fiona and the girls voted the squid too rubbery but they all loved the crabs and the prawns were delicious and huge. Charles and Fiona washed the food down with beer, the two girls with Fanta orange. For dessert they had a kind of pancake with honey drizzled over it. Pippa asked the girl who served them about the fish tank and was told that people picked out the fish they wanted to eat. The big ones were garoupa and had to be shared among a number of diners. Nancy was aghast at the poor fish being meals and not pets and was heard to announce to Pippa that she would never eat fish in Penang again.

The butterfly farm was only a short ride away and it was even hotter than before. The bicycle seats had got hot in the sun and they could hardly sit on them.

Charles started singing, "Mad dogs and Englishmen go out in the midday sun." The words drifted back to Fiona at the rear and she thought how lovely it was to be with Charles when he was so carefree and not anxious about work.

They paid their entrance money. Nancy was worried about not having any money with her apart from about ten ringgits but Charles said that her parents would do the same for Pippa when she went with them one day and she went in happily. The atmosphere was steamy inside and the colours of the butterflies varied and breathtakingly beautiful. Pippa pointed out her favourite which was black with bright yellow markings.

"Look Dad. It's a Batman Butterfly," she said and they all laughed. There was food out for the butterflies, some banana and other fruits, and masses of them collected on these food trays, quivering along their tiny bodies as they ate and unafraid of the people watching them. They saw a pit with scorpions, black tails held aloft. The pit was covered by a wire mesh, the holes large enough for viewing the insects but too narrow to allow them to escape. They saw an iguana, green coloured to help it blend in with the lichen - covered rock on which it was sitting. Charles explained to the girls about camouflage and told them the joke about the chameleon which went mad when placed on a piece of tartan.

Coming out of the enclosure which housed the various creatures, they found themselves in a shop. Fiona took Nancy and Pippa aside and gave them fifty ringgits each to spend. Nancy looked doubtful but Pippa said, "Take it Nancy. Fiona's not my Mum either but I'm taking it. Thanks Fiona."

As they walked off towards the colourful array of items for sale, Fiona heard Nancy say, "Who is Fiona then, if she's not your Mum?"

"She's Dad's girlfriend. They both work together. My Mum's in England. I stay with her sometimes. I'll probably be going in the October holiday because my friend Hazel wants me to go with....."

They moved out of earshot and Fiona turned to look at the brightly - coloured blouses and tee-shirts for sale. Charles had soon lost interest and had probably gone outside to wait for them as he was nowhere to be seen. She picked a tee-shirt in turquoise with PENANG in black on the front and handed over the money asked for, being unsure of whether she should barter in a shop. She collected the two girls with their purchases and they went outside. Charles had found a drinks' machine and was quaffing cola. He asked if they wanted a drink and they all said yes.

Back on their bicycles, they headed off to their hotel and were just in time for afternoon tea. The dress code for the lounge was smart casual but when she asked, Fiona was told that shorts were OK in the afternoon. Nancy had told Pippa excitedly what they would get and the little three- tiered cake stand lived up to expectations, holding one tier of tiny sandwiches, one tier of small scones with a dish of cream and another of strawberries and a top tier of little cakes. Fiona chose a tea she had never tried before, with Charles opting for a coffee latte and the girls for lemonade. They chatted about their day and Nancy told them that they left in ten days' time, just the day before her new friend. They had been here a week already and she had been into Georgetown.

"It's quite scary in there," she told them. "There's lots of traffic and trishaws. We went in one. It was a squash with three of us. They're called the Kings of the Road and all the other traffic has to give way to them but it was quite scary being so low down with all the big trucks and buses passing us."

"Can we try one Dad?" demanded Pippa and Charles promised her that they would go into Georgetown one day. Fiona said she would give it a miss and look round the shopping arcade that she'd read was in Georgetown.

"It's quite near where the hotel bus lets you off I think," she told them. "There'll be more room for you if I don't come too."

Across his daughter's head, Charles smiled at Fiona. She was so easy to be with, he thought, entering into everything, offering to give him some space and now suggesting he go off with Pippa. She smiled back.

At that moment, Nancy's parents arrived in the lounge, just in time to have their afternoon tea. Nancy chatted excitedly to them telling them all about her day and they thanked Charles, Fiona and Pippa for taking her with them. They had gone to the batik factory which was quite near the butterfly farm. Hope White showed Fiona what she had bought, a lovely blouse in a cerise colour with the batik pattern beautifully etched on the front and back.

"They put the material over banana leaves," she told them, "then put on the colour."

As Charles and Fiona had hoped, Rory and Hope offered to look after Pippa the following day and they agreed, trying not to appear too pleased.

"You know that loud-voiced man who was complaining this morning when we met you? Well he was so unpleasant to the young girl at reception. He demanded to see the manager and she called for him. The resident manager came and tried to calm him down but that didn't work. He still wanted the general manager. Well he came next and he was brilliant. He managed to calm the man down without giving into him. Talk about Irish blarney. He was great to see in action," Rory informed them.

"It's his wife I feel sorry for ...not the manager's wife...I mean the complaining man's wife. She just looked embarrassed throughout it all and went off in his wake, giving the manager an apologetic look," said Hope.

She had just finished speaking when into the lounge came the same man and his wife. She was carrying a large bag which was bulging. They sat down and the man demanded tea, only to be informed that afternoon tea was between three and four o'clock and that it was now well after four o'clock.

"Bollocks! I want tea now," shouted the man.

The waiter, the man who had spoken to them last night, explained very politely that they were now getting ready for canapés and that if he insisted on having afternoon tea, he would be charged for it.

"Bloody sure I'm not paying. The brochure said that it was free to Rasa Wing guests," bellowed the man. His wife sat silent at his side.

"Get me the organ grinder. I don't want to argue with the monkey," he roared and Charles had had enough. He got up and approached the table where the couple sat.

"Excuse me...Sir," he said to the man. "I've had enough of you and your loud voice, spoiling my peace. Either leave now or I'll be the one complaining to the manager. I could have you arrested for breach of the peace."

"Who do you think you are?" blustered the man.

"I don't need to think about who I am. I know who I am. I'm Detective Inspector Charles Davenport," Charles said quietly, very quietly and Fiona recognised the signs of a very angry Charles.

"Come on, Jean, I'm not staying here to be insulted," the man said and he got up and strode off.

"I'm so sorry, Mr Ping," said the woman, reading the waiter's name tag and she smiled gratefully at Charles as she scuttled off after her irascible husband.

"Are you? A police inspector I mean?" asked Rory White.

"Yes, I am."

"I'm a lawyer, criminal defence, so I guess we're in the same line of work," laughed Rory. "Come on young Nancy, time to get off to our room. Thanks for looking after her. If we don't see you before, we'll see you down here at ten o'clock tomorrow morning. What will you do with your free day?" he asked.

"Don't know yet. Need to look at the leaflets in our room. See if we can find something Pippa wouldn't want to do," replied Charles, winking at Fiona who hoped that the red in her cheeks would be seen as sunburn.

They all headed off for their rooms, the Whites making for the nearest lift as they were on the fourth floor, almost above the lounge

Having been at the Pool restaurant and the Spice Market, Charles decided that they should dress up and have a meal in the Feringgi Grill that night. He phoned and booked a table at the window and at seven o'clock they made their way up the stairs from the lounge having said no to the canapés.

They were escorted to their table at the top of the room, looking out over the spa village towards the sea. The red of the sunset bathed the restaurant in its warm glow and the quiet music was a pleasant background. Pippa sat back to have her napkin placed over her lap and was handed a large menu, bound in dark-brown leather. They were silent for a few minutes.

"What's beef cheek, Dad?" asked Pippa.

"I've no idea love, sorry. Ask the waiter when he comes back. What are you having, Fiona?"

"I'm going to try the three-soup starter then have Beef Wellington. I know I won't manage a dessert after that but never mind. What about you? "

"I think I'll have tomato soup. It's seemingly made at the table, then sea bass. Pippa?"

At that moment the waiter whose name tag read, 'Safari, came up and Pippa asked him about beef cheek. She liked what she heard so decided to try that, starting off with her favourite prawn cocktail.

They all sat and watched Charles's tomato soup being prepared at the table, flames rising high as the waiter put the gin in it.

"We'll need to come again and remember the camera next time," said Fiona.

Half way through, the chef came to ask them how they were enjoying their meal. He was from America and had just started at the Rasa Sayang two months ago. He was young and friendly and teased Pippa when she said she was going to have a dessert.

"You'll get fat," he said, then recommended that she tried the Rasa soufflé.

Tired and very full, they made their way to their room, not even Charles wanting to stay and have his nightcap.

It had been another lovely day in paradise.

CHAPTER 6

Fiona was first up the next day and she spent longer than usual in the bathroom, having washed her honey-blonde hair. When she came into the main room, Charles was on the phone.

"Sorry, Gopal. We can't manage the temple trip today. Can we give you a ring when we want to go... thank you...sorry again."

He put down the phone.

"Hi love. Just remembered that we'd booked Gopal to take us to that Kek-something temple and Pippa won't want to miss that. Is there anything special you want to do with our day of freedom?"

Looking quickly over to Pippa's bed and seeing that young lady still fast asleep, Fiona sang quietly, in a mock, sexy voice, "I just want to stay here and love you."

"All day? Please woman. Have some thought for an old man's heart."

"It's not your heart I'm after," she laughed.

"We'll talk about this after breakfast when you're less light-headed," was his laughing response and as Pippa started to come round, they left that conversation and began another one, asking her if she had any idea what she would be doing and what clothes she wanted to wear.

"Just shorts as usual. Don't think we're going anywhere fancy. Nancy said she didn't want to see any temples and neither do I, except that one with all the shops and the turtles. Dad, we were going to go out with Gopal today to that temple..."

"...Don't worry. I've rung him and cancelled it till another day. We won't go without you."

Fiona blew her hair dry, using the drier which was conveniently plugged-in inside the top drawer of the desk.

They were seated for breakfast at the table next to the loud-voiced man who did not look their way. His wife smiled at them. He was sitting across from her and had The Straits Times held up in front of him, making no attempt to talk to her.

"Dad, that's bad manners," said Pippa indignantly.

"Sh, Pippa. It's not good manners to talk about someone either!" said Charles, quite sharply. Pippa blushed and went off to get her cereal and fruit. On her way back, she caught sight of Nancy and her parents at the other side of the large room and went over to them. She came back, looking excited.

"Dad, Mr White's hired a car and he's going to take us to the mainland, over a large bridge, to a bird sanctuary."

In her excitement she had forgotten that her Dad had been annoyed with her. Fiona smiled at her, thinking what a nice child she was.

"Is he? That'll be the bridge which is supposed to be the third longest in the world. Do you want to take our camera with you?"

"Oh yes please, Dad. I'll be really careful with it."

Then her face fell.

"But will you and Fiona not want to take photos of whatever you're going to do?"

"No, we don't need it for what we want to do, pet," said Charles and Fiona could see that he was trying hard not to grin. For the umpteenth time in her life, she wished she did not blush so easily as she felt the warm red tide flood her face. Luckily, Pippa was too interested in the planned trip to notice and soon they had finished breakfast.

At the bottom of the stairs to the Grill restaurant, they met Leong Ping who was happy to comply with Pippa's demand for another Bahasa word to add to her vocabulary of one word.

"How about, 'apa ghabar'. That means, 'Hello, how are you?.' "

The Whites came up to them at that moment and Pippa greeted them with her new phrase, then had to explain what it meant.

"We're just going to set off right away as soon as Pippa's sure she has everything she needs," said Hope White.

Charles explained about the camera and rushed back to the room for that, sun lotion and one of the small bottles of water which were in the room every evening. He handed the bag containing these things to his daughter, along with a 50 ringgit note which she tucked into her shorts' pocket.

Rory White spotted this transaction and was quick to point out that they would pay for Pippa as Charles and Fiona had done for Nancy the day before. Charles thanked him and said that in that case it could be for any extras, such as postcards or a present for her friend, Hazel, as she was always looking for something suitable for her.

Fiona and Charles went with them into the grounds at the front of the hotel, saw them into the little car, a bright yellow Proton, and waved them off.

"I hope he knows what he's doing, driving on these roads with all the motor bikes cutting in all over the place," said Charles as he tucked Fiona's arm through his.

"Don't worry. I spoke to Hope while Pippa was doing her Bahasa bit and she said that they had lived here for a few years in the 1990s and he was used to the cyclists," Fiona replied, smiling up at him.

Charles asked the young man at the door whose name tag read, 'Jaz', about the Proton car.

"I haven't seen that at home," he said.

"We say it's made out of seven-up cans," laughed Jaz. "One little bump and it looks as if it's been in a crash."

Seeing Charles looking worried, Fiona turned his attention to the screen showing the top hundred hotels in the world. The Rasa was twenty-third.

They strolled back to the hotel and leisurely made their way back to their room which was usually made up by the time they had breakfasted. As luck, bad luck, would have it, the girl was still doing their room. She apologised and said that she would not be long. Fiona blurted out, "It's OK. We just came back for our swimming stuff" and hastily took a bikini out of a drawer and put it in her holiday bag.

Charles did the same, adding his swim shorts to her things and they made a quick exit.

"Better have that swim then," he laughed.

There was more laughter when they got to the Rasa Wing pool and Fiona went off to a nearby rest room to change, only to come back to tell Charles that in her haste she had gone into Pippa's drawer and pulled out a bikini belonging to the eleven year old.

"I'd love to see you in that," he said with a mock leer.

Charles swam a few lengths while Fiona sunbathed on a lounger and about half an hour later, they were back in their freshly-made-up room. Charles went into the bathroom to take off and hang up his swim shorts to dry and when he came back into the room he was naked and putting on one of the dressing gowns provided by the hotel. It was the work of seconds to divest Fiona of her shorts and tee-shirt to reveal her skimpy black bra and lacy knickers.

"Is this all you've been wearing under your shorts, madam?" he asked.

"No, I bought them specially for a day when we were on our own," she said shyly.

The bell rang.

"Get into the bathroom. I'll see who this is," said Charles.

Fiona could hear voices, then the voices receded but whoever it was did not leave for some time. At last the door closed and she came out to find Charles standing by the balcony door which was open.

"I ordered a bath for us. Come here, darling," he said and she went to join him.

The blinds were down on the balcony and the massive marble bath was full of foam and rose petals.

"Your bath awaits, madam," he said and, taking off his robe, he unfastened her bra straps and peeled her panties down. They stepped into the bath and sat down amongst the fragrance of bath oil and flower petals. The water came only to their waists. Charles leaned over his side of the bath and produced a bottle of champagne and two long-stemmed, crystal flutes, brought by the man who had run the bath.

They lay and sipped their wine, then Charles took Fiona's glass from her and placed both glasses on the wide rim of the bath. He kissed her lips then her throat and worked his way down to her nipples which were already erect. She moaned a little in pleasure, moans which intensified as he put one hand between her legs and gently rubbed her there. In minutes he was inside her and their climax when it came was tumultuous for them both. Gently he rolled over so that she was on top and looking into her soft brown eyes which were now looking sleepy, he murmured, "I love you, Fiona Macdonald."

"I love you too, Charles and I never thought I would ever find this kind of love," she confided.

They sat up and finished the glass of champagne and he poured them another.

The bath water was getting cold so they got out and dried each other, then Fiona put on Charles's robe and they went into their room. He fetched the other robe and they sat together on the middle bed and talked. Fiona rested her head on his shoulder and a few minutes later she was asleep, so he gently laid her down and got up and dressed. When she woke about half an hour later, he told her to get some clothes on as he had ordered a room service lunch.

"Oh Charles, they'll guess about what we've been doing, inside the room on a lovely day at this time," she said blushing.

"I love the way you blush, Miss Macdonald and who cares? I don't. I want the world to know how I feel about you."

A smiling waiter brought their lunch on a pull-out table. There was a rose in a vase and beautiful white napkins along with another bottle of champagne and covered plates. The waiter removed the plate covers to reveal a meal of prawns, scallops and salmon in a white wine sauce with creamy mashed potato. He smilingly took the tip Charles gave them and left.

"More champagne! Charles Davenport are you trying to get me drunk?"

"Yes I want to have my wicked way with you."

"Again?" she said in mock horror.

They finished their meal, drank some more wine and then he pushed the table away and pushed her back against the pillows of the middle bed where they had sat for their meal. He took off her dressing gown and bending down he kissed her on the mouth, then moved on down till he reached her clitoris and then his tongue found her special spot and she begged him to enter her but he refused, bringing her to the brink of orgasm then teasingly withdrawing his tongue, only to start again. When she thought she would die of desire, he entered her with force. On the few occasions when they had had sex he had been very gentle but this time he was more forceful and she responded with enthusiasm. When they had climaxed, they lay back, sweating and breathless and this time it was Charles who fell asleep with his head on her breast.

It was about three o'clock when she woke him.

"I think we'd better get dressed, love. Pippa might be back at any time and we should get this room tidied up."

They got showered and dressed and wheeled the table out into the corridor. Fiona spotted a little card saying to ring room service to have the table removed so she called them. Charles remade the middle bed and Fiona made the finishing touches to it. They emptied the balcony bath and after a few minutes, worked out how to use the gizmo which opened the blinds.

They had just ordered afternoon tea in the hotel lounge when Pippa and the Whites arrived back, tired but happy.

"Fiona, you should have seen this stuff they gave us to feed the birds. Nancy's Dad bought us a tub each. We all thought it was seeds but when we opened the tubs they were full of tiny wriggling worms."

"Yeuch!"

Fiona shuddered.

"We went down this wee path and held up the tubs and lots of birds came down and took the worms," added Nancy.

"I was at the other end of the path."

Hope White shuddered.

"Birds and butterflies are not my favourites."

"We saw a baby deer too," said Pippa. "Rory, tell them about the meal we had."

"Did Mr White say you could call him Rory, Pippa?" asked Charles.

"I did. I hope you don't mind," said Rory White.

"Not at all and you can call me Charles," Charles turned to Nancy as he spoke.

"And I'm Fiona," said Fiona.

"Well we went into the inevitable shop which was beautifully set out with expensive items such as

Selangor pewter and a sign pointed to a cafe so we decided to go in there for lunch. It turned out to be a very basic eating place so we decided to play safe and have something we knew and we all chose omelettes."

"Rory's came first," said Pippa, grinning, "and it looked like scrambled eggs."

"Then mine came with cheese and it looked a bit better," added Hope.

"Nancy and I had asked for prawns in ours and when they came they looked quite like omelettes. The two girls behind the counter were giggling and then they told us that the chef had gone for his lunch and these were the first omelettes they had ever made," finished Pippa.

"Mum, tell Mr D...sorry... Charles about the loo," said Nancy.

"I went to the toilet and it was just a hole in the floor. I went back for the video camera and took a picture of it. The cafe and toilets were a shock after the expensive-looking shop," said Hope.

"The rest of us managed to wait till we got home," laughed Rory.

"What did you do, Dad?" asked Pippa.

"Had a swim, had lunch and just lazed about," said her father. "We enjoyed it, didn't we, Fiona?"

Fiona sputtered and coughed.

"Yes," she managed. "We enjoyed it."

Hope was looking at her strangely, so she added, "We didn't want to go anywhere that Pippa would like to go to."

"How would it be if we all ate out tonight, together, at the hawkers' stalls?" asked Rory and the girls excitedly said yes to that.

"It's just along the road. We can walk back through the markets which'll be up by the time we've eaten," he added.

"We meant to go last night but went to the Feringgi Grill instead," said Fiona.

"Dad, can I have my afternoon tea now?" asked Pippa and Nancy declaring that she too was hungry, the Whites ordered tea for four.

They met in the foyer having had their complimentary drinks from 6-7pm at separate tables and made their way through the men and women setting up their stalls. At the area where the eating stalls were, there were hundreds of tables. It was like the restaurant, "The End of the World," with red plastic seats and Formica tables each with a number on them.

Rory pointed out the stalls. European food, steaks, chops and the like was being served down the right hand side, Chinese food was on the left and in the middle at the back were the Indian stalls. One whole section was devoted to fish and another to various kinds of rice.

"We take turns to go and order. Just give them the table number and you pay when the food arrives. Off you go, all of you, and I'll wait till the first person gets back then I'll go," said Rory.

Pippa wanted to try something new so Charles took her to the Indian section and recommended that she try a chicken or prawn korma which was very mildly curried. She decided on chicken and he chose a chicken Madras. Claiming that she didn't like curries, Fiona went to a fish stall and ordered sea bass then they all went to the rice section, Fiona being unable to see potatoes anywhere, and ordered three portions of fried rice. They got back to the table and Rory went off to choose his meal. In about ten minutes, they were all happily eating, washing the meals down with Tiger beers for the adults and Sprites for the two girls.

After the meal, they made their way back to the hotel, passing through all the night stalls. Stall owners tried to get them to buy their various wares but it was all done good-naturedly. Fiona stopped beside a stall with fake watches and bought one for Caroline Gibson, a friend from one of their early cases together, Charles following her lead by buying one for John who made up their foursome at bridge. They haggled as they were expected to and came away laughing. Pippa spotted a DVD which she wanted and had enough money left over from the trip to pay for it herself. The young man tried to encourage her to buy nine more at a very good rate but Charles told him that one was enough and he smilingly accepted that.

Then Fiona spotted a wall hanging ,picturing a beach scene painted on what seemed to be velvet and she bought that. It was wrapped and put between two pieces of cardboard.

"How on earth are you going to pack that, Fiona?" asked Pippa.

Fiona looked worried.

"You can put an address label on it and put it through with your case," offered Hope.

They arrived back at the hotel at about 9.30 and decided that, after coffee, they would all have an early night. Pippa was too tired to have a drink though Nancy managed her favourite mocktail.

They were leaving the lounge when they heard some commotion in the lobby. One of the young doormen was trying to placate the man Charles had nicknamed, "The guest from hell".

"Mr Grant. You can't go into the lounge in your shorts, I'm afraid."

"I'll go in how I like, young man," retorted Grant.

"I can give you a sarong to wear, Sir."

"A sarong! Are you trying to make a fool of me? I'll be reporting you to the manager."

Fiona pulled Charles away down the corridor leading to their room and saw Hope doing the same to Rory. Pippa and her new friend were already ahead of them, being too engrossed in their own conversation to have noticed the argument.

"It would seem that Mr Grant is in complaining mood again," said Rory. "I hope we don't have to listen to him moaning for the rest of our holiday."

They went on down the corridor and to their separate rooms, agreeing to meet up the next evening.

CHAPTER 7

Over breakfast in the Spice Garden, they discussed their plans for that day. They wanted to go to the temple with the shops but Charles had heard of the daily putting competition in the hotel grounds and wanted to have a go at that. Fiona wanted to book herself in for a spa treatment. In the end they decided to leave the temple till the next day. Fiona would swim with Pippa while Charles putted, then after lunch at the Pool Bar, Charles would swim and sunbathe with his daughter and Fiona would go for her massage. Pippa was undecided about whether or not to go putting but in the end chose to swim.

Charles walked through the grounds towards the golf course and putting green which were where the Rasa Sayang and The Golden Sands Hotel met, well almost, as they were before the Rasa gates which were locked in the evening. He actually passed by the course, taking the wrong path and found Mr Foo who was a local masseur who practised on the beach. He called out to

Charles and offered him a reflexology massage, an hour for 60rm which was about a tenth of the price that Fiona would be paying for her massage in the spa. He told the smiling little man who had a toothless grin, that he would certainly let his girlfriend know about him and retraced his steps.

When he reached the putting green, there were about twelve people seated under a wooden structure which he found out later was called 'the clubhouse' and which had a table-tennis table upstairs. He paid his 10rm, gave his room number and his surname and chose his putter and ball.

"Ah you are new?" asked an elderly woman with a white pony tail and a foreign accent. "I am Vilma. You can practise till time is called."

Feeling obliged to practise, Charles tried a few holes then quickly came back and sat down as the young lad in charge called, "Time!" They were called by name to come and try four holes.

Charles was embarrassed when he was called Davenport as all the others were called by their first names. After he had played his first round, he went over to the young lad in charge and had his name changed to Charles. He sat down beside a woman who said she was from Australia and came here twice a year. Her name, she said, was Joan and she pointed out a tall man who was her husband, called Richard. She had noticed Charles's embarrassment and told him of the time the young boy had called a man Agnes when it turned out that it was Angus.

One woman got a hole in one and everyone clapped. When everyone had finished, their scores were called out and the woman was given a voucher. "It's for a free drink, wine if you want it," she told Charles who was looking puzzled.

One man was standing in front of those seated. The elderly lady called out, "Don, you are not a window."

Don sat down looking sheepish.

There were three rounds and in the end Charles was in a play-off for second place with Vilma who had been taking the whole thing very seriously. He had heard during play that she was from Germany and came every year to stay at The Golden Sands for six months.

Vilma, who turned out to be Wilma, took three strokes in the play-off and Charles took only two so he was awarded two vouchers for second place and Wilma one, for being third. First was a gentle-looking man called David who apparently often won. He'd had four holes in one. The play was rounded off by a jackpot round for all those who were not placed. Nearest to the hole got a voucher.

Charles and one other man were the only Rasa residents and he walked the man back through the grounds, saying cheerio as the other man branched off to the Rasa Wing pool.

When he got back to the Garden Wing pool, Fiona was lying in the shade with Pippa beside her, engrossed in one of her Chalet School books.

"Dad, Rory and Hope will look after me this afternoon if you want to go to the quiet pool while Fiona has her massage." She looked up from her book to impart that information. He picked up one of his two towels from the third lounger, took off his polo shirt and made for the ' busy' pool, stopping by the Whites on the way to check that they really were happy to watch over Pippa for the afternoon.

"We'll do it tomorrow and you can go to the quiet, child-free pool," he said and laughingly they agreed.

Charles swam and cooled himself off and then went back to his womenfolk in time for them all to go for lunch.

"Apa ghabar?" Pippa said to one of the young waiters and he said something that sounded like, "ghaba baik" and told her that that meant, "Hello, I am fine."

Fiona tried the fruit basket and was delighted when it came and contained all the Malaysian fruits, white dragon fruit with its black seeds, red dragon fruit which had a purple flesh, mango, rambutan, jackfruit and her favourite, pineapple. Pippa had ice-cream and Charles had fish and chips.

"Terima kasih," Pippa chanted as the dishes were laid in front of them. The chef must have heard her from his kitchen which looked out onto the deck of the Pool Bar because a man with a tall white chef's hat came over to them and introduced himself as Amir. He congratulated Pippa on her Bahasa and asked her what room she was in.

"2246," she told him.

"That is dua, dua, empat, enam," he informed her and she chanted it after him till she got it right.

Lunch over, Pippa went back to the Garden Wing pool, getting a new lounger beside her friend and asking for two fresh towels and Fiona and Charles made their way across the vast grounds to the Rasa pool. They were fortunate to find plenty of empty loungers under sun umbrellas in the little garden area which meant they were not right beside the pool. The pool attendant brought them four towels and some water and they took a sip gratefully. Fiona said she would just lie in the shade till it was time for her spa treatment and Charles said he was going to have a snooze after his large lunch. Soon he was snuffling gently and Fiona glanced over at the nearest set of loungers to find herself smiling at the little, shy lady who was reading and looked up from her book to smile back. Wishing that they had taken time to choose somewhere far from the domineering man and wondering if he was the reason for the empty loungers, Fiona was pleased to note that he appeared to be sound asleep, his huge stomach moving up and down rhythmically.

At three o'clock she went off to the spa village, not waking Charles who would know where she had gone.

Charles woke to find the timid woman in conversation with another woman, a slim, very tall, younger lady. 'Statuesque' was the word which came to his mind. He had seen her in the Spice Market a couple of times, at breakfast. She had been alone and it was good to see that the two women had struck up a friendship. They were both sitting on the lounger of the woman he now knew was called Mrs Grant.

About an hour later, he got up to have a swim and was halfway down the pool when a scream rang out, disturbing the peaceful calm of the sun-filled afternoon. Charles swam across, pulled himself out of the pool and hurried to the sound which had come from near where he had been sitting.

The two women were standing looking down at one of the loungers. The younger woman had her arm round the older one who was ashen-faced and shaking.

"What is it?" demanded Charles, the first to arrive.

"It's my husband. Someone's stabbed my husband."

The older woman collapsed onto her lounger and the other one sat down beside her. Charles went across and looked down. The man was lying on his back as he had been before but was now covered by a hotel towel through which blood had seeped in a number of places. A knife was sticking up out of one gory spot.

"Keep everyone back!" he shouted at the pool attendant who had arrived next, "And phone for the police."

He took a napkin that was lying on the table between the loungers and lifted the towel back as far as he could with the knife pinning it down. The wounds without the knife in them were still pumping out blood and he felt the man's pulse at his neck. It was there, faint but there.

He put the napkin over one of the open wounds and pressed down heavily, knowing not to touch the knife in the nearby wound

He heard the attendant telling someone to get the police.

"Everyone go back to your loungers," Charles said to the little group of bystanders. "But please don't leave till the police have spoken to you."

He saw Fiona at the back of the group and motioned her to come forward which she did as the others moved obediently back, parting to let her through. Only one man remained.

"Who are you, telling us all what to do?" he asked a bit truculently.

"I'm a detective inspector at home," Charles replied. "So bear with me if I take charge. The local police will be here soon."

Looking mollified, the man went to join his female companion..

Fiona looked flabbergasted. She had seen the knife and the blood.

"I can't leave you alone for an hour but you stumble on a ...is it a murder? Is the man dead?"

"Not yet, at least he wasn't a few minutes ago," Charles replied. He went over to the lounger, bent down and once again felt the pulse at the man's neck. The younger woman came up to him.

"Is he dead?"

"No, not yet but he's losing so much blood, I don't think he'll survive long."

As if in response to his words, there was a sigh from the man and one arm which had been across his stomach, flopped down towards the ground.

Charles felt the pulse as two men arrived on the scene, one in police uniform, the other the manager whom Charles had seen once in the grounds and been introduced to.

"He's dead," said Charles, standing up. He stood back to let the policeman through. The man bent down and felt for the pulse at one wrist. He put his hand out towards the knife.

"Don't touch that!" Charles shouted.

The policeman straightened up.

"I'm sorry. I don't know what I was thinking about. It's my first day you see and..."

His voice tailed away.

Charles took pity on the youngster.

"Anyone could make the same mistake. I won't tell anyone."

He said softly, so that no one else could hear, "Ask for a room the police can use and get all these people into it. Ask the manager to stay with them and make sure that they don't discuss what has happened."

The young man thanked him. He went over to the manager who was standing beside Fiona.

"I've called my superior but meanwhile, Sir, I'll need a room for all the people here to wait in. Don't let anyone disappear and please ask them not to discuss this until they've been interviewed. If you have a hotel doctor or nurse, get them down here for the man's...wife is it?"

"Yes that one, the older woman, is his wife," said Charles.

"What's your name, Sir?" the policeman asked him.

"My name's Charles Davenport. I was first on the spot after the two women over there. I'm a

DCI in Scotland so I sort of took charge. I've told the other guests who were at the pool not to leave. Should we perhaps cover his face?"

On being given permission to do this, Charles took a clean towel from his own lounger and placed it over the dead man's face.

The manager went over to the two women.

"Mrs Grant, would you like me to get the doctor down here or would you like to come with me to his room? I take it that would be OK?" he asked the policeman who agreed that it would be as long as she was not left alone at any time. Fiona offered to go with her.

"I know where the doctor's room is, Mr Grafton," she told the manager and when Charles told the policeman that she was also in the police force, the man nodded gratefully.

Mrs Grant got up shakily.

"Is he dead, Mr Grafton? There was all that blood."

The manager looked at Charles.

Charles broke the news.

"I'm sorry, Mrs Grant. He is dead now."

She swayed where she stood and her companion took hold of her arm.

"Can I go with her, please?" she asked the policeman.

The man took out his notebook.

"And you are?"

"My name is Annabelle Kilbride. I met Jean Grant the day before yesterday and we've been talking quite a bit since then when her husband was asleep or not with her. We've just been in the lounge having afternoon tea. We got back and sat chatting then Jean looked across at the other lounger and noticed the blood."

The policeman wrote in his notebook, then said she could go with her friend as long as she stayed there with her till his superior arrived.

The threesome moved off, Mrs Grant in the middle, supported by the other two women. The rest of the guests were summoned and after picking up their belongings, they too left the area with the manager, one young woman wrapped in a hotel towel and dripping water as she went.

"I'm in room 2246," Charles told the policeman. "I'll collect my daughter from the other pool and I'll stay in our room till your superior wishes to see me. We'll take room service if we get hungry."

The young policeman thanked him.

"I am Constable Ravanathan, Sir. Thank you for your help."

Charles picked up his clothes and their beach bag and left the scene. He looked back at the prone figure under the gaudy umbrella.

Alan P Grant would not cause trouble ever again.

CHAPTER 8

Deciding to leave Pippa at the Garden Wing pool, Charles went back to his room, thinking about what had happened. He would have liked to have had time to explain to Fiona what had happened. He was pacing the floor, wondering what he would do to pass the time before he was needed by the police, when he suddenly remembered that Pippa would expect him to come for her at the pool for afternoon tea. Even if the Whites took her with them up to the lounge, she would wonder where he and Fiona had got to. She was not usually a worrier but in a strange country, away from home, she might get anxious.

He picked up the room phone and phoned the Rasa Wing reception desk, asking the cheery young woman who answered if she could ask one of the doormen if he would go to the Garden Wing pool and tell Pippa Davenport to come up to her room right away.

"That's OK Mr Davenport. I know your daughter. I can describe her to Farez who's on duty just now."

It was only about ten minutes before Pippa arrived at the room. He heard her card in the door and she burst in.

"What's up Dad? I'd dried off for afternoon tea and was expecting you any minute. Nancy and her Mum and Dad have gone up now. Are you ready?"

"Whoa, pet. Sit down while I talk to you."

They sat on Pippa's bed and Charles told her about the murder and about how he had been on the scene so had to stay in his room till the police came to talk to him.

"I think they'll see me before the other guests. That's why I came here instead of going with the rest."

"Where's Fiona?"

"She's in the doctor's room with the murdered man's wife."

"Who got murdered?"

Pippa, used to her father's involvement in murders, was interested, rather than frightened.

"That loud man, Mr Grant."

Whatever Pippa thought about that was never spoken, as at that moment there was a loud knock on the door.

Charles went across and opened it.

A policeman in uniform stood in the corridor.

"Mr Davenport?"

"Yes."

"The manager told me I'd find you in your room. I don't know why you were allowed away from the rest of the guests. It was sheer incompetence on the part of Constable Ravanathan."

The police officer, his round chubby face at odds with his severe expression, stepped over the threshold. Ravanathan hung back, looking sheepish.

"Do come in," said Charles, sarcastically but the sarcasm was lost on the man who perched himself on the desk which divided both sections of the room, taking off his hat to reveal shiny black hair. Charles smiled at Ravanathan who also removed his hat, showing black, wavy hair. Charles sat on the edge of the settee. Both police officers wore immaculate uniform.

"My name's Cheng, Sergeant Cheng. Tell me please your version of what happened at the swimming pool area."

Charles told his side of the story.

"So you took it upon yourself to keep the other guests away and you covered his face? What was Constable Ravanathan doing at the time?"

"He hadn't arrived on the scene when I told the guests to keep away and I asked his permission to cover the dead man's face. Would you rather have had the guests milling round the lounger?"

Cheng ignored this question.

"And the man was alive when you reached him?"

"Yes but he died almost immediately."

"Did anyone touch the knife?"

"No they didn't. Constable Ravanathan saw to that. He took charge as soon as he arrived."

"When you went for your swim did you see the murdered man?"

Charles closed his eyes and thought.

"Yes, I did look back at him. His skin was reddening and had he been a nicer man, I might have woken him up and warned him about getting burned. Anyway his wife was beside him so she could have told him."

"So he wasn't a *nice* man?"

Charles felt that the sergeant was making fun of him by emphasising the word 'nice' but replied simply that any time he had seen the man, he was causing trouble.

"But I don't see any of the staff stabbing him because he was a constant complainer. I..."

"I don't need your opinion... Sir."

Charles felt his skin reddening. It was like being in school, he thought and being ticked off for some demeanour. He wondered in what way he had got this man's back up. He was like a porcupine defending its young! He glanced at the young police constable and noticed that he was looking sympathetic.

"What are your smirking at, Ravanathan?"

"Me, Sir? I wasn't smirking."

It appeared that this was the sergeant's normal way of treating Joe Public and his colleagues. Charles thought how different was his own rapport with his younger colleagues and wondered if the sergeant got any respect from his staff.

Pippa had been listening to this exchange. She came forward and shook Ravanathan's hand. He smiled at her. She offered her hand to the sergeant who looked down at it with disdain.

"I'm Pippa Davenport. Is it OK if my Dad and me go for afternoon tea now?"

"Pippa!"

Charles had to hide a grin. Trust his daughter to get straight to the point.

"One further question. Was there a towel covering Mr Grant when you passed him?"

"I didn't pass him. He was further inside the garden than I was. I just glanced back at him and no, there was nothing covering him. As I've just told you, I noticed that his skin was reddening. He had nothing on except a pair of swimming shorts, black ones."

Reluctantly the sergeant agreed that they could go to the lounge.

"OK Mr Davenport...Miss Davenport. Please don't leave the hotel until you're told you can. Come Ravanathan, Inspector Hussain will be waiting for us in the library with the other guests."

He stood up, opened the door and swept out. The young policeman gave Charles a grateful smile, put on his hat and went after him. The door closed behind them.

"What a rude man, Dad!" said Pippa, indignantly. "Doesn't he know it's bad manners not to shake someone's hand when it's offered to him?"

"Obviously not, pet. Come on. Let's get downstairs for tea. Hopefully, Fiona will be able to join us soon."

"I don't suppose I can tell Nancy about this, can I?"

"No. We can't discuss it right now, not till it becomes common knowledge. I'll just tell them that there's been an accident and that the police are involved. OK?"

Outside the door, Pippa slipped her small hand into his.

"Will you be working now, Dad? "

"What do you mean?"

"Will you and Fiona be trying to solve this murder?"

"I doubt it, pet. I don't think the police will want me sticking my nose in, somehow."

"Good -oh."

He smiled down at her as they walked down the corridor.

CHAPTER 9

There were very few people in the lounge when Charles and Pippa walked in, so they were served very promptly by Leong Ping, or Mr Chang as some guests called him.

Pippa was, as usual, hungry and wolfed down her sandwiches. Charles found that his appetite had left him, so contented himself with one small scone with cream and strawberries.

"Pippa, can I sit with you?"

Nancy had arrived.

With a warning look at his daughter, Charles told her to go and sit at another table with her new friend and he invited Nancy's parents to join him.

"Where's Fiona?" asked Hope.

"She went off for a spa treatment," Charles replied with honesty. "I don't know if she'll manage to join us this afternoon."

They were soon in lively discussion about other sights that should be seen in Penang.

Charles wanted to go up Penang Hill and they still had the temple visit to do. The Whites said that both trips would be suitable for Pippa. The funicular train journey up the hill was interesting but there was very little to do once at the top of the hill and the temple was very unusual, having shops at the bottom and a reservoir at the top.

Charles went over to his daughter's table.

"...and Hazel and I tried to help once..."

Wondering what Pippa and her best friend had tried to help with, Charles apologised for interrupting them and asked Pippa whether she would like to go up Penang Hill or go to the Kek Lok See Temple the next day.

"The train's fun, Pippa," said Nancy. "But then so's the temple. There are turtles in a pool there about half way up."

"Will you come with us?" asked Pippa. She looked up at her father.

"Dad, can Nancy comes with us wherever we decide to go?"

"Pippa, maybe if Nancy's already been to both places she won't want to go again."

"Oh no, Mr Davenport...sorry, Charles. I loved both and I don't think Mum and Dad want to go again so if you'll let me I'd like to go to either one."

"Right, go over and ask your parents if it's OK if you come to the Temple with us. We'd already mentioned it to Gopal so we'd better go there first."

Nancy bounced over to her parents and came back saying that they would be delighted to get rid of her for at least part of the day. The Whites grinned over at Charles and when he returned to sit beside them, they said that they really wanted to chill out this holiday so would welcome a day by the pool.

"Hope's mother died a couple of months ago," Rory explained. "We've been clearing her house and that was emotionally and physically draining. Nancy loved her Nan but children recover quicker than adults, don't they? She always wants to be doing something on holiday so this way we can all get what we want."

At this point, some guests began to appear in the lounge and Charles recognised the man who had questioned him about his taking charge at the murder scene. The man saw him and came across.

"Phew! They're pretty officious these Penang policemen. They made me feel guilty of the crime, rather than just an innocent bystander. Are Scottish police so unfriendly?"

"No. I insist that my team treat all people involved, including suspects, with politeness," laughed Charles. "Was it the sergeant who questioned you?"

By this time, the man's wife had joined him.

"Hello there. The young policeman questioned me. He was very gentle with me. Jim must have been unlucky. Unless he got your back up, Jim. You can be bristly, you know you can."

"I didn't get "bristly" as you call it until he became bordering on rude and it was a sergeant who questioned me. He seemed not to believe that I had seen nothing and acted as if I was being deliberately obstructive."

Hope and Rory Hood were looking interested in this exchange. Charles took the man aside and asked him if he had been told to keep quiet about what had happened. On hearing that they had not been told to say nothing, he returned to the Whites and between him and the other two guests, they recounted the events of the afternoon.

"Can't say I'll miss him," Rory remarked drily.

"Oh, Rory. That's cruel," exclaimed Hope.

"It's his poor wife I'm sorry for," said Jim. "We were way across the other side of the pool to get away from him and it was deserted at their spot until you came," he observed to Charles.

Their little knot of people became larger as two other couples joined them. The women sat down beside Hope and Rory. Rory got up to let Jim's wife sit down and joined Charles standing.

"Who could have killed him?" said one man. "I'm Jack Bennett, by the way and this is Mike Jamieson."

The men shook hands with Charles, Jim and Rory. Charles explained that he had only just told

Rory about what had happened as the police might have wanted it kept secret for the time being.

"The four of us were caught by Grant the day before so we were sitting in the grounds and just passing when the screaming started and we came into the pool area to see what had happened. His wife must have felt like a leper," said Jack ruefully.

"Probably used to it, poor soul," said Mike.

"I think she had managed to get friendly with one other guest, a Mrs or Miss Kilbride," said Charles, remembering the woman talking to the police constable. "I don't blame you for wanting to keep away from the man. He was a loud-mouthed bully as far as I could see."

"But surely no one would kill him for that?" said Jim. "I mean we're only here for a while and would never have to meet up with him again. Murder is a bit drastic, surely?"

"Well that's up to the Penang police to find out," said Charles. "Not my pigeon, thank goodness."

He saw Jack Bennett and Mike Jamieson looking a bit puzzled so he explained that he was a chief inspector at home in Glasgow.

"Maybe they'll let you help," laughed Rory.

"You obviously haven't met the sergeant. He wouldn't let me help if he was single-handed, though the young policeman was very nice. Wonder what their DCI is like?"

"I think you might find out quite soon," said Jack. "I think this might be him now."

Charles turned to glance in the direction Jack had been looking towards and saw Sergeant Cheng coming across the lounge towards them accompanied by another, older man in plain clothes.

Cheng beckoned rather imperiously to Charles who separated himself from the group of men and walked over to the police officer and his companion.

"Mr Davenport. This is DCI Hussain. Sir, this is Charles Davenport who took charge when the murder was discovered."

The words 'took charge' were emphasised slightly, in a rather sneering manner and Charles felt his hackles rising. He turned from Cheng and smiled at the other man.

The DCI was immaculately dressed in a dark grey suit with white shirt and dark grey tie. Taller than Cheng, he was lean-faced and his dark hair was cut short.

He did not return the smile.

"I didn't really take charge, Sir. I just asked folk to stand away from the body."

"And according to one witness, you also covered the body with a towel."

"After asking PC Ravanathan if this was OK," Charles said.

"Mr Davenport, I must insist that you do not take it upon yourself to do any investigating in this murder. My colleagues and I are able to conduct this enquiry ourselves and need no help from the UK. Is that understood?"

"Perfectly. And now if you'll excuse me, I will return to my friends."

The Asian DCI bowed stiffly from the waist then he and the sergeant walked out of the lounge.

Feeling like a reprimanded child, Charles went back to the group he had left. Professional etiquette stopped him from commenting on how he had just been treated. He satisfied himself with two words:

"Stuffed shirt."

The next folk to arrive were Fiona and the other woman who had accompanied Mrs Grant to the doctor.

"Fiona," said Charles, "how is Mrs Grant?"

"The doctor and his nurse are accompanying her to her room. He's going to give her a sedative to help her sleep after the police have questioned her. I guess that's them going to see her now. Did they speak to you?"

"They did. I'll tell you about that later."

He turned to the other woman.

"Are you a friend of Mrs Grant's?"

"Not really. We just met here. We've had the odd coffee together when her husband was asleep, that's all. We came up here to the lounge this afternoon because he was well away and snoring for Britain. Sorry, that seems callous when he's dead but I didn't like the man. He bullied her all the time, as far as I could see. I'm going to my own room now. I've been asked to stay there until the police have questioned me."

"Are you here on your own, Annabelle?" asked Fiona.

"Yes, I am."

"Well, why don't you join us for dinner tonight? Is that OK, Charles?" Fiona looked at Charles appealingly and he said immediately that that was fine.

"No one wants to be alone after a thing like this and I don't imagine that Mrs Grant will be up to eating tonight with you," he said.

"Thank you. That's very kind. Will I meet you here for drinks?"

This was agreed and Annabelle Kilbride went off to her room.

Charles, anxious to talk to Fiona, made his excuses to the other men, explained to Rory about not meeting them that evening and arranged to meet them with Nancy in the foyer after breakfast for the Temple trip.

"It seems odd to be carrying on with our holiday in the face of this tragedy," Fiona said to Charles, after they had collected Pippa and were on their way back to their room. "Don't you want to get involved?"

"Oh I've been warned off, love, in no uncertain terms. No interference from a UK Inspector."

"Who said that? Oh don't tell me. Sergeant Cheng! He came across as being one of the most insensitive people it's been my misfortune to meet. He showed no compassion for Mrs Grant and treated Annabelle and I as if we were idiots."

"That might be the culture thing but I didn't think the Malays would be guilty of sexism. The ones we've met so far have been so friendly. Mind you his superior is Muslim and I don't imagine that he has much respect for women! He doesn't even show much for some men! It was he who warned me off."

In the lift, Charles told Fiona about how he had been treated by DCI Hussain. She was indignant but Pippa was incensed.

"Dad, that sergeant man was dreadful to you too. You would never treat anyone like that!"

"Come on, you two. It's our holiday remember. Who wants to be involved in a murder anyway? Some busman's holiday that would be!" Charles laughed.

By the time Charles had explained to his young daughter what a busman's holiday was, they were back in their room.

As Pippa got washed, Charles explained to Fiona what he had seen at the pool and about how he had helped the young policeman. She, in turn, told him what had transpired when Mrs Grant had seen the doctor.

"I was surprised when the sergeant questioned us all together," she informed him. "I had seen nothing of course, coming along as I did after it had all happened, but he grilled the other two. Poor Jean - Mrs Grant - was in a state of complete shock. She said they had left her husband sleeping, had coffee in the lounge and returned to see the blood on the towel."

"Did she say whether or not the towel was over him when they left?"

"She said it wasn't and Miss Kilbride confirmed that."

"He was uncovered when I went for my swim, so the murderer must have put the towel over the man before he killed him. The knife blade was through the towel so it couldn't have been done afterwards. There were a number of knife entries so it looked as if the murderer wanted to make sure the man died."

"Charles, you're talking like a policeman. Stop it!"

"Sorry, force of habit."

As Pippa came out of the bathroom at that point, Fiona took her place. Soon they were all washed, dressed and ready to go to the lounge for their evening drinks.

They passed the Bennetts and the Jamiesons at one table and said hello, stopped for a few words with the Whites and settled themselves at a table by the window. It was not long till Annabelle Kilbride came into the lounge, spotted them and joined them. In spite of the tragedy, she had taken time with her appearance and looked very attractive in a pair of silky, black trousers topped by a cerise blouse. Her raven black hair was shining and newly washed, piled up on her head, making her look very regal.

During drinks, they agreed that the best idea tonight was just to remain in the hotel, so they chose the Spice Market which meant that Annabelle who had declared that the events of the afternoon had taken away her appetite, could have something small from the a la carte menu and Pippa who declared herself starving, could opt for the buffet. Fiona decided to take a main course from a la carte and Charles joined his daughter in the quest for his favourite foods in the buffet.

Naturally, the talk at the table turned to the murder but only briefly as the adults seemed to agree tacitly that it was not right to discuss such grisly subjects in front of Pippa whom Charles at least knew would be disappointed when the talk turned to more mundane things.

The evening passed uneventfully. They met the Whites in the lounge and Charles asked Annabelle if she would like to come with them the next day to the Temple but she had already been there and anyway declared that she wanted to stay around the hotel in case Jean Grant needed her.

When they reached the lift to their corridor, they said goodnight, Annabelle having a garden room on the ground floor.

CHAPTER 10

For once, Pippa woke first. She went quickly into the bathroom and had her shower then returned to the main room and shook her Dad awake.

"What time is it?" he asked her sleepily.

"It's just after nine, Dad and we asked Gopal to come for us at eleven. I thought you wanted to have a swim before we went to the temple."

Davenport groaned. What had seemed a good idea last night, had suddenly lost its appeal. He shut his eyes.

Pippa got up from his bed, looking disgusted and went out onto the balcony from where she could see the entrance to the Spa and the pool, and the sea if she looked to her right. She spotted a figure she recognised coming from the pool area and called out to him.

"Mr Rav...Rav... she stuttered to a halt, not being able to remember his name.

The young policeman came up to stand under her balcony.

"Ravanathan, Miss Davenport but why don't you just call me Rav. I like that but not of course in front of either of my superiors," he added quickly.

"What's a superior, Rav?" asked Pippa.

"Someone who is above you in your job as Sergent Cheng and DCI Hussian are above me," he answered, smiling.

"So my Dad is superior to Fiona."

"Who's superior to me, Pippa?" came a voice from behind her and Fiona stepped out onto the balcony in her white towelling dressing gown, her fair hair rumpled from sleep.

"Rav was telling me that his DCI is superior to him so I was telling him that Dad must be superior to you," Pippa informed her.

"Rav?"

Fiona looked down and the young constable gave her his full name.

"PC Ravanathan....is it Mrs Davenport?"

"No constable. Miss Macdonald...Fiona. I'm Mr Davenport's DS at home which is why Pippa was telling you I was his inferior."

She laughed loudly as she turned to see Charles joining them on the balcony.

"Who are you inferior to, Fiona?" he asked.

"You, of course, Sir."

Charles looked at his daughter who was now waving to the constable as he walked away.

"Was that PC Ravanathan, Pippa?"

"Yes, Dad."

"What did he want?"

"He didn't want anything. I called down to him and he came to talk to me. He called me Miss Davenport and said I could call him Rav if his superiors weren't there."

"Better not to talk to him at all pet, if the sergeant or the DCI are there. I don't think they'd approve."

"Why not, Dad?"

Pippa's small face was puzzled.

"They don't want me to get involved in the murder case here so I think the less we see of them the better."

"But that's stupid. You and Fiona and Penny and the others are good at murders."

Fiona laughed.

"That sounds as if we're good at killing people!"

"You know what I mean, Fiona," Pippa giggled.

"It would be like someone trying to help you with....with a solo talk, when you know you can do it yourself," Charles explained. "DCI Hussain thinks he can manage without any help from us and he's probably right. Now come on you two, time you got dressed and ready to go to breakfast."

At the foot of the stairs to The Feringgi Grill, they met Leong Ping.

"Apa ghabar?" Pippa greeted him.

"Salamat pagi. Terima kasih. Anda ialah?"

"I know,' thank you'. Is Anda ialah, how are you? No it can't be, that's apa ghabar."

Pippa looked confused.

"I said - good morning - that's salamat pagi and - anda ialah means, and what about you?"

"So what do I say for, fine?"

"Ghabar baik."

"Oh I remember. I was told that the other day so - salamat pagi. Ghabar baik, terima kasih," chanted Pippa..

"Oh to be young," said Fiona, as they walked up the stairs. "I could never remember all that but I bet Pippa does."

They all decided on blueberry pancakes with maple syrup for their main course, Fiona bemoaning the fact that too many breakfasts like this would prevent her from getting into her bikinis. After a round of toast and a cup of tea each, they went back downstairs and Charles left to collect their beach bag and water for their trip. Fiona and Pippa went over to the main entrance. It was a new young man at the door this morning and he asked if he could get a taxi for them.

Fiona told him that they had already booked their own taxi.

Pippa looked at his name tag.

"Hello, Yous," she said. Where's Sugu?"

"It's his day off," the man said. "There are six of us doormen. Would you like me to tell you all our names?"

"Oh yes please," said Pippa.

"Well, there's me - Yous - maybe it'll help if I tell you that one Scottish guest calls me Useless," he laughed good-naturedly. "Another one is Sham. Sugu you know. The other three are Amin who's quite small like Sugu, and Farez and Jaz. Where are you from - England?"

"No, Scotland," said Pippa.

"Well if you see Jaz tell him that and he'll say some Scottish words to you," Yous grinned.

"We've met Jaz," said Fiona. "He told us about Proton cars being made out of..."

".. drink cans," finished off Yous.

At that moment another red -uniformed man came across to join them and Yous introduced Sham.

"Do you like wearing a skirt?" asked Pippa bluntly.

"It's more of a sarong," Yous said, pulling it aside to show his black trousers underneath.

Charles and Nancy came round the corner and joined them at the door just as a taxi was drawing up. It was Gopal. He got out and came into the foyer.

"Hi Gopal!" welcomed Sham.

"We know Gopal well," explained Yous. "Before the hotel was renovated two years ago, he worked here as a waiter in the gardens."

"Cheerio!" Pippa called out as she climbed into the back of the taxi with Fiona and Nancy, leaving Charles to get into the front.

"Salamat tingaal," called Sham and Yous.

"That must mean cheerio," said Pippa, settling back in the seat and putting on her seat belt.

It was a long journey to the temple and they went back towards the airport this time. Again Pippa exclaimed with delight at seeing small monkeys on the telephone wires.

Charles and Fiona were interested to hear from Gopal about the land which had been reclaimed from the sea for an expensive development of houses on one side and they commented on the other side of the road where houses were being built on the hillside.

"Not very safe," remarked Charles. "Heavy rain and they could slide downwards."

They laughed when Gopal called some newly built houses 'bungalows' when they had three storeys. Fiona explained that they were laughing because in Britain, bungalows were on one level.

Gopal pointed out Island Plaza as they passed it on the left.

"It was the first shopping mall," he told them. "It has a big food supermarket inside called Cold Storage."

"Are there other malls then?" asked Fiona with interest.

""Yes there's Gurney Plaza..."

"Is that near Gurney Drive? Sorry for interrupting Gopal," said Fiona. " I was told we could eat there at the hawkers' stalls."

"What a hawker's stall?" demanded Pippa.

"They have lots of stalls selling different foods," explained Fiona. "The girl who did my massage told me about them. "You get fish at one, meat at another, rice at another and each stall owner charges you what you owe them and the meals are very cheap, a bit like that place we went to along the road from the hotel. Sorry, Gopal, you were telling us about the malls."

"No problem, Miss," said Gopal. "Yes, Gurney Plaza is in Gurney Drive where the food stalls are. Gurney Plaza is more modern than Island Plaza and has more shops. A new part has just been added on, so my wife Usha told me. Some shops are very expensive but there are stalls with cheaper things. Queensway Mall is the newest and biggest but it's away across the island near the airport. There's also Prangin Mall in Georgetown and the new First Avenue there too."

Now they were turning off the main road and the shops became smaller and less modern. Most were really just stalls and the traffic was much more congested here. Gopal stopped.

"We are at the entrance to the temple," he said and pointed out a hand-written sign with an arrow pointing, "To Kek Lok See Temple."

Seeing their amazement, he added, "I could take you further up the hillside to another entrance and you could walk down to here, if you like."

"What happens if we get out and start from here?" asked Charles.

"I can meet you back here or meet you higher up, even at the top if you want to climb the whole way up. There is a reservoir at the top."

They were causing a traffic jam so Fiona made a quick decision.

"We'll go right to the top. Yes Charles? But we'll come back down to here, Gopal."

"Suits me," Charles replied.

They got out, thanked Gopal and made their way to the narrow entrance between two stalls. Steps faced them, rickety steps flanked by more stalls. Pippa was fascinated. She went across to one stall which seemed to sell lots of medicines. The stall-holder picked up one small tin, saying that it was tiger balm and cured sore muscles.

"Lots of people buy many tins to take home for friends," she told them.

"We always take some home," volunteered Nancy.

Fiona bought one tin.

"We don't have many aches and pains," Charles laughed.

They climbed steadily, stopping only to buy Pippa and Nancy brightly-coloured tee-shirts with Penang written across the front. Pippa's was a vivid blue and Nancy chose purple. At the first level, they stopped to look into an area which had some huge gold-coloured Buddha figures and were persuaded to drop money into slots labelled, Health, Wealth and Happiness. There was even one for success in exams. Some people had lit joss sticks and the perfume filled their nostrils.

"I can smell vanilla," said Fiona.

"No, it's like that perfume old ladies wear," said Charles.

"Lavender," put in Fiona.

They came out and climbed on. Pippa was the first to reach the next level.

"Oh Dad, look at all the turtles!" she exclaimed.

Fiona and Charles joined her on a bridge, Nancy hanging back. They looked down and saw masses of turtles, some swimming in the dirty water, some resting on a slope down to the water. At places there were turtles on top of turtles. The smell was unpleasant. Charles took a quick photograph.

"I can smell why you didn't come too close, Nancy," he said.

Fiona took Pippa's arm and pulled her off the bridge, moving over to some slits in the wall from where they could look down towards where they had left the taxi. The air coming through was not exactly fresh - it was too hot for that - but the musty, foetid water smell was absent here.

"Those poor turtles, Dad," said Pippa. "There are too many of them in that small pool."

"Did you notice that it was called "The Pool of Longevity"?" asked Nancy..

"What does that word mean? Long something?" Pippa asked..

"Longevity means long-living." Nancy told her.

"Don't think they would live long in those conditions," said Fiona, in disgust.

"Maybe it means if you look at them, you'll live long," Charles suggested.

On they climbed, the adults marvelling at the artefacts, Pippa looking increasingly bored. Then they were at the top and could look at the female figure they had seen from the bottom. It overlooked the temple from up the hillside and looked enormous now.

"We should have bought a guidebook to tell us what that is," said Charles.

"Maybe we can get one at the bottom on the way back," said Fiona.

They took a little funicular that they operated for themselves to the topmost level where there was a huge, new statue of a goddess and a pool full of carp with a misspelt sign, reading, " Do not crowed the pool by putting fish into it". Further along there were stone figures representing all the Chinese Years – the pig, the tiger and the snake being three of them. They tried to find a leaflet which would tell them what year they were but with no luck.

They took the funicular back down, then walked back down through the shops. The steps were broken in places and it was quite dark so they had to be careful not to trip.

Gopal was there, on the road, waiting for them.

They piled in gratefully; glad to be back in the air-conditioned taxi.

"Will I drive you up to the reservoir?" he asked.

Pippa looked fed up but Fiona explained to her that they would probably never be here again so should see all that there was to see and she accepted with good grace, especially when Nancy said that she had not seen the reservoir. The journey took only minutes and they were glad that they had come when they saw the view.

"It's like a Scottish loch," said Charles.

"Only in sunshine and heat," laughed Fiona.

They got out and took some photographs, grateful for their digital camera as they had taken so many pictures that day. The heat was intense, even more so than at their hotel poolside so they got back into the taxi quite quickly and Gopal drove them back down the winding road outside the temple.

"Would you like to stop for a drink at one of the stalls?" he asked them.

The stall did not look too hygienic and Fiona was surprised when Charles said yes. They got out and all chose cans of coca cola. Charles offered Gopal a drink too and he chose his drink from an open container.

"What is it?" Pippa asked.

"It's a soya drink - banana flavoured," he told her.

Drinks over, they clambered back into the taxi. It was nearly 1 o'clock by this time so when Gopal asked if they wanted to go anywhere else, Charles said that they had had enough sightseeing for the day and wanted just to go back to the hotel.

It was four tired, hot travellers who were deposited at the hotel entrance.

"Lunch folks?" asked Charles.

"Ice cream for me, Dad," said Pippa, brightening up.

"And me please," said Nancy.

"Fiona?"

"Yes me too. Penang Bar?"

They made their way to the bar. It was quite empty, it being now nearly two o'clock.

The young man who brought the menu was new to them. Pippa, as usual, read his name tag and pronounced, "Salamat pagi, Sunny Tan." The man grinned at her and said, "It is now salamat tengah hari, madam."

Pippa giggled.

"Not madam - I'm just Pippa."

"Well Miss Pippa, salamat pagi is good morning, salmat tengah hari is good afternoon. Do you want to know what good evening is?"

"Yes please."

"That is salamat petang and goodnight is salamat malam."

"Help," said Fiona. "I'm lost already."

They ordered their ice creams and long cold drinks. Charles had a tiger beer and was told by Sunny Tan that that was called what sounded to them like 'harimou'. Fiona, Pippa and Nancy settled for lemonade with lots of ice.

Sunny Tan brought their bill to be signed and asked their room number.

"Dua, dua....empat, enam," recited Pippa.

"Is that 2246, Miss Pippa?" he asked, looking impressed when Charles confirmed that that was indeed their room number.

They made their way along the ground-floor corridor to the lift, agreeing that what they wanted most now was a nap, even Pippa declaring that she couldn't do another thing.

They said cheerio to Nancy who said that her parents would either be in their room or in the lounge having afternoon tea. She looked indignant when Charles offered to come with her to find them so he let her go, telling her to come back if she could not find them.

She did not return so the three collapsed on their beds and silence reigned in room 2246.

CHAPTER 11

Refreshed after their doze, they made their way down to The Spice Market at 7 o'clock, feeling quite hungry with having foregone their afternoon tea and canapés. The part of the restaurant which was inside was crowded so they made their way outside.

"Why is it so busy?" Charles asked the little girl who came to give them the a la carte menu.

"It is Friday, Sir. We are always busy on Fridays - and Saturdays," she added. "The local people come to eat here at the weekend."

She smiled and left them.

"What do you think, Fiona, buffet or a la carte?" inquired Charles.

"Well it's Mongolian Night. It said that on the board as we came in and I don't like spicy food much so I'd prefer a la carte but we can each choose what we want. What about you, Pippa?"

Pippa had been scanning the other tables, no doubt hoping to see her friend. She turned back to Fiona.

"I'd like the buffet, please."

"And you, Charles?"

"I'll go in with Pippa and have the buffet. I'll tell someone on the way in to come and see what you want from the menu. OK?"

The two went off and minutes later a waiter came to take Fiona's order of lobster bisque soup followed by linguine prawns.

Charles and Pippa returned with laden plates and Fiona told them to tuck in without waiting for her. They had gone back for seconds by the time her soup arrived and when they came back, they had Nancy White in tow. She was carrying a dessert plate full of various flavours of ice cream, sprinkled with chocolate flakes.

"Hello, Fiona," she said as she sat down.

"Hello, Nancy. You must have started before us if you're at the pudding stage."

"No. I met Mum and Dad in the lounge and had a huge afternoon tea and I wasn't very hungry so this is all I'm having. The waiter said it was OK and he'd just charge me for the one course."

The two girls became engrossed in each other.

"I wanted to lift some turtles out and take them away," Pippa was confiding in Nancy when the manager, Mr Grafton, approached the table.

"Mr Davenport, could I interrupt your meal for a few minutes?" he asked.

"Of course, Mr Grafton."

Charles smiled at him and invited him to draw up a chair and sit down. A waiter approached and asked if the manager would be eating.

"Thanks, Prakesh. Would you bring me a plate of the same soup that this lady's having and a bottle of wine and three glasses. Would you prefer white or red, Sir?" he asked Charles.

"We prefer white thanks," said Charles.

"A bottle of sauvignon blanc, Prakesh, please."

The girls were finishing so Charles suggested that they go back to the Rasa Lounge and have a mocktail each.

"We'll join you there soon, pet."

"No problem, Dad. Come on, Nancy."

When they had gone, the manager apologised again for interrupting their meal and asked if Charles wanted to go for his dessert before he spoke to him. Charles went off and came back with a plate of trifle.

"Now, Sir. What can I do for you?" he asked, smiling.

"It's about this murder, Mr Davenport...."

"Please call me Charles and this is Fiona. As well as being my...partner, she's my detective sergeant at home so she will be interested in what you have to say, if you don't mind her being present."

"No problem and please call me Sean. Well, the thing is, I've tried to find out how the investigation is going and been told to mind my own business.

Not in those words but that's what it came down to. I'm afraid the police in Malaysia are a bit autocratic but my guests are asking me questions too, naturally, and I don't like being side-lined. I wondered if there was any way that you could find anything out, you being on the same side as it were."

Charles smiled ruefully.

"I'm afraid I was warned off in no uncertain terms, Sean. The DCI, Mr Hussain, told me not to interfere and his sergeant was almost rude to me. PC Ravanathan who was on the scene before them, was friendly but then I think he was grateful for my advice."

Seeing the disappointed look on the manager's face, Fiona said, "Is there no way we could do a kind of behind the scenes investigation? Talk to Mrs Grant for instance? I don't suppose she'll have been treated very well by those two either."

"Not unless she specifically asked us to get involved, love and even then I might get hauled over the coals by..."

"Mr Knox," she supplied.

"That's my chief constable, Sean. He does things very much by the book and would probably take the side of Mr Hussain if a complaint was to be filed against me," said Charles.

"If I spoke to Mrs Grant and she was willing, would you try some undercover sleuthing?" asked Grafton.

Charles and Fiona looked at each other.

"I must admit to being very curious. What do you think, Fiona?" asked Charles.

"Could we do it without them finding out?"

"Only if the people we spoke to were OK with it, otherwise they might complain to the police here."

The bottle of wine and glasses arrived and Prakesh poured them half a glass each.

"Can I have my bill to sign, please?" asked Charles.

The waiter left.

"Tell you what, Sean, you speak to Mrs Grant and see if she feels uncomfortable with the way the local police are treating her. If she does, ask if she would mind me trying to help, under cover as it were, and if she is agreeable I'll talk to her at least. I can't go further than that I'm afraid, not yet anyway."

Prakesh arrived with the bill and the manager took it from him and signed it.

"It's my treat, Charles. Even if you can't help further, I'm grateful to you for listening at least."

He got to his feet.

"Now I'll leave you to join your daughter in the lounge. Enjoy the rest of your evening."

He walked off.

"What a nice man," said Fiona. "I know you'll be itching to find out the murderer but please be careful, Charles. You know how Knox would crucify you if he received a complaint from the police over here."

They walked through the hotel grounds, arm in arm. The stars were clearly visible in the black velvet of the night sky and they stopped to look up.

"Is that Venus?" Fiona asked, pointing to one particularly bright star.

"I think so, my love. Make a wish."

Fiona closed her eyes and said nothing. They could hear the sea breaking on the sand.

"What did you wish for?"

"I can't tell you or it won't come true," she laughed.

They walked on till they came to the flight of steps leading up to the Rasa Wing and stopped again. Charles put the fingers of his right hand under her chin and, lifting her face upwards, bent to plant a soft kiss on her lips.

"Whatever I do or don't do, I won't let this murder spoil the rest of our holiday, my love."

"Whatever you do or don't do, I'll be helping you, remember, so I won't blame you if it interferes a bit with our holiday," she said, returning his kiss.

They climbed the stairs slowly, sniffing the air as the scent from the flowers on either side of them reached their nostrils.

In the lounge, Pippa and Nancy were sitting with Rory and Hope. All had drinks in front of them and Leong Ping came over immediately to ask what the new arrivals wanted.

"Just coffee for me," said Fiona.

"The same for me," said Charles.

Talk turned to the day's events. The Whites had gone to Gurney Plaza.

"Did you go in on the hotel bus?" asked Fiona.

"Yes but we came back on the local bus," said Hope. "You should try it. I love the old, blue one. There's no glass in the windows and you can sit with your elbow out. We used to get a taxi back but we prefer the bus and it's cheaper too, only one and a half ringgits instead of about thirty. There's also a new service with Rapid buses. They're more modern."

"Taxi and bus are dead easy to say in Bahasa, Pippa," volunteered Nancy. "Bus is bas and taxi it teksi."

"And, Pippa," said Rory.... Pippa had obviously been regaling them with her new words, Charles told Fiona later... "Police is polis."

"Just like they say it in Glasgow," said Pippa with a giggle.

"Charles. We're going to the Botanic Gardens tomorrow morning. There's a man there who takes clever photos of you with the monkeys. Can Pippa come with us?" asked Rory.

"Oh please Dad, can I?" asked Pippa.

"Of course you can. That's kind of you, Rory. Maybe we could do some shopping, Fiona."

Nancy yawned and Pippa joined in.

"Time these young ladies were in bed, I think," said Hope.

The girls ran ahead of the adults till they reached the corridor which led to the Whites' room, then Pippa hugged her friend and ran off ahead towards her own room. Charles and Fiona said goodnight to Rory and Hope and, more slowly, made their way after Pippa.

"Shopping, Charles or sleuthing?"

"Depends on whether or not we hear from Sean about Mrs Grant being willing to talk to us, I guess."

By this time they had reached Pippa who was waiting at their room having forgotten to take her key card, so talk of sleuthing had to stop.

CHAPTER 12

Nothing was forthcoming from the manager the next morning, so after seeing Pippa off in a taxi with the Whites, Charles and Fiona decided to try the local bus. Rory White had told them to ask for Jermail Began and get off after the bus rounded the corner at the massive McDonalds which was a good landmark.

"Walk back towards McDonalds and take the street just before it. Gurney Plaza is along that street, not far along. Take water with you. Even that short walk can be very tiring in the heat."

So, armed with two bottles of water and the beach bag, empty for shopping, they walked down the hotel drive to the bus stop. Two local men were waiting there and smiled at them. Fiona risked a "Salamat pagi" and got one back.

After about three very hot minutes' wait, the old, blue bus rumbled up. Charles motioned for the two men in front of them but they smiled again and one said, "We wait for the new bus, Sir. It has aircon."

Fiona went on first, leaving Charles to pay the aged driver who smiled, showing toothless gums.

"Three ringgits," he said holding up three fingers.

Charles handed him a five ringgit note and the man motioned down to where lots of coins rested on the front facia. Charles helped himself to two ringgit coins and went to join Fiona halfway up the bus.

As each person got up to get off, he or she pressed a bell above their seat and the bus which went quite fast for its age, shuddered to a halt.

"We're only just doing that on our buses now," commented Fiona.

"What?"

"Ringing the bell and not getting up till the stop," she informed him. "I suppose someone as important as you never gets on a bus at home!"

He looked sheepish.

"I haven't been into Glasgow itself for years, except in the line of work. I'm not a lover of shops."

"So why are you coming into Gurney Plaza?" she inquired.

"Well the shops will at least be different, surely. I mean they won't have Marks and Spencers or Debenhams, will they?"

"I hardly think so."

"I think that's McDonalds I can see coming up ahead. I wonder if there are any stops before it or should I ring the bell now?" Charles asked her.

"We've to wait till the bus turns the corner, remember," she answered him.

After quite a lengthy stop at the traffic lights, the bus rounded the corner, passing McDonalds on the left. Charles stood and pressed the bell. Fiona waited in her seat till the bus pulled up at the stop. Charles put one foot on the ground and quickly pulled it back up as a motorbike whizzed past the bus, almost on the pavement. Looking a bit shaken, he glanced to his left and, seeing that it was now safe, he stepped down and reaching back, gave Fiona a hand down the step.

Safely on the pavement, he admitted that he had forgotten this habit of Penang motorcyclists of passing on the inside.

"We could book them for that at home," Fiona laughed.

They set off. The heat seemed to bounce off the pavements and they were glad of the water they had brought and very relieved when they reached the air-conditioned Plaza.

The part they went in at was obviously very new, marble-floored and spacious and housing designer shops with exorbitant prices. A sign pointed to "More shops" and when they went in that direction, they found stalls with reasonably-priced jewellery and watches and racks of clothes.

"I must buy a fake watch, Charles," said Fiona and spent the next half hour trying on various watches, deciding eventually on one which said, "Gucci" on the face. She persuaded Charles to buy the matching man's watch and the stallholder lowered the price for the double purchase.

They went up the moving staircase to the top floor and, discovering that all that was there was a cinema complex, took the escalator back down one level where they found a little craft shop called Arch which specialised in carved, wooden pictures. Fiona bought a small one with a pig carving under which read "Sincere, diligent, obliging, generous". On the back was what the owner told them was the Chinese horoscope for the year of the pig which was every twelfth year from 1923.

"I'm going to give that to John. He was born in 1971. It's his fortieth birthday next year, I'm sure. Did he not tell us that at Jean's birthday meal?"

John and Jean were their bridge friends and Charles agreed that John would like this present.

"Will we get Jean one too?" Charles asked.

"No, I think I'll get her a shawl. She feels the cold and there were some lovely pashminas downstairs. I was going to get one and then forgot. Remind me when we go back down."

They strolled round that floor and the next two, found the stall with the pashminas and bought a beautiful peacock-blue one which they were sure would suit Jean Hope.

"Only the basement left. Can you manage another floor?" Fiona asked.

"Yes but just one more then I must have a coffee," Charles stated.

In the basement, they found Cold Storage which Fiona found fascinating. She bought shampoo just because she said she liked its name, "Feather" and some Cadbury's chocolate in flavours which she had never seen at home. Charles followed her round but obviously did not share her enthusiasm for the shop.

"It's just like Morrison's," was his dry comment when they reached the checkout.

He cheered up when they discovered a quaint little shop which sold many varieties of doughnut, two of which they tried, sitting in, with a latte for Charles and iced mango tea for Fiona. Knowing that Pippa would love these doughnuts, Fiona bought a box of four, with different coloured icing and fillings.

"Had enough of shops, love?" she enquired sympathetically as they finished their drinks.

"God, yes," he said. "Take me home please."

There were rows of taxis outside the exit which was on the opposite side of the mall to where they had come in and they decided to do the touristy thing this time and pay for a cool ride back to the hotel. Charles remembered to ask the price before they got in and thought that thirty-five ringgits was near enough to the thirty mentioned by Rory.

The drive back was quicker, with no stops to be made this time. Charles asked the receptionist for the day who was Anissa, the girl who had welcomed them some days ago, if Pippa and the Whites had returned but they were still out so they walked back to their room, tidied up and went down to the Penang Bar for some lunch, deciding to share twelve satay sticks of beef, lamb and chicken.

Over lunch, the talk turned to the murder.

"Lucky for Mrs Grant that she was up in the lounge having coffee when it happened," said Fiona, "otherwise she might be the main suspect."

"The only suspect, I imagine. Who else out here would hate Alan Grant enough to kill him?" said Charles. "I mean he was a nasty individual and a bore but murder...that takes real hatred usually, unless the murderer is someone unhinged. I wonder how the police treated Mrs Grant under the circumstances."

"Surely they would be gentle with her, given that she wasn't at the scene," Fiona conjectured.

"It's possible that she stabbed him and then left for coffee, I suppose," mused Charles. "I didn't see her leave the poolside and there was no one else on the loungers nearby, remember. No, that couldn't have happened. I'd have seen the blood when I looked back at him him, surely."

"Would she not have had blood on her?"

"Not necessarily. Whoever did the two stabbings could have put the towel over the body first to stop the blood from splattering out.

Lunch over, they went back to the room and changed into their swimming clothes. Fiona emptied the beach bag and refilled it with their books and suntan oil and they made their way to the grounds, having decided to sit outside the Rasa pool area and swim in the Garden Wing pool as it was cooler in the afternoons, though often busier with children. They were fortunate this time as there were only two other people in the water, both young adults so they were able to take a leisurely swim round the pool.

Back at their loungers, Charles rubbed suntan oil into Fiona's back for her and she did the same for him and then they settled down, Fiona to read and Charles to do the crossword in his copy of The Straits Times. There had been no problem getting two copies of the paper sent up each morning.

It was about two o'clock when Pippa and the Whites arrived back. They had not had any lunch while out at The Botanic Gardens and were on their way to the Penang Bar when they spotted Charles and Fiona.

Pippa ran over to them, exclaiming excitedly about the great time they had had.

"Dad, there were heaps of monkeys, some with babies underneath them clinging on. We bought food to give them and ...."

"Pippa, Pippa, slow down. Look, go and have lunch then go and get into your bikini and come and join us here. You can tell us all your stories then," laughed Charles.

Pippa ran back to join the Whites, returning about an hour later to tell her father and Fiona about the photographs which would be arriving the next day and which would show her holding out her hand with a monkey sitting on it.

"Surely not!" exclaimed Fiona.

"No, not really. I stood with my hand out and he took a photo of me then he took a photo of a monkey sitting and he'll super... something the picture onto the one of me."

"Superimpose," volunteered Charles.

"We saw lots of really weird photos of people lying on top of planes or flying over famous buildings and I could have had one like that. Nancy chose one of her flying over the leaning Tower of Pisa and she had to lie down on the grass with her arms stretched out as if she was flying and he'll super...impose that onto one of the tower. I chose the monkey one."

"How much did that cost? Did you have enough money with you?" asked Charles.

"It was only 50 ringgits for one picture, Dad and Rory bought me a drink but you buy a drink for Nancy when she comes with us, so that's OK."

"Right, settle down now and give us some peace. Did you bring your book down? Read for a bit then we can go for a swim together."

"Ok, Dad."

Pippa produced her latest book, "Murder on the Orient Express," and was soon engrossed in it. She was currently trying to read all of Elinor Brent-Dyer's Chalet School books and all of Agatha Christie's crime novels. Fiona shared her love of the former books and had been able to supply some which had not been available in Glasgow bookshops. Pippa had read about twenty-three of the school series and about five of the Christie mysteries which featured Hercule Poirot.

Seeing the crime novel, Charles remarked quietly to Fiona that he wondered if Sean Grafton had had a chance to talk to Mrs Grant about involving them in the investigation into Alan Grant's murder.

"Well, apart from going up Penang Hill, we've managed to see all the sights we wanted to see so far so we could be free to do some sleuthing if she does agree to us getting involved," said Fiona.

"And the trishaw trip in Georgetown. I don't imagine that Pippa will let me forget that," Charles said.

"True. I'm sure the Whites would take Pippa with them on any other trips they make. It probably makes things easier having two kids along and Pippa's no bother, is she?" said Fiona.

"What's that you're saying about me?" demanded that young lady, hearing her name mentioned.

"Just saying that if Fiona and I do some detective work in the next few days, Rory and Hope will probably be happy to take you along with them on any trips they make," said her father.

His daughter's eyes lit up then clouded over.

"They're going to go to somewhere called Cameron Highlands to stay for two nights at a hotel called Strawberry Park but that might be too dear."

"When are they going?"

"Rory said he was going to book it up tonight but I didn't really pay attention to when they were going as I didn't think I'd be allowed to go. Would you let me, Dad?"

"I'll think about it, pet. See how expensive it is first."

Content with that, Pippa went back to her murder mystery.

CHAPTER 13

"What do you think, Fiona? Should we let Pippa go on this trip to the Cameron Highlands?" Charles asked when Pippa was in the bathroom, getting ready for bed that night.

"I'd wait and see how much it costs and then decide if you can afford it. It seems a waste of money to have her room here unused for two nights and be paying for another two nights somewhere else but then again, if we do hear from Mrs Grant and she'd like us to do some investigating for her, it would be a lot easier with Pippa out of the way."

"Good point. I'll need to find out the price first and if Mrs Grant does want us to get involved, I'll ask Rory and Hope if Pippa can go with them. They might not be too keen to have the responsibility of looking after someone else's child for two nights and three days."

They all slept well as usual and rose to another cloudless, blue sky. The Feringgi Grill was busier than usual, it being the weekend, and service was slower but none of them minded as they were not rushing off anywhere.

"Just a lazy day, today? Does that suit both of my women?" asked Charles as they were finishing off the toast.

"Ok by me," said Fiona.

"Me too. My book's getting really exciting," said Pippa.

"Is 'Murder on the Orient Express' that one where all...."

"Don't say it, Charles. You'll spoil the end for her," interrupted Fiona.

Charles looked surprised at her interjection.

"I've read it too and I think I know what you were about to say, so don't say it," she laughed.

Govan came across when they were about to leave.

"I saw you looking at the lovely pastries," he said to Pippa.

Pippa blushed.

"I know. They look lovely but by the time I've eaten everything else I'm too full to eat one," she confessed.

"Would you like me to put two into what you call a 'doggy-bag', I believe?" Govan asked her.

"Oh yes, please," said Pippa.

"Come on then and choose which two you want."

Pippa followed the young man to the table and pointed out three pastries and they waited a couple of minutes while he had them wrapped in tinfoil for her.

As they were walking to their room, they passed the gymnasium where some energetic people were exercising. One of the staff was standing at the entrance. He was holding a tennis racquet. Charles stopped.

"Excuse me," he said, looking at the name tag. "Wadi, could I play tennis tonight at six o'clock. I saw that there was Fun Tennis on then. I haven't played for some time but would quite like a game."

"Certainly, Sir. You just meet here at about five fifty. "

"I haven't brought a racquet."

"That's OK, Sir, we have racquets and balls."

"I didn't know you played tennis, Charles," said Fiona.

"Neither did I, Dad," added Pippa.

"I haven't played since before you were born, Pippa. Your Mum and I actually met at a tennis club. Do you play, Fiona?"

"No. I did at school but preferred netball. Pippa and I will just get some extra drinks in while you get all hot and bothered tonight, won't we, Pippa?"

As she said this, she linked arms with the girl and they skipped down the corridor together,

Fiona looking for all the world like the youngster's older sister in her white shorts and colourful top.

Back in their room, they packed the beach bag with everything necessary for a day's lounging and swimming and were lucky to find three loungers halfway between the two pools and not far from the back stairs leading to their room.

Charles and Fiona took turns of swimming in the warm water of the Rasa pool in the late morning. They all had lunch at the Penang Bar as usual and read after that. At about three o'clock, after a swim in the Garden Wing pool, Pippa suggested that she and Fiona went up to the room, made tea in the kettle provided there and brought down three mugs of English Breakfast tea to drink along with the doggy-bag of pastries.

"I asked for three - one each, "she told them proudly.

"I take it that we're missing afternoon tea, today," Charles commented.

"It means that we'll maybe be ready for a bigger meal tonight," said Fiona. "We haven't tried the Chinese place across the road yet. We could go tonight. Maybe Nancy would like to come too or all of them perhaps."

Pippa was delighted with that suggestion and sped off through the grounds to the spot where the Whites usually sat. She was away for some time then returned to say that the Whites all wanted to come.

"Rory said they'd been to Kampong when it was further away down the road we cycled along. It's moved to just across the road and it's great.... and cheap," she added. "Dad, would it be OK if Mai Lee came too? She was going to eat with Nancy tonight."

"Of course, if her parents don't mind."

Pippa ran off again, coming back to tell them that they would all meet in the lounge after drinks.

"And after your tennis, Dad. Rory said he might play too."

At five o'clock, Charles went up to the room to lie on the daybed on the balcony which was now in the shade, to cool off a bit before getting changed for tennis. Fiona and Pippa sat for a while longer and had the skewers of fruit brought round by Tony and the cold towels brought round by a small girl who said she was a trainee. Fiona asked her where she was training and found out that her family paid the hotel to take her on for a few weeks during holiday from college. The Rasa, it appeared, was a good hotel to have on her cv, the girl explained.

By the time they got back to the room, Charles was dressed for his tennis and, promising to meet up with them after a shower, he went off, whistling happily.

"Nice to see your Dad so relaxed and happy, isn't it?" Fiona said and Pippa agreed. They took turns of the bathroom, Pippa opting for a shower and Fiona for a relaxing bath and at 6.30, they made their way down to the Rasa lounge where they joined Hope and Nancy. Mai Lee and her parents were sitting quite near them. Hope said that they were happy for their daughter to join them that night at Kampong as it would let them have a meal by themselves at The Feringgi Grill.

"They had their honeymoon here," Hope told Fiona, "and they love the Grill but Mai Lee has a small appetite and going there isn't so good with her."

It was little Maz, or Masnoon as her name tag read, who served them this evening. A diminutive girl who had told them that her home was in Borneo, she often looked quite sad, as she did tonight. Fiona asked her if she was happy at the hotel and she smiled and said that she was but that her friend Yante who had started at the Rasa with her two years ago had gone on to housekeeping and she was missing her. The other girl, Emma, who also served in the lounge, was older and not as friendly towards her as Yante had been.

Just before half past seven, Rory appeared in the lounge, looking quite red-faced. He claimed that he was exhausted after almost an hour's tennis but he looked pale and cool compared with

Charles who arrived shortly afterwards, his face shining like a beacon.

"I can almost feel the heat coming off you," said Fiona as he sat down beside her.

"We played two sets. Rory was with Wadi and I was with a man from the Golden Sands who used to be a tennis coach in England. I haven't run so much for years. Even a cold shower hasn't cooled me down completely."

"Well sit down, have a drink and cool down a bit more," she advised him and he and Rory chose a beer each. Nancy, Pippa and Mai Lee had moved off to another table. Most tables were arranged for four people so this left room for the two men to join their partners.

"Hello, Mr Davenport, any news on the murder front?"

It was Annabelle Kilbride.

"Sorry, no. I was told in no uncertain terms to keep my nose out," Charles answered.

"How is Mrs Grant?" asked Fiona.

"Very upset after another meeting with the police this morning, I'm afraid. She thinks that they suspect her of killing Alan. She's over there, talking to the manager right now about keeping her room. They were due to leave tomorrow to go to Langkawi for a week but the police say she can't leave yet."

"Look, Annabelle, why don't you and she join us for dinner tonight. We're going to a Chinese restaurant across the road, Charles, Rory, Hope and I with the three girls. They can sit at a separate table which will suit them fine I imagine. It might be good for Mrs Grant to get out of the hotel for a wee while."

Fiona looked anxiously at the others but she need not have worried as all of them added their pleas to Annabelle Kilbride to join them.

The manager left the lounge and Mrs Grant came slowly across the room towards them. She looked wan and older than she had looked on the plane, said Fiona said in an aside to Charles. "I thought that this might give her an opportunity to talk with you... if she wants to," she added.

The woman agreed that it might be good to get out of the hotel.

"I've felt like a prisoner since it happened," she told them. "Mr Hussain told me not to go far from the hotel so I've kept to my room. I didn't want people looking at me and pointing me out as the murdered man's wife."

The two men having downed their beers, Fiona and Hope rose to their feet. Charles called the three girls over and they came immediately.

"At last, Dad. I'm starving," said Pippa.

"Me too," echoed Nancy.

Mai Lee just smiled shyly.

They walked out of the hotel and, turning left, made their way to Kampong which was now situated beneath the only high-rise apartments in

Batu Feringgi. They climbed some steps and found themselves at a swimming pool round which tables were laid for meals. Fiona explained to Pippa that they were to have their own table.

"Order your own meal. You know how to do it and remember to order drinks too. No, not wine," she smiled as she saw the look on Pippa's face.

They found two unoccupied tables with an occupied one between them and sat down. "You'll love Andrew, the owner. He's a real character," said Rory. A woman brought them menus and asked what they wanted to drink, telling them that they had French wine which was only thirty ringgits a bottle, very cheap for Malaysia.

"Wine everybody?" asked Rory and when everyone said yes, he ordered two bottles, one white and one red.

"Alan didn't like me to drink," said Mrs Grant. "He didn't like me driving either but he had to put up with that if he wanted to drink when we went out."

She gave a nervous laugh.

"Shouldn't be speaking ill of the dead, should I? You'll be thinking, like that Inspector, that I murdered him."

"Surely not" Hope White was indignant. "Why does he think that?"

"He said murders were more often than not committed by the husband or wife."

She looked at Charles. "Miss Macdonald told me that you're an inspector too. Is what he said true?"

"I'm afraid he is, sadly, correct, Mrs Grant. I'm Charles Davenport by the way. Fiona here you've already met and the others are Rory and Hope White."

"It really is kind of you to invite us, especially me, to share your meal. Tell me all about yourselves and let's not discuss Alan or his murder any more this evening."

As Andrew came up to their table at this point, she got her wish. Rory recommended sizzling prawns and they all took his advice and Charles explained that the three girls were going to order their own meals but that this table would foot the bill.

"No problem," said Andrew and minced daintily off. Given that he was a rotund figure, carrying a lot of weight round his midriff, this was no mean feat. As the man approached the girls' table, Charles could hear them giggling at him and hoped that Andrew would not be offended but he heard what was obviously Andrew's stock reply, "No problem" as he stepped away from their table and made his way to the kitchen, greeting people at other tables as he went.

Charles went over to Pippa and her friends.

"What are you lot having?" he asked.

"Nancy and me are having sweet and sour prawns and Wai Lee's having chicken and sweetcorn soup. She's not as hungry as us."

"Nancy and *I*, Pippa. Why were you all giggling?"

"Nancy told us that the waiter was... you know... gay and then he walked really funny, Dad."

"Ok but don't do it again. You might embarrass him."

"Sorry, Charles. It was my fault," said Nancy looking guilty.

After the meal, they walked back to the hotel. The Whites wanted to go through the night markets so they left the others at the entrance. Fiona, trying to leave Mrs Grant alone with Charles, walked ahead with the two girls and Annabelle.

They walked into the foyer in silence. Behind them, Mrs Grant coughed gently and said, "Mr Davenport..."

"Charles, please."

"I'm Jean. Charles, could I talk to you about what happened to Alan, please? You've dealt with things like this before and could maybe give me some advice."

Overhearing this, Annabelle Kilbride said that she wanted an early night and would leave them together to have a chat.

"Why don't you find a secluded table and I'll tell the others what's happening."

She suited her action to her words, going across to where Fiona had just seated herself with Pippa and Wai Lee, then leaving the lounge.

Charles steered Mrs Grant into a small alcove with four chairs in it.

"Would you like a drink, Jean?" he asked the woman who was once again looking a bit anxious.

"Oh yes please. I'll have a small brandy if I may."

Charles went off to find someone to bring them drinks and returned almost immediately.

"Now, Jean, how can I help you"

"Well, should I get a lawyer?"

"I would think so, yes. Mr Grafton will perhaps know of someone who would help."

"Yes, I wondered that. I also wondered while we were eating, if you would be able to do some investigating for me."

"Well, not officially. I've already been warned off but if your lawyer agrees, I can do some rooting about for you, I suppose."

"I'd be so grateful if I felt that I had someone on my side," said Jean Grant.

"Do you want to meet me somewhere private tomorrow then?"

"Maybe you could come to my room after breakfast. We have a suite as Alan was always telling anyone who would listen, so there's a wee sitting room we could use."

"Maybe better if we asked the manager for a room, Jean, just in case the inspector or sergeant came to your room and found me there."

He laughed.

"It all sounds a bit cloak and dagger. Sorry, dagger was maybe not a tactful word to use under the circumstances."

"Look Charles, before we go any further, I'm shocked, really shocked that Alan's been brutally murdered but I'm not going to pretend that it isn't also a bit of a relief to have ...escaped from him so don't worry about upsetting me."

"I understand but I would advise you not to say anything like that to Inspector Hussain who might mistake your relief for a murderer's satisfaction."

"Oh don't worry, I'm going to be very circumspect around him and his sergeant. The only one who seemed at all sympathetic was the young constable."

"Yes. PC Ravanathan is a nicer person, I think. Still, better to keep your guard up with him too, as he has to obey his superiors."

After Jean Grant had gone to her room, Charles admitted to Fiona in a quiet aside that he felt vaguely guilty about recommending that Mrs Grant kept up a grieving widow pretence in front of the police.

"She might, after all, be guilty, though in that case asking me to help would have to be a double bluff."

They waited in the lounge until Wai Lee's parents came down from the Feringgi Grill, before going off to their room, Charles telling Fiona on the way that he would be asking Sean Grafton for a private room somewhere for himself and Jean Grant to talk in. Then he remembered his promise to Pippa to find out the price of two nights at Strawberry Park, Rory having been unsure of the exact cost when he had asked him over their meal.

"I don't think money's an object with the Whites," he said now. "You carry on back to the room and I'll go back to reception and ask Jill if she can find out the price for me."

Jill had finished her shift and gone home but Anne, another diminutive, slim young lady, told him what he wanted to know. She also rang the manager for him to talk to.

Pippa was getting into bed when he went into the room, Fiona coming out of the bathroom, in her white, towelling dressing gown.

"I can afford two nights at the hotel in Cameron Highlands, pet and Nancy's parents are OK about you going with them. They're going on Monday. I met them downstairs as they came in from the night markets."

Pippa gave a whoop of delight.

Charles motioned to Fiona to come out onto the balcony.

"I told the Whites that Jean Grant has asked me to do some investigating for her and that having Pippa out of the way would be a help, just in case they thought that I was foisting Pippa on them."

"Good idea. What time are you seeing Jean?"

"I'll ring her tomorrow. I asked the receptionist for her suite number. It's on the floor above us. I also phoned Mr Grafton and he's giving us a room in the Garden Wing. He'll contact her if the police come calling for her."

"Don't feel guilty, Charles. From what you say, the police, apart from the PC, aren't very likeable characters."

"I know but my professionalism balks at the idea of going behind their backs."

"Come on, let's get to bed. With one thing and another it's been a tiring day."

They went back into the room. Charles told Pippa to stop reading and when she had closed the book, he kissed her and switched off the main light, leaving on the bedside light between him and Fiona long enough to blow her a kiss.

CHAPTER 14

Charles rang Jean Grant at 8.30 the next morning while Pippa was in having her shower. He told her that the manager was providing them with room 1207 in the Garden Wing, free of charge and available to them for the next week if necessary.

"That's so kind of him!" exclaimed Mrs Grant.

"Well, he was hoping that you might ask me to help as he's being left in the dark by the Penang police and wants to be kept abreast of things, so we're doing him a favour really," explained Charles. "The only thing I would say is that I'd like to postpone our talk till tomorrow as Pippa will be going off then to the Cameron Highlands with Mr and Mrs White and Nancy and I'd rather she was out of the way before I get even slightly involved in this case."

"Oh I understand, Charles and I'm so grateful," said Mrs Grant and Charles rang off just as Pippa came out of the bathroom.

"Dad, can we play putting today? Nancy's going with her Dad."

"As long as you don't mind looking an idiot in front of other folk. I know you like to be good at things you do but you've never putted before."

Pippa laughed.

"It can't be that hard if Nancy can do it."

Fiona was coming in from the balcony so Charles told her that she would be able to go into the Rasa pool this morning as he and his daughter would be away at the putting competition.

"Good. I'll be able to get on with my book," she said.

They had their usual large breakfast in the Feringgi Grill. Govan must have passed on news about the pastry doggy bag, as Istvan approached Pippa as she finished her toast and asked if she would like to choose some pastries again.

"No, Pippa, I think not today," Charles said.

He smiled at the waiter.

"I think we'll be having afternoon tea today so it would be greedy to have pastries as well."

The waiter returned his smile, grinned at Pippa and walked off.

They chose their loungers, then Tony came over to them to say that he had already put two towels on each of the three sunbeds which they had chosen the day before. His round face was creased in his usual big grin.

"Once I learn where people like to sit, I try to have the seats ready every morning."

"What happens if we go away for the day?" asked Fiona. "Do we come and tell you?"

"Not at this time of year. It's only at busy times such as Christmas and Chinese New Year that we take towels off seats in the grounds if nobody sits on them for an hour," he explained. "It's different at The Rasa Wing pool as there are often not enough loungers there," he added.

The three moved over to where they had been before, halfway between the two pools.

"I like this place Dad," said Pippa. "It's easy to get to our room and to both pools."

They all settled down, Charles and Fiona with their Straits Times' crossword and Pippa with her Agatha Christie murder mystery. The murder on the Orient Express had just been discovered and she was totally engrossed when her Dad told her that it was time to go putting.

"I like to have a wee practice first," he told her, "and it would be good for you to try a few shots too."

He got up from his lounger and put his dressy shorts on over his swimming shorts, suggesting to Pippa that she should cover up a bit as the putting green was not in the shade. She pulled on the shorts and tee-shirt which she had worn to breakfast.

"Are you sure you don't want to come, Fiona?" she asked.

"No thank you. Putting is the worst part of my golf game as your Dad can tell you, so it would be too much like hard work. I'll be quite happy to relax here till you come back then we can have lunch."

Pippa and Charles walked away across the grounds and Fiona saw them stop at the loungers where the Whites were sitting and saw Nancy and Rory get up and join them. She was soon engrossed in her crossword again.

There were fewer people at the putting green than when Charles had gone the last time. He counted only eight other people apart from themselves. He picked up two putters and two balls for himself and Pippa and took her out onto the green to give her a quick lesson. Nancy and Rory got their clubs and balls and sat down, having paid for the competition.

Pippa had a few hits and after some wild shots, began to get nearer to the holes she was aiming at. Charles left her on the green and came off to pay for them both and give their room number.

"Hello, Miss Nancy," said the young man in charge, a different man from the last time, Charles noticed.

"Hi, Hari," returned Nancy. "I've brought my friend Pippa today."

Pippa was coming off the green so Nancy introduced her to Hari who shook her hand.

"Good morning, Miss Pippa. Welcome to putting."

He put his whistle to his lips and blew once. The two people still on the green, came off.

"We'll be last to play, pet, so watch what the others do and try to learn about the green. It's what we call, running fast, so you won't need to hit the ball too hard at any of the holes."

As beginner's luck would have it, Pippa was the only one to get a hole in one in the first round. Hari congratulated her and handed her a voucher with her name and room number on it.

"That'll get you a free drink, Pippa," Nancy informed her.

Hari read out the scores and Pippa was last, in spite of her hole in one, having taken four at one hole and six at another. There had been three holes in that round and would be the same in the next three. Nancy had netted eight, Charles six and Rory the same.

"Rory and I have got what is called 'par', Pippa," Charles informed her. "That means that we took two strokes at each hole. Nancy is two over and you're five over."

They played two more rounds, Charles remaining par with a score of eighteen, Pippa finishing with six over having taken twenty-four,

Rory with seventeen and Nancy with nineteen. Another woman had taken the same as Rory so they had a play-off. Hari chose a hole and the winner was the one who got nearest to the hole. This was Rory and he got two vouchers, the woman being given one.

They had a chat to two of the Welsh putters from The Golden Sands Hotel. One of them, Ralph, had on a funny hat which turned out to have a wig attached to it and he took it off to show the girls his bald head. His friend, Selwyn, was good fun too. He had shouted encouragement to the two girls each time they had putted.

They walked back through the grounds, stopping to tell Hope how they had done, then Pippa and Charles continued on to where Fiona was sitting. The Whites were going to have lunch in the Spice Market and they agreed to meet up for drinks at 6pm to discuss what Pippa needed to take to the Cameron Highlands the next day.

"How's the crossword doing?" Charles asked Fiona when they got back to their loungers.

"I'm stuck for one."

"Which one? I didn't get far but I might have it," said Charles.

"2 down. Vehicle for half mad proposer."

"No, sorry. I haven't got that one. I'll get stuck into it after lunch. What do you both feel like having?"

"I feel like having that fruit basket I had a few days ago," said Fiona. "Pippa, what about you? Ice cream as usual?"

"Yes please. Amir gives me loads of chocolate sauce," replied Pippa, her eyes lighting up at the prospect.

"Oh to be young and not have to think about your weight," moaned Fiona.

They went over to the Penang Bar, choosing a seat near the sea. Sunny Tan came to take their order. Charles was the only one who needed the menu and he debated between fish and chips or potato skins, choosing the latter when Fiona suggested that they might go to The Park Royal's 'Tiffins' restaurant that night as it would be the last night for a while that they were all together.

"Better have a smaller lunch then," he said.

Lunch over, they went back to their loungers.

"Did you have a swim in the Rasa pool while we were away, Fiona?" asked Pippa.

"No. I got too engrossed in the crossword."

"Lie for a while, pet, before you have a swim. Let your meal get down," warned Charles.

At about two-thirty, Fiona declared herself ready to cool off with a swim and Pippa went with her to the Garden Wing pool, Charles declaring that he wanted to continue with the crossword.

"I haven't got that clue either," he said, "and another one too."

He was smiling like a cat who'd stolen the family's fish dinner when they returned.

"OK, you've finished the crossword," said Fiona, laughing, good-naturedly.

"Think of Daisy."

"Daisy who?"

"Daisy who was proposed to."

Fiona sat for a while then gave in.

"You win! Give me the answer."

"Daisy, Daisy, give me your answer do…"

"…Bicycle!"

Pippa did not understand so Charles explained to her about the man proposing marriage to his girlfriend Daisy and telling her that he could only afford a bicycle - a bicycle "built for two" and saying that he was "halfcrazy" with love for her.

"So he was the "half mad proposer" in the clue and the vehicle is the bicycle. Get it?"

Pippa declared that she had indeed 'got it'.

At three o'clock, they went up to the Rasa lounge for afternoon tea. There was no sign of the Whites or Wai Lee and her parents but they waved over to Jean Grant and Annabelle Kilbride on the other side of the lounge. Having decided on what they wanted on their way there, Fiona asked Leong Ping for a plate of scones only and he brought them four each instead of two. Luckily they were small. Pippa had decided to try an unusual tea and asked for orange pekoe which was on the afternoon tea menu, Charles and Fiona settling for lattes.

When they had finished, they went back to their loungers and all three read contentedly until it was time to go back to the room to shower and change. After her shower, Pippa fell asleep on her bed. Charles found that there was some golf on TV and Fiona went down to the business centre to email a friend, after washing her hair.

They met up with the Whites in the lounge for drinks at six o'clock. Hope had written a short list of things for Pippa to take and she handed it over.

"We'll take our smallest suitcase and put everything into that," she said. "Now we'll see you in the lounge at eight o'clock as the hired car is being brought to the hotel then."

"I'll see that she's up in time," said Charles, "and I'll come down to see you all off."

They parted company after that, the Whites declaring their intention of going to Gurney Drive hawkers' stalls. Charles asked the doorman, who was Sugu once again, to get them a taxi and when it came, asked to be taken to the Park Royal Hotel.

It was only a short drive. The taxi driver offered to come back for them but having seen how short a journey it was, Fiona said she would like to walk back through the street stalls and Pippa seconded that.

The restaurant, Tiffins, was upstairs and they were shown to a table at a window. As they waited for their meal, they were treated to a spectacular sunset as the glowing orb slid over the horizon in a blaze of orange and red. Charles had brought his camera and took several pictures.

While they were eating their main course, a young man sat down at the piano near them and began playing softly. Their waiter came up and told them that they could make a request for their favourite songs.

"Have you got a favourite song, Dad?" asked Pippa.

"Yes. I like Kenny Rogers singing, "The Coward of the County". Will I ask for that one?"

Charles went over to the pianist and came back.

"He asked me what country in the UK I was from," he said.

The pianist played the Kenny Roger's song extremely well then he paused before giving a rendition of, "I Belong to Glasgow".

Pippa was delighted and clapped loudly when he was finished. A man sitting on the other side of the room, got up and spoke to the pianist and they heard the familiar tune of, "Land of Hope and Glory".

Fiona and Charles laughed heartily as did the man and they had to explain to Pippa that the man was obviously English.

The bill arrived, showing that the meal had been the most expensive they had eaten so far but they all agreed that it had been superb. The waiter seemed delighted with the extra they left for him even though the usual 10% service charge and 5% government tax had been added to the bill.

They walked back through the markets. Pippa persuaded her Dad to buy her another DVD and a pair of shocking pink flip flops, while Fiona bought a handbag, a fake designer one. She was tempted to buy perfume but Hope had told her that the fake perfumes were useless, the scent hardly lasting at all so she managed to walk past and ignore the woman trying to encourage her to buy.

A quick coffee for the two adults and a lemonade for Pippa and they were ready for bed after Fiona had packed Pippa's clothes into a carrier bag to be transferred into the Whites' suitcase in the morning.

CHAPTER 15

"Now Jean, I have to ask you this so let's get it over with right away."

Charles had seen Pippa off at 8am, ensconced in the back of a black Mercedes with Nancy. He had, at the last minute, decided to give her the camera and reminded her to take lots of pictures to show him and Fiona when she got back in three days' time. He had waved until the car turned the corner, then gone back to their room where he had found Fiona stirring sleepily. They had made love, unhurriedly, secure in the knowledge that they would not be interrupted by Pippa, then had washed, dressed and had breakfast in The Spice Market. Charles had suggested room service but Fiona had reminded him that Pippa had still not experienced that and they agreed that they should wait till she was back.

Coming back to the room, he had rung Jean Grant and was now seated across from her at the desk in their allocated room, 1207, on the second floor of the Garden Wing.

At his opening statement, Jean looked apprehensive but Charles smiled at her and she physically relaxed into her chair.

"I know Alan was a bit of a bully. We all heard him with the staff but did he also bully you?"

"Yes he did bully me, verbally and I'm sorry to say, physically," Mrs Grant replied. She touched her cheek just below her left eye.

"I noticed a bruise under your eye when we saw you on the Emirates' flight from Glasgow," he said, gently. "Had he hit you often?"

"No, not often, just when he'd had too much to drink and I annoyed him. I got wise to that and made sure that I didn't say anything controversial when he was drunk. The main trouble was that I had to drive him home when he'd drunk a lot and he found my driving too easy to criticise. I used to retaliate but learned not to."

"Did you never think of reporting him to the police?"

"What could they have done, Charles? It would only have inflamed him even more."

"Was he always abusive?"

"Oh, no. The man I married was kind and considerate, if rather distant at times. He became a bit of a dictator when the children were growing up. His mother confided in me that his father had been very much the boss in their household and I think Alan became like his father. I suppose I became a victim when I gave up work and never went back so I relied on his wage and that gave him power over me."

"Did you not want to go back to...what was your job?"

"I was a teacher at our local comprehensive. I taught English and yes I did want to go back but Alan kept persuading me not to and in the end, I grew away from it and lost my independence."

"Did he hit the children?"

"He smacked them both when they were wee but not hard. It was later that he became quite violent towards Peter, though not Denise. She stood up to him and I think he admired her for that. They both left home as soon as possible and I think then that I bore the brunt of his quick temper."

"And the last time he was violent towards you was...?"

"...a few days before we came away. I was collecting him from a function in town and I scraped the car going into the garage when we got home. He punched me in the face."

"Have you told DCI Hussain this?"

"No. He hasn't asked me if Alan was violent towards me. The bruise has gone now as you can see."

"Is there anyone else who had reason to hate your husband? "

"Back home there were a number of folk but not here, Charles, not here."

Jean slumped down in her chair as if someone had slit her open and let her stuffing out. Charles went to the mini bar and took out the miniature brandy which he knew would be there. He unscrewed the top and poured the contents into one of the glasses provided in the room. She drank the amber liquid gratefully and some colour came back into her thin cheeks.

"Who are these people at home?" he asked gently.

"Well, he sacked his accountant, Phil Soames, about seven months ago. Alan's secretary told me that at the firm's annual dinner in December."

"Why did he sack him?"

"Phil had borrowed some money from the company to pay for his wife's private medical treatment."

"Mr Soames could hardly hate the man who sacked him for theft, surely!"

"He had promised to repay the money. He had been with Alan for years, in fact they were at school together."

"So he hated your husband for not letting him off with stealing from the firm?"

"There was more to it than that. Alan sacked him and Ellen Soames died. Phil blamed Alan, said it was the scandal and the thought of them being financially ruined which finally killed his wife."

"Right. Anybody else?"

"Alan also sacked his ex-partner, well didn't sack him, bought him out."

"How did that come about?"

"Louise, Bill's wife told me. We had been really close friends, the four of us - holidays together that kind of thing. She told me that Alan had blamed Bill for loss in production. He told Bill he wanted him out but for old times' sake he would buy him out. The money didn't last long. Bill started drinking heavily and couldn't get another job. Louise said that Alan wouldn't give him a reference. Louise got a job, I think. We lost touch."

"So we have three people back home who probably hated your husband?"

"Four if you count my son," she whispered.

"For bullying him?" asked Charles.

"Yes that and he hated Alan because Alan had made Peter afraid to stand up to him. Peter has always felt inadequate. He has refused to see Alan since he left home."

"Which was when?"

"He stayed till he left university and found a job. Denise left while at university. She got two jobs while she studied and shared a tiny flat with a friend. Pete now wishes that he had stood up to his father earlier. He hated Alan for making him fear him."

"How do your son and daughter get on?"

"Denise tried to stand up for Pete, took the blame when she could. Although she wasn't abused, she had no love for Alan either. They recently decided to share a flat."

"Could she have felt murderous towards her father?"

"She often told him he'd be found dead with a knife in his back one day...."

Her hand flew to her mouth.

"...It was only said in anger. She wouldn't mean it...would she?"

The last two words came out as a whisper. She took another sip of the brandy.

"Now are you sure there's nobody else?"

"Nobody that I know of but Alan had some affairs over the years. I don't know who with, though I suspected quite recently that one fling was with his secretary. I was grateful if you must know, as it stopped him making love to me. If you call what he began doing to me, making love," she added bitterly.

"Sorry to be personal, Jean, but I have to know the worst that DCI Hussain can find out. What did your husband do to you at these times?"

Jean Grant rose and walked to the window where she stood with her back to Charles.

"He made me take him in my mouth. Sometimes that was enough but at other times he used his belt on me. He had a large mirror put up in the bedroom and forced me to watch him taking me from behind."

"Buggery?"

"Yes."

"Recently?"

"I think he must have finished the current affair because he ordered me back to our bedroom about two weeks ago and the abuse started up again."

"Did your children know about this?"

"How could I tell my son and daughter such things?"

Charles had been writing on the notepaper he had found in the desk drawer.

"Right, so we have a bought-off, bankrupt, ex-partner; his wife; a sacked accountant; your son, your daughter and perhaps at least one jilted lover."

"Yes but all at home, Charles. Not here," she said, as she had earlier.

Charles rose to join her at the window. She turned to face him.

"Jean. This is your last chance to tell me and I'm sure a court would be lenient with you. Did you murder your husband?"

"No, Charles. I did not."

"I suggest that you tell the police here what you have told me..."

"...I'm not going to incriminate my son and daughter, and Bill and Louise and Phil Soames have suffered enough."

"Well in that case, you'll just have to hope that the police close the case through lack of evidence."

"You won't tell them what I've told you?"

"Luckily, I'm sure they won't ask me, as they hopefully won't find out that you've spoken to me but of course if by any chance they do ask me, I can't lie to them."

"I understand that," she replied. "But I won't be telling them I've talked to you and Mr Grafton has no reason to tell them, has he?"

She seemed calm again.

"So what do you want from me, Jean?"

"Help to prove that I couldn't have killed Alan, I suppose."

"OK. You'll need to get names of staff who were in the lounge that afternoon and saw you having afternoon tea or coffee. See if anyone at the poolside saw you leave with Annabelle. Offer the police the clothes you were wearing - I expect they'll ask for those soon anyway."

"It was Mr Ping who served us tea and the sergeant came with me to my room after they'd questioned me at the Dr's. He asked me to change my clothes and he took away the ones I'd been wearing. Why?"

"Well with the towel covering the wounds, it's unlikely that the murderer would be splattered with blood but there's a chance, so you need them to know that there is no blood on the clothes you wore that day."

"There couldn't be blood unless I accidentally touched the towel when I discovered him."

"Did you cover Mr Grant with a towel before you left?"

"No."

"Did the staff not see you leave the pool?"

"I don't know. I didn't speak to any of them. Will the police not question the staff at the pool?"

"They should but if they're convinced that you are the only suspect, they might not try too hard to find witnesses for you. I'll ask though. Now you won't mind me trying to find out the whereabouts of ..." He looked at the paper he had written on... "Phil Soames and Bill and Louise - what's their surname please?"

"Elliott, with two ts. Will you have to tell the police if you find out that they were away from home at the time of the murder?"

"I can't answer that. It'll depend on the circumstances. I couldn't let you be accused if I thought there was any chance that someone else did it, could I?"

"I don't know then whether I should give you the addresses."

"I can quite easily find them out you know. I have staff at home who could get the addresses for me."

She looked stricken.

"I also need those of your son and daughter... and also the address of the company."

"I thought that you would want Pete and Denise's address so I brought my handbag, luckily."

She felt in her black bag and brought out a tartan - covered address book. Charles wrote down what she told him.

"I felt really disloyal to my profession, telling her that the police might not try too hard to prove her innocent, Fiona," Charles told her when he had met up with her in the grounds.

"I like to think of police as trustworthy and honest but somehow I don't like the DCI or his sergeant," he added.

"Don't feel guilty, Charles," comforted Fiona. "I was speaking to Sean Grafton while you were away and he has a friend who was an ambassador here and he said a lot of the police are corrupt."

"As some are in Scotland, love, unfortunately."

"So what will you do now?"

"Well, Jean gave me names of some possible candidates for wanting Alan dead, so I'm going to phone the team at home and ask them to try to find out if any of them are out of the country. Not in police time, of course. Drat! I forgot to ask the name of Grant's current secretary!"

"Oh love, that's risky. What if one of them lets slip something and Knox finds out?"

Fiona forehead was wrinkled, a sure sign that she was anxious.

"I'm only asking if these folk are at home and I'll emphasise that it's to be done out with work time."

"OK. When will you phone?"

Charles looked at his watch. It was just after midday.

"It would be too late now to phone the station but maybe that's as well. Do you have any of their private numbers, Fiona?"

Fiona went off upstairs to get her diary and came back to announce that she had Salma's home number as she had rung her at home recently when her mother had died.

"I don't have Penny's or Frank's," she said, apologetically.

"Well that's at least one. Not your fault. I don't have any, not here. I do have all their private numbers at home."

Armed with Salma's number, Charles went off to their room. It took him a few minutes to find out the number to use from Penang but he did find it and dialled his sergeant's number.

"632 1251," said a young girl's voice."

"Hello. Is your sister Salma in please?"

"Yes, who's calling?"

"It's Mr Davenport, her boss."

The phone was put down and he could hear voices in the background. Then the receiver was lifted.

"Sir? Is something wrong? Are you home?"

Salma sounded anxious.

Charles put her mind at rest, then told her what he wanted her to find out for him.

"All I want to know is whether these people are in Scotland right now. No more."

"Are you on a job over there, Sir?"

"No I'm not. This it totally unofficial so I'd be grateful if you kept it to yourself, Salma. Don't even tell Frank or Penny."

"Well, that should be easy as they were seconded to other departments almost as soon as you left, Sir. I'm on my own in our department, a kind of skeleton staff," she laughed. "I haven't seen either of them this week."

"Right then, try and find out but don't let it interfere with your day to day work, OK?"

He dictated the addresses he had and there was silence as she wrote them down.

"Ok Sir. Do you want me to e-mail, or phone when I have results?"

"Phone the hotel around...7.30a.m, from home. That will be 2.30 in the afternoon here and

I'll make sure I'm in the room then from now on. Here's the hotel number. Just ask for Mr Davenport in room 2246. Have you got that?"

Charles hung up. Of the three stay-at-home team, Salma was the one he thought he could trust most. She was quiet and not a gossip and it seemed as if she was not likely to see the other two.

He went back down to the gardens and told Fiona.

"I'd have chosen Salma if I'd had a choice," she said. "She's competent and discreet."

They went for a swim in the Rasa pool, found the water too hot and went across to the other pool to cool off there. The pool was quite busy so they did not stay in for long. Coming back, they decided to lie for a while to dry off, then have lunch as usual at the Penang Bar. Fiona had finished the crossword and remarked that they had not had much of a competition recently, either one or other of them getting it done before the other began. She picked up her book. It was called "The Lovely Bones" and was about a girl who had been murdered and her body hidden. The book was telling of her thoughts - unusual but enjoyable all the same, she told Charles.

"I wanted to get it read before I started on my Anne Perry crime novels. Caroline recommended it and gave me her copy, so I thought I'd better read it first."

"I don't imagine that Pippa will guess the murderer or murderers in her Agatha Christie book," she laughed.

"Yes, thanks for stopping me from giving part of the game away," he replied.

After lunch they sat back on their loungers. Charles fell asleep though he denied this when Fiona teased him about it later. They went for afternoon tea at 3pm and went back down to the gardens around 4. This time it was Fiona who dozed off and Charles woke her to tell her he had finished the crossword without her help. Something about his demeanour made her suspicious so she quizzed him and he admitted to cheating by looking at her paper to get his last two clues.

"You're a cheat, Charles Davenport! What did you say about corrupt police?" she said with a twinkle in her eye. He flicked his towel at her and when she got up to get out of his reach, he grabbed her hand and ran off towards the back stairs. In their room, they collapsed giggling like two schoolchildren on her bed and minutes later they were undressed and in each other's arms.

Afterwards, both fell asleep. Fiona was first to wake up. She looked at her watch and shrieked, "Wake up, Charles. It's after six o'clock. We're missing our free drinks!"

They hurriedly got showered and dressed and made it to the lounge in half an hour.

They saw no one they knew.

"I'm glad that Jean Grant isn't here. I don't want to talk shop tonight," said Charles. "Where will we go to eat?"

"I fancy the Chinese place again," said Fiona. "Those sizzling prawns were wonderful."

Charles agreed and added that they had better not go anywhere new without his daughter. They were shown to a secluded table at the pool and spent a leisurely couple of hours there, even having a dessert of pineapple fritters this time. They strolled back to the hotel and went into the lounge for coffee, deciding to treat themselves to a brandy each as neither was tired after their sleep in the afternoon.

Sean Grafton found them there when he went off duty at eleven.

"Did you get a chance to talk to Mrs Grant?" he asked Charles.

"Yes I did."

"Can you tell me anything?"

"Well under normal circumstances I wouldn't tell you a thing," laughed Charles. "But these circumstances are anything but normal."

"Look, don't start now. Tell you what. It's my day off tomorrow. I'll send my driver for you at

7pm. He'll bring you to my house and I'll do a BBQ for us and you can tell me then. That will make it totally unofficial for both of us. How about that?"

Charles agreed.

CHAPTER 16

Promptly at seven o'clock, a silver grey BMW drove up to the Rasa Wing entrance and a swarthy, heavily-built man got out. The doorman, a small man whose name tag told them he was Amin, welcomed the man.

"Hi, Ishmael. Who are you looking for tonight?"

Charles walked forward and introduced himself.

"I think he might be looking for me. I'm Charles Davenport. Fiona is just in the ladies' room. She won't be long."

Ishmael put out a large hand which Charles shook. Fiona joined them and all three said cheerio to Amin and got into the lovely car. The journey took them past the now familiar McDonalds' landmark, not far past, into an area which Ishmael said was called Bagan which they remembered from their bus journey. From there it was only minutes till he pulled up outside a large house. He pressed his key fob and the gates opened automatically, letting Ishmael drive into a roomy courtyard.

Fiona got out first, leaving Charles to tip Ishmael who said that he would be returning for them. As he reversed the car, the front door opened and two dogs rushed out, followed by Sean Grafton in shorts and polo shirt.

"Hi there, come along in. Hope you don't mind dogs. They're very friendly. Ishmael is going home but will bring you to the hotel whenever you want to leave.

"Why does everyone here say "bring" instead of "take"?" asked Fiona, sounding puzzled.

"I know. It confused me at first but now I obviously say it too," Sean laughed.

Charles shook his hand and handed him a bottle of red wine which he had bought locally in Batu Feringgi. The first thing he noticed in the hallway was an enormous wine rack full of bottles and he laughed.

"Talk about bringing coal to Newcastle!"

Fiona was patting the dogs. One was a golden retriever and the other a smaller dog which looked a bit like a golden spaniel but which Sean told her was a cross between a spaniel and a spitz. Being both the same colour made them look like father and daughter, she thought, then discovered her mistake.

"The big boy is Habibi and the wee fellow is Lucky," Sean informed them, leading them out of the hall, through a sitting area and out again into the pool area where a table was beautifully set for three. A young woman came out and was introduced as Marianna. She went back inside and the three of them sat down in armchairs, arranged facing the pool which was lit up.

"Marianna's my treasure from The Philippines," said Sean. "She looks after me and my house, though this house is one which Shangri-la rents for me, so it's not really mine."

"Do you not have a home then, Sean?" asked Fiona curiously.

"I have a home in Ireland and a house which I bought in Bali. The last manager lived nearer the hotel but it wasn't suitable for my boys, having only a small garden."

He bent to pat Habibi who had sat down beside him, Lucky having lost interest and gone to ferret in the bushes which fringed the pool.

"Are the dogs your only family?" Fiona asked.

"I have a brother and sister in Ireland and four nephews and nieces there too, but I'm not married if that's what you mean. Is Pippa your only daughter?"

"Pippa is Charles's daughter, not mine. We aren't married."

She blushed as she always did when embarrassed and Charles took her hand.

"Fiona"s my treasure at work and outside work. I'm divorced from Pippa's mother, amicably divorced I'm happy to say. Pippa's my only child."

"So you're a policewoman, Fiona?"

"Yes, for my sins."

"Detective Sergeant Macdonald, to give her her full title," said Charles, sounding proud.

Sean rose to get them drinks.

"If I'm having a large number of guests at my house, I bring in one of the waiters. He works in The Feringgi Grill in the mornings. You may have met him. His name's Specially. He is always discreet and never tells stories of what is said or done here."

"Specially! How lovely and how unusual. I haven't seen anyone of that name yet. We know Katherine and Govan, the one who offered Pippa the pastries...maybe I shouldn't have told you that Sean," Fiona said.

"Don't worry. The staff are encouraged to do everything they can to make our guests happy," Sean reassured her. "We have cards at reception which we call "extra-mile cards" and guests can fill them in for any member of staff who goes out of his or her way for them. The only trouble is that guests fill them in saying that a member of staff has been pleasant and helpful when that is their job, not an added extra."

He left them. Lucky trotted round the pool and went into the house after him but Habibi stayed where he was, under Sean's seat.

"Some pad", Charles commented. "I love the pool. Wonder what the rest of the house is like."

Sean returned with a whisky and water for Charles and a gin and tonic for Fiona. He had poured himself a glass of white wine.

"I was saying that you have a lovely house," repeated Charles.

"Come on and I'll show you round the rest of it."

Sean took them round the ground floor with its three kitchens, two lounge areas and four bedrooms.

"One of these is Marianna's. There's a maid's room next to one of the kitchens and a toilet with a hole in the floor," he grinned. "She was disgusted when the man showing us round pointed it out as her room. I use another bedroom as my study and the others are storage rooms really. Come on upstairs."

The staircase was impressive and was made of lovely wood. It curved round the hallway beneath and led to a landing which led off to three more bedrooms, two sharing a shower and toilet room and the other a massive room with ensuite which was Sean's bedroom.

They thanked him for,"the tour", as Charles put it and were soon back outside, sipping their drinks.

Talk, as they expected, turned to the murder of Alan Grant. Charles told Sean that Mrs Grant had indeed asked him to do some sleuthing for her, though she understood that it would have to be done without the knowledge of the local police.

"I've asked my sergeant at home to find out where some people who had reason to, shall we say, dislike, Alan were at the time of the murder. It seems hardly likely that it was a local here as the Grants were not sitting at the pool laden with expensive jewellery and although he already had guests who disliked him, they merely took evasive action when they saw him coming."

"Will the local police not investigate people at home, Charles?" asked Sean.

"Hopefully they will but according to Jean Grant, they seem to have almost decided already that she is the murderess. Have you ever had a murder at any of your last hotels, Sean?"

"No, never, thankfully. The worst thing to happen here was two people coming off a plane which had on board someone suspected of having swine flu!"

"What did you do?" asked Fiona.

"I quarantined them in their room for three days. They had room service and we provided them with DVDs and CDs... all free of course. Luckily they were a honeymoon couple so they were quite happy to be in their room all day. Then we got our doctor in and he declared them free of the virus and they were able to get on with their holiday."

It was getting dark now and insect noises came from the undergrowth. Fiona sprayed herself with Jungle Formula having realised that this was the time when she got bitten most. Charles had had only one bite, then, as he said, they were sick and passed on the message to their pals.

"Here comes Marianna with our BBQ ingredients," said Sean and his maid came into view carrying a tray laden with food. Sean got up to take it from her and excused himself saying that he liked to do the next part himself. They heard the sizzling as meat and fish were cooked and he came across with plates of prawns, sausages, chops, steaks and another fish which he said was garoupa.

"That's the big one we saw in, 'The End of the World' restaurant," exclaimed Fiona.

"Tuck in but leave room for some bacon - pork bacon," he added.

Charles looked delighted as he had found the chicken bacon and beef bacon at the hotel quite tasteless. He asked Sean about this.

"My predecessor had the hotel ethnically cleansed," was the reply. "Pork bacon years ago was on display in the breakfast outlets, then it was available but only if asked for, then the Muslim workers asked for it to be banned altogether so the hotel was cleansed and now bacon is not on offer but of course the Chinese love it so you can still buy it in the markets. I thought you might be missing it, so I bought some today."

"You did the shopping?" exclaimed Fiona.

"Yes, I enjoy the markets, except perhaps the chicken area as you can hear the live ones squawking."

"Ugh. I'd hate that. I think I'd be vegetarian if I had to kill my own meat," Fiona shuddered.

They tucked in and ate heartily, washing their food down with expensive red and white wine. The white wine was Cloudy Bay which they had seen on the wine menu in the Feringgi Grill.

"I sometimes buy Oyster Bay," said Charles. "When it's on offer in the supermarket but this is even smoother."

Talk returned to the murder. Sean asked if Charles would keep him up to date with his enquiries and Charles said he was happy to do this though under normal circumstances if he had been the DCI in charge, he could not have done it.

"I would never have been rude to you as it appears Hussain and his side-kick have been but I wouldn't have given you details either."

"Do you think Mrs Grant killed her husband?" Sean asked as the dessert dishes were brought to the table.

"My gut instinct tells me she didn't..."

"...and why would she ask Charles for help if she was guilty, unless that was a double bluff?" said Fiona.

"So if it wasn't her and it wasn't a thief and it wasn't a cheesed-off guest, then someone else from home was here or nearby?" queried the manager.

"Those are my thoughts," agreed Charles. "Though why come all this way to kill him!"

"Maybe for that reason, Charles, to throw the police off the scent," suggested Fiona.

"Or to throw blame on Mrs Grant," said Sean.

"A bit cruel, given her nice nature. She hasn't hurt any of them, I'm sure," said Fiona

"Lucky that she had an alibi then, with Annabelle Kilbride", Charles added.

"This dessert is fantastic, Sean. Don't tell me you made this yourself."

Fiona had been delving into the creamy meringue and fruit concoction.

"I cheat with desserts and have some brought from the hotel. Ishmael brings them in the car along with the guests. I pay for them, just as I pay Ishmael for our- of -hours' work and Specially for being wine-waiter on occasion."

About half an hour later, Marianna came out to tell them that Ishmael had arrived. It had been a lovely evening and Charles voiced his only disappointment.

"Pippa will be so sorry that she missed seeing the dogs."

"Are you still here next Sunday?" asked Sean.

"Yes we go home on the following Tuesday," answered Charles.

"Well, I'll bring them to the hotel on my day off...better still why don't I invite you for a swim here on Sunday. Yes, come next Sunday. It's Ishmael's day off but you could get a taxi or risk the local bus which passes the foot of this road."

Thanking him again for his hospitality, Charles and Fiona went out to the courtyard. They were back at the hotel just before 11.45.

"Our latest night yet, love," said Charles as they walked arm in arm through the hotel to their room.

CHAPTER 17

They woke up in the same bed just after nine o'clock. Charles's arms were round Fiona and he kissed her gently, enjoying the way she made little murmuring noises as she surfaced from sleep.

"Time for work, Miss Macdonald!" he said sternly.

"Wha...what's the time?"

She sat bolt upright in bed then hastily pulled the sheet up to cover her breasts.

"Too late, madam. I've seen them," he teased her.

Realising where she was, Fiona lay back down and Charles stroked one breast, feeling the nipple harden, then taking the other one between his teeth and nibbling it. She moaned and felt for his hardness.

An hour later, Fiona was scurrying about getting dressed in yellow shorts and white tee-shirt on top of her white bikini and Charles was singing in the shower.

"Hurry up, Charles. Breakfast stops at 10.30!" she called to him.

"We're becoming like a honeymoon couple," he said, as they hurried along the gym corridor.

The Grill was almost empty and they were shown to a table with a lovely view out over the spa village.

"Where is Miss Pippa?" Safari asked and they told him.

"No need for pastries today, Safari," said Fiona.

Over breakfast, they discussed what they should do that day and decided that they would go to Fort Cornwallis as although it was historically interesting for them, it was not something that Pippa would mind missing. At reception, they asked Jill the best way to get there and she said by taxi.

"You could take this map and walk back to The Traders' Hotel and get the hotel bus back," she suggested, handing them a colourful leaflet. They decided to do this and Jaz phoned for the taxi.

"Jaz. What's that short for?" Fiona asked the smiling young man.

"Jazmizzen," he said.

"We were told that you knew some Scottish words, Jaz," said Charles.

The man grinned.

"It's a braw, bricht moonlicht nicht tonicht," he chanted in an almost perfect Scottish accent.

"That's fantastic!" Fiona sounded amazed.

Amin came up and added, "Good morning quinie; good morning loon."

"Cockaleekie soup," Jaz said.

"How on earth did you learn all this?" asked Charles.

"A returnee guest from Glasgow taught us," Jaz informed them.

"We are only to say quinie and loon to people who come from Aberdeen," Amin added.

"I say, "right" to his wife," Jaz told them, sounding Glaswegian as he said the word. "She is always saying it and we have a good laugh."

"I'll give you a new one to try out on them the next time they come back," said Charles, adding, "There's a wee moose loose aboot the hoose."

Both young men repeated it after him, Jaz copying the accent skilfully.

"What does it mean?" asked Amin.

"There's a small mouse running about the house," laughed Charles.

"Tikus is mouse or rat in Bahasa," said Amin. "There's an area on the way to Georgetown called Pilau Tikus."

At this point, Jaz moved to open the door and Gopal came in.

"Have you got your new taxi yet?" asked Jaz, informing Charles and Fiona that Gopal was buying a people carrier.

"I get it next week, man."

Jill came across from the reception desk and told Gopal that the guests wanted to go to Fort Cornwallis but just to leave them there as they had a map and wanted to walk back to The Traders' Hotel. She had written them out two tickets for the bus home and handed them to Charles.

Fort Cornwallis was historically interesting with the large canons facing the sea and a small museum where, among other things, they read that what was now a girls' school on the outskirts of Georgetown, had been a prisoner of war camp. They looked at their map and started out, using the tall Komtar as their landmark. Lots of the streets had Scottish names, Farquar Street for example, and they laughed out loud when they passed a temple in whose grounds there was a notice saying, "Please do not feed the pigeon."

"Only one pigeon! I wonder what it's done to have to go unfed," remarked Charles.

There were lots of little shops. The owners called out to them to come in but accepted it good-naturedly when the pair walked on. They had almost reached Komtar, when they came to a three-storeyed shop which sold only materials and Fiona dragged Charles in. She came out with enough material to have a tunic blouse made for herself. It was in vivid colours, greens, blues and yellows and very inexpensive.

"I'll get it made up at that Parmenand shop across from the hotel," she said.

A few streets later, they arrived at Komtar with its numerous steps leading up to the first level. Fiona took pity on Charles and told him that she did not want to visit the numerous levels of shops and they turned the corner and found themselves outside The Traders' Hotel, a Shangri-la, city hotel.

"Are you ready for a drink, love?" asked Charles and when Fiona said that she was, they went into the hotel where they discovered that they could transfer the bill to The Rasa Sayang. They had about half an hour till the hotel shuttle bus arrived, so decided on a Tiger beer each.

The bus was about three-quarters full and Charles recognised some of the people who putted and remembered that this was a non-putting day. The journey took about forty minutes, there being a stops at one of the malls. They picked up another dozen or so guests, making the bus full apart from one seat in the middle.

They arrived at The Rasa Sayang at 2.20 and Charles, reminding Fiona that he had told Salma that he would be in the room at 2.30, hurried ahead of her, with her trotting along to catch him up. The phone was ringing as he inserted his card key and he ran across to the desk and picked up the receiver. Fiona heard him say, "Hello Salma.

What have you got for me?" before she went into the bathroom and shut the door. She had a quick shower, feeling sticky after the walk in the burning sun. The bus had aircon but it had not cooled her off much. She came out to find that Charles had changed out of his long trousers into shorts.

"What did Salma say?"

"She's only managed to find out about the Elliotts, that's the man who was a partner till he was bought out. There was no one in at their flat in Pollokshields but the woman across the landing was in and told Salma that they were on holiday in Cornwall. Salma asked how she knew this and the woman said that they had come to tell her.

She told Salma that she was surprised as they'd been quite snooty, especially Mrs Elliott. The neighbour, a Mrs Scott, had found out that they used to live in a big, detached house in Bearsden. She told Salma they must have come down in the world. She thought that maybe they wanted her to water plants or something but they didn't ask her to do anything, just told her where they were going but left no telephone number or address. The only other thing they volunteered was that they were going with another couple who had been workmates of Mr Elliott."

"Odd that they were so forthcoming after being standoffish," remarked Fiona.

"My thoughts entirely, love," said Charles. "It's almost as if they thought that someone would come asking."

"Not really any way we can find out if they really are in Cornwall, is there?"

"I suppose we can get Sean to find out if there are any Elliotts in The Rasa Sayang..."

"...or Golden Sands, or The Park Royal, or any of the other hotels along the strip," said Fiona, pessimistically, adding that she did not think that they would register under their own name if they were indeed the murderers of Alan Grant.

"I'll ask Sean anyway. He'll be glad of something positive to do, I imagine," grimaced Charles. "Let's go down for afternoon tea."

They thanked Jill for her map and told her that they had found their way easily and enquired if the manager was available.

"I'll ask his secretary, Shirley," Jill said, picking up the phone.

They wandered over to Jaz who met them with his rendition of the 'moose' and Jill came across to say that Mr Grafton would meet them in the lounge in about ten minutes. In the end it was about twenty minutes and they were tucking into the scone section of their cake stand when he arrived and sat down beside them. He agreed to find out if there were any Elliotts in either of the Shangri-la Hotels, adding that it would be more difficult to find out in the other hotels although he did know someone in The Park Royal.

"Leave it with me and I'll get back to you as soon as possible," he said.

CHAPTER 18

"No Elliotts here or in The Golden Sands and I also found none in Traders either."

Sean Grafton had come up to the Grill room while they were having breakfast. He now sat at their table. A member of staff had brought him a coffee.

"Could they be in a hotel under an assumed name?" asked Charles.

"Not a bona fide hotel like this one and the others on the Batu Ferniggi strip, though they might get away with it in a downtown flea pit," Sean said, rather dejectedly.

"As you know, we ask for your passport the day you arrive and you fill out a form with your address on it too."

"Yes. I remember we both had to do that," said Fiona and Charles nodded in agreement.

"I should have asked you to find out about a Phil Soames too although Salma might find out that he's been at home all the time. I know you're a busy man so don't bother about him till I let you know one way or the other," Charles sounded apologetic.

Sean Grafton agreed, finished off his coffee and left, after making a firm date with them for the following Sunday.

"Shirley, my secretary will confirm it in writing," he said.

Charles and Fiona opted for a quiet day at the Rasa pool and found two loungers under a large umbrella further into the garden that Charles had been in on the afternoon of the murder. Now that Alan Grant was no longer around to bore them, people had chosen to lie here again and Charles said hello to the two couples who had spoken to him a few evenings ago, the Bennetts and the Jamiesons. Jack Bennett asked if the police were any further forward and Charles gave his stock response.

"I was told to butt out."

"I've never been questioned by the police before," Jack stated, "but I didn't realise it would be so formal and a bit scary, if I'm honest. The man, a sergeant I think, seemed to think I was lying to him when I said we had seen nothing, not even been by the pool."

"I was quite scared too. Would police back home make you feel like that?" asked Sylvia.

"Not my staff," said Charles. "I'm Charles Davenport by the way and this is Fiona. You told me your names the other evening but I didn't return the compliment as the DCI came looking for me. If it's any comfort, I was made to feel like a naughty child for trying to be helpful at the pool that day."

"So you really did see nothing?" asked Fiona.

"Well I saw the two ladies walking away from the pool area and I said to my wife that I was glad the soul had found a friend. Sylvia said she had seen them do the same the day before. They were obviously having afternoon tea together."

"They didn't stay away for long that day either. She was probably scared he would wake up and give her hell for going away without his permission," laughed Lorna Jamieson.

"I read in a detective story that all the hotel guests were forbidden to leave. Could that happen to us, Charles?" asked Mike Jamieson. "Not that I'd mind an extra week here but no doubt the insurance company wouldn't cover our costs. Probably call murder an act of God!"

"At least they couldn't call it a known condition," laughed Sylvia. "We got caught out on that one two years ago when we cancelled a holiday to Tenerife as I took a bout of anxiety. Then when I tried to mention it the next time I took out insurance, the girl said they couldn't cover me for that or depression."

Fiona slipped away from the group and went into the pool. She burned quite easily and had not used her suntan oil yet, having decided to leave it till after her swim. Even the short chat had made her shoulders red. Charles soon joined her.

"No witnesses then?" Fiona asked him.

"No, but unsolicited proof that Jean Grant and another woman did leave the pool area around afternoon tea time There was nobody in the wee garden part except Alan Grant and myself and those four only saw Jean Grant leave with Annabelle Kilbride. I vaguely remember other loungers being in use and some couples were lying reading, I think."

"There's another entrance to the wee garden part," said Fiona. "Look!"

She pointed to the top of the pool.

"I suppose one of those couples could have gone round that way, murdered Mr Grant and simply slipped back to their lounger."

"They could even have showered in that shower there."

It was Charles's turn to point.

"That makes more sense than someone coming into the pool area in full view of anybody who could have been watching and gone into the garden, knifed Grant and gone back out the same way."

He looked thoughtful.

"If say, one of those couples was the Elliots, they could have seen Jean go off with Annabelle the day before, seen them leave again that day and realised they had time to murder him and go back and lie down on their loungers," Fiona sounded excited.

"That would mean that they had a knife, quite a large one I would think by the size of the wounds, with them just in case. A bit unlikely, surely?"

Charles sounded cynical.

"Well, if they came over to Penang bent on killing him then they would want to be prepared, would they not?" Fiona argued.

"But then why was their name not on the hotel register?"

"Just came here during the day, hoping that no one would challenge them?" posed Fiona.

They swam in silence for a time

Charles got out of the water and went up to the pool counter to ask for a soft drink. Kamerol, the cheery-faced attendant, opened the can for him and handed over a tall glass.

"Kamerol, it wasn't you who called the police on the day of the murder. Where were you that day?" Charles asked him.

"I was there, Sir. I was at the top end of the pool serving drinks to a young couple there when I heard Mrs Grant scream."

"Was there not another couple? Can you remember what they were doing?"

They were sleeping I think. I looked over at them in case they wanted to order something but neither of them said anything. They sat up when Mrs Grant screamed."

"Can you tell me anything about the two couples, Kamerol?"

"The young couple only arrived that day, I think. He was American and she sounded English. The other couple were older and had been coming to the pool for a few days. I'm sorry, Sir. I can't remember their names."

Kamerol looked upset so Charles hastened to reassure him that he had not been expecting him to know their names. He explained to the man that the manager had asked him to do some private investigating and asked him not to tell the police that he had been asking questions.

"I understand, Sir," he said, smiling. "I heard that you were a policeman too."

Fiona came to the counter and Charles asked her if she wanted a drink. She asked for a diet coke.

"One coke light, madam," said Kamerol, handing her a can and a glass.

They took their drinks and walked back to their loungers.

"Kamerol said that one of the couples at the pool that day was older," Charles informed Fiona. "I wonder if they or one of them did commit the murder the way you suggested. It makes sense."

"Rather cool to stay on after committing murder," countered Fiona.

They lay for a while, then sat up and started their crossword, deciding to join forces after some time but still not managing to complete it. They had their usual lunch at the Penang Bar and then went back to the loungers. It was Muru from the Rasa pool counter who came over to collect their glasses.

"Sir, Kamerol was telling me that you asked about who was at the pool the day of the murder."

"Yes, that's right," said Charles, sitting up.

"Well Sir, there was also a single lady. She left just after Mrs Grant came back."

"Did you tell the police, Muru?"

"No, Sir."

Muru looked mulish.

"Why not?"

"They didn't ask me if anyone else had been there and they were rude to me when I said that I had left before the murder was discovered. They suggested that I was trying to avoid doing any work. That's how I know there was another woman. She went out of the pool area just in front of me."

"Do you know who she was, Muru?"

"I'm sorry, no, Sir. She was new to me. I don't remember seeing her before. I wondered if she was from the Garden Wing and had sneaked in for a quick swim. Some guests do that."

"How old would you say she was?" asked Fiona.

"About twenty-five to thirty, madam," Muru said.

He picked up the dirty glasses and the empty can and went off, Charles thanking him for his information.

"So, Fiona, we have two couples, one young and one older and a young woman on her own so there were people who could have committed the murder. I wonder if the police have found this out."

"Not about the young woman on her own anyway. We'll ask Kamerol on the way for afternoon tea whether or not the police questioned him about who was round the pool."

At three o'clock they packed the beach bag, took their towels across to Tony where he was teaching three people to play mah-jong under the trees and made their way to the Rasa pool counter. Kamerol and Muru were standing behind it, folding towels.

"Kamerol, did the police ask you about who was round the pool that afternoon?"

"Yes, they questioned me and Nasrool - that's the boy who called the police for you, Sir. I told them about the two couples."

Fiona and Charles walked up the steps to the hotel. It was hot work in the afternoon heat and they were glad of the cool of the air-conditioned lounge. Once they had ordered tea and coffee, they resumed their conversation about the murder.

"I think the police should know about the woman who left just before the murder was discovered," said Charles. "It's one more person who could be guilty but I can't tell them or they'll know I've been investigating."

They sat silently for a minute or two.

"Rav!" said Fiona.

"What?"

"Can you not see Rav and let him know? He can pretend to have found out somehow."

"Good idea but how can I see him?"

"He's bound to be in the hotel at some time, surely. Ask the boys at the door to let you know if he appears on his own."

Anissa, one of the receptionists came across the lounge towards them.

"Mr Davenport. There was a message left for you from a Salma Din."

She held out a slip of paper.

"Drat, Fiona, we forgot to be in the room at 2.30," Charles said.

He thanked Anissa who went back to her post. He looked at the note.

"I will ring you again at my lunchtime, around 1pm, my time," he read out.

"That's...8pm here. We'll go back to the room after drinks."

"What time are you expecting Pippa back, Charles?"

"Rory wasn't sure but he said early evening. I'm sure he'll bring Pippa to the room if we're not in the lounge."

Agreeing that they had had enough sun for the day, they walked through the hotel to their room. Fiona decided to get some more postcards from the small hotel shop and by the time she got to the room, Charles was in the bath.

"You can scrub my back if you like," he called through the bathroom door.

"Scrub your own back," she laughed. "I'm going to sit in the shade out on the balcony and get these cards written."

"Rotten spoilsport," came the reply.

Clad in his white towelling dressing - gown, he came to join her on the balcony, bringing his book.

At 6pm they went down to the lounge and had some canapés.

"We might not get a meal tonight if we want to get Salma's call," Charles said.

"And if we do, we can have something small or share a meal," agreed Fiona.

They saw no one they knew and left the lounge before 8pm, not wanting to miss Salma's phone call again. On the dot of eight o'clock, she rang, sounding excited.

"Sir, I went to the factory and spoke to the secretary. She's only been there a few weeks and told me that Mr Grant had made some suggestive remarks to her already. She'd mentioned this in the canteen and had been told that she should watch out as he had just broken up from his last affair."

"I don't suppose you got a name?" Charles asked.

"I'm sorry, Sir. This secretary, Mary Graham, felt that being new, she shouldn't ask too many questions. Do you want me to go to the canteen tomorrow and ferret around?"

"Only if it doesn't interfere with your own work and remember, I don't want anyone else to know about this, Salma."

"Any luck with Phil Soames?" mouthed Fiona.

"Salma, did you find out anything about Phil Soames, the ex-accountant?" asked Charles.

"No, Sir. Mary Graham, being new, didn't know anything about him and the new accountant was out of the building. She did suggest that I saw one of the factory workers, an older man called Leonard Brown who'd been there for ages and could probably tell me anything I wanted to know but by that time the factory hooter had gone and I imagined he'd have gone home."

"Well, when you have time, go back and speak to him and if you can manage to go in your lunch time, try the canteen for a woman who might share some gossip with you. Maybe the last secretary left because she'd been having an affair with him and the affair ended."

"If anyone asks me why I'm doing this, Sir, what should I say?"

"Well, I imagine that the news about Grant's murder will have reached home, so just say that you've been asked to find out and hope that they assume by the police over here."

"Yes, Sir. Even the new woman had heard about the murder. She said that Mrs Grant had rung the factory and asked to speak to her husband's new deputy."

Thanking Salma, Charles rang off. He looked worried.

"What's the matter, love?" Fiona asked him.

"I'm just hoping that DCI Hussain doesn't find out from the factory that the Glasgow police have been in questioning them."

"Well, it's done now. No use worrying about something you have no control over," Fiona said, putting her arm round his shoulders.

They went back to the lounge. Jean Grant was sitting by herself. They went up to her.

"No Annabelle tonight?" asked Charles.

"No. She left last night. I thought that the police might refuse to let her go but they simply took her address," said Jean.

"I meant to ask, where was she sitting that day? She wasn't in the pool area, was she?

"No, she had started sitting just outside in the gardens. She found it too hot round the pool, she said."

"You contacted the factory?" asked Charles next, knowing the answer.

"Yes. I thought that David Hamilton, the new deputy should know. I'm afraid I don't even know who Alan will have left everything to. I feel such a fool, not knowing."

Charles reassured her, saying that in his experience this was often the case with a sudden death.

Seeing Leong Ping across the lounge, he left the two women and approached him.

"Leong Ping. Can you remember serving Mrs Grant and another woman on the afternoon of her husband's murder?"

"Yes, Sir. I did serve them. I remember that they were a bit early but I served them anyway. She is a nice woman, Mrs Grant."

Charles thanked him and went back to join Fiona and Jean. Shortly afterwards, the Whites and Pippa arrived back and the talk turned to the Cameron Highlands.

CHAPTER 19

Pippa's only complaint about The Cameron Highlands' trip was that it had been colder there and she had had to borrow a cardigan of Nancy's at night.

"The hotel was lovely but small. There weren't many people there so we had the pool to ourselves all the time. What did you two do while I wasn't there?"

"Had peace and quiet!" replied Charles with feeling. "You've never stopped talking since you got back."

Indignantly, his daughter got up from the breakfast table and went over to the laden table to get some fruit. When she came back she ate without speaking, looking almost huffy which was unlike her as she usually bounced back after a criticism. When Fiona asked her what she wanted to do that day, she received a short, "Don't care," and they all walked in unaccustomed silence to their room.

Charles picked up the phone and rang reception, asking if he could speak to the manager and when Sean came on the line, he asked if he could be informed if the young policeman was ever in the hotel as he would like to speak to him alone.

"He's having a staff meeting shortly and will ask to be told if the police return," Charles told Fiona.

Pippa, usually curious at all times, asked nothing but busied herself getting her swimming things and book ready. She spent all morning with her nose in the book, not even cheering up when lunch was mentioned.

"Are you OK?" her father asked.

"Fine," was the short response.

After lunch, Nancy came over to them to ask if Pippa wanted to come for a putting competition, "Mum and me against you and Dad," she grinned.

"No thanks," said Pippa. "We're going off shortly."

Nancy left looking disappointed.

"Did you two fall out when you were away?" asked Charles.

"We're not kids!" retorted Pippa.

"So why tell her we were going away somewhere?"

" 'Cos I can't be bothered doing anything."

She buried her head back in her book, not even going with them when they told her that they were going for a swim.

"She was OK last night, Charles," Fiona pointed out. "So it's not something that happened while they were away."

"It's so unlike her to be moody," he pointed out.

"Soon she'll be a teenager and they're always moody, well the girls are anyway. I know I was," was Fiona's contribution.

Pippa was a bit more forthcoming when they got back and imparted the information that Nancy was in secondary school already.

"She's done her first year," she told them.

"Are you worried about going to the new school, pet?" asked Charles.

"A wee bit but I've got Hazel, and Ronald's already there."

They left her reading and went up to the room in time for a possible phone call from Salma.

"Maybe she's more worried about starting secondary school than she's letting on, Charles," Fiona said on their way upstairs.

This time Salma told them that she had got Phil Soames' address from the factory but that when she had gone there it was to be told by the new inhabitant that he had left some months before and had left no forwarding address.

"I had a day off, Sir, so I went back to the factory and went to the canteen, as you suggested and asked for Leonard Brown. He was having his lunch at a table with other men but we moved to an empty one. He was very helpful. The last secretary was called Ethel Kelman. They all thought that there was an affair going on and then she suddenly left. She was a lot younger than Mr Grant and opinion was that she had found someone better and he had let her go quickly to prevent her gossiping about him. Phil Soames has moved to a house in Wemyss Bay, Leonard said, a flat very near the sea, on the Greenock side. He said he could get the address from the woman who had been Soames' secretary before he was sacked so I asked him to do that and contact me - on my mobile Sir, after 6pm."

Charles thanked her and rang off. He told Fiona what had been said.

"Do we add this Miss Kelman to our list of possibles?" she asked.

"Well, it's possible that he tired of her, though with his age, looks and personality, I'm sure it would be as the staff thought."

They were just about to leave the room when the phone rang again. This time it was Sean Grafton with the news that PC Ravanathan was to be round the pool this afternoon. DCI Hussain had asked that the pool area be kept empty of guests that afternoon as he was sending his PC to do some looking round.

"Bit late for that," said Charles. "He should have sealed it off that afternoon and not let anyone use that pool for the time being. I wondered at us all being allowed in the next day but it's their funeral if evidence has been tampered with or taken away."

During the afternoon, Charles went over a couple of times to the Rasa pool. Although there was the ubiquitous blue and white police tape sealing the entrance now, it was not till nearly 5pm that he caught a glimpse of the young policeman. Looking over his shoulder to make sure that Sergeant Cheng and DCI Hussain were nowhere in sight, Charles called out to him and he came over to the tape.

"I've been told not to interfere but I think you should ask one of the pool guys who was present at the pool that afternoon."

"There were two couples, Sir," replied Ravanathan.

"Yes and........"

"Someone else? I see. Thank you, Sir."

Ravanathan looked round furtively and then he ducked under the tape and drew Charles aside.

"A hysterical woman came to our station this morning. She claimed that her life was in danger. Said that she knew who had killed Mr Grant and that she would be next."

"What happened?"

"I only heard it from the desk sergeant. He told Sergeant Cheng, then a message came back saying to send the woman away unless she had any proof of what she was claiming. The desk sergeant asked if she had proof and when she said no, he asked her to leave. She looked scared but she went away."

"Surely they talked to her!"

"No, Sir. I'm afraid that my DCI is convinced that the killer is Mrs Grant. They found a couple of spots of blood on her skirt."

"Is he arresting her?"

"I don't know, Sir. I only heard from the other policemen. The DCI and Sergeant don't take me into their confidence."

"Do you know this woman's name?"

"No, sorry, Sir, I don't."

"What have they got you down here for?"

"Just to see if there is anything incriminating lying around."

"Any luck?"

"No. Nothing except a few cigarette ends, a black comb and a used condom."

"Look, is there any way I can get in touch with you if I find out anything else that might help?"

Ravanathan looked thoughtful.

"That's kind of you after the way you were treated," he said when a few seconds had passed.

"Well I don't want someone who might be innocent locked up for something they didn't do," Charles said.

"Ok, Sir. You can contact me on my personal mobile. I don't have it on me during work hours but you could leave a message on it."

He took his notebook out of his top pocket and wrote on an empty page, tearing the page out and handing it to Charles.

"Just one more thing, Constable. Were there any fingerprints found on the knife?"

"Apart from nearly mine, Sir?"

The young man grinned and Charles smiled back.

"No, Sir, no fingerprints."

Charles strolled back to the loungers, looking preoccupied. Pippa had gone and Fiona, looking a bit anxious, told him that his daughter had gone up to lie down as her tummy was hurting.

"I wanted to go with her but she said to stay and tell you where she had gone," she told him.

"Maybe that's what's been making her grumpy, though it's not like her to get a tummy upset." Charles looked worried now too.

"The heat perhaps?" Fiona wondered.

Charles said that he would go up to the room and suited his action to his word, returning about half an hour later to say that Pippa did not feel sick, just sore. He had given her two paracetamol.

"Two paracetamol....sore..." said Fiona musingly. "I wonder...."

"What?"

"Could she be starting her period, do you think?"

"She's only eleven," Charles protested.

"Girls seem to be starting earlier these days. I'm sure I read that somewhere recently. It would explain the grumpiness too."

"So what do we do now then?" Charles looked a bit helpless.

"I'll go up and explain that it might be this. I'm sure she'll have been told all about it at school."

"Her Aunt Linda's talked to her about it. I know that because she asked me if she could and I said, yes please," Charles laughed.

Fiona went up to their room. Pippa was lying on her bed, curled in a tight ball.

"Pippa, love. This sore tummy might be the start of your periods. You haven't been bleeding, have you?"

Pippa looked up. Her face was pale through her tan and she looked a bit frightened.

"No, Fiona, no bleeding but I've never felt my tummy sore like this...ever."

"Does the pain come and go in kind of waves?"
"Yes."

"Well, the paracetamol will ease the soreness. I've got some wee pads with me and we can buy more. I use tampons but that's not for you yet, I don't think. Don't be embarrassed, please. Just tell me if you do start to bleed at all."

Pippa put up her hand and grasped Fiona's, holding on tightly.

"If I can't have Auntie Linda, you're the person I'd want next, Fiona. I feel a bit sleepy now."

"That'll be the pills working, love. Get under the cover and I'll pull the curtains and let you have a doze. I'll come back up in an hour. OK?"

Pippa wriggled under the cover. Fiona drew the curtains and left the room, going back to the gardens to tell Charles that things were under control.

CHAPTER 20

" . . . and he said that a woman had come into the station this morning, almost hysterical, saying that she knew who'd murdered Alan Grant and she would be next," concluded Charles.

"What else did she say? She gave them a name, I imagine," Fiona said.

"Incredibly, the DCI sent word that she was to be sent packing unless she had proof!" exclaimed Charles. "According to Ravanathan, Hussain is convinced that Jean Grant is guilty as they found some spots of blood on her skirt. The constable didn't hear the woman's name, if she ever got as far as giving it!"

"I wish there was more we could do except wait for Salma to come up with something relevant about the folk back home," Fiona said fervently.

"Me too. I got Ravan...think I'll do a Pippa and call him Rav...to give me his mobile number and said I'd contact him with anything we do find out. I hinted that he ask the pool boys about who was there that day. His superiors have only found out about the two couples, not the single woman."

"Will he contact you if they find out more?"

"I didn't ask him that, love. It didn't seem fair. He'd get into terrible trouble if it was found out that he'd been in touch with me."

After an hour of reading under the shade of one of the beautiful, old trees in the gardens, Fiona went up to the room to see how Pippa was. She had told Charles that she would wait there till 3pm in case Salma rang and she did this but there was no call. Pippa was sound asleep, so, going over to the desk, Fiona took out a sheet of hotel notepaper and wrote a note to Pippa, saying that they would be in the lounge till 4pm and she should join them for afternoon tea if she felt like it.

"I'll come back to the room after that," she wrote. "Hope you had a good sleep."

She went back down and reported the lack of phone call and Pippa being asleep, to Charles and they made their way across the gardens and up the flight of steps to the hotel lounge.

Nancy and her parents were in the middle of their tea. They waved over and Fiona went across to say that Pippa wasn't feeling too well and had gone to bed earlier in the afternoon.

"If she wakes up, she'll join us here probably," she added and went back to join Charles.

However, Pippa did not arrive, even though they stayed till after 4pm. Fiona left Charles at the top of the steps to the gardens and walked through the corridors to their room. It was still in darkness but Pippa was tossing about on the bed this time, though still asleep. Fiona found the sanitary towels she had brought with her and put them into Pippa's underwear drawer. She was debating whether or not to write another note when Pippa woke up.

"How do you feel now?" Fiona asked her.

"Sore again."

She got up to go to the bathroom and came back looking scared.

"I've got that blood, Fiona. Not much but some."

Fiona took one of the small pads out of the drawer and showed her how to take off the protective strip covering the sticky part and attach it to a clean pair of pants.

"How long will it last, Fiona?" Pippa asked in a small voice.

"Probably not long the first time and maybe it won't be what we call a heavy period at first either."

Fiona took her into the bathroom and showed her the little bags at the side of the toilet. Put the used pads in here. I've put clean ones in your underwear drawer."

"Does it come at the same time every month?" was Pippa's next question.

"Probably not, at first. Some people can tell to the day when it will come but others can't and some people miss months."

"What are you like, Fiona?"

"I'm one of the lucky ones who can tell to the day usually. Now do you want to come down to the grounds? You can't swim with the pad on but you'll be able to when you can manage the tampons."

"No. Think I'll just stay up here. Can I take some more paracetamol?"

Fiona looked at her watch.

"Not yet, love. Another hour I think. When you're at home you can hold a hot water bottle on your tummy but I don't think that'll be something the hotel will have here!"

Telling Pippa that she and Pippa's Dad would not be staying down for much longer, Fiona left the room.

"Whew! Never thought I'd have to deal with that," she said laughing, telling Charles that his daughter had indeed started her periods and that she just wanted to be left in the room for now.

It was about 5 o'clock when they made their way back to the room. Fiona gave Pippa two more paracetamol and then went to have her shower. Charles, feeling a bit embarrassed, patted Pippa on the shoulder and she smiled a bit wanly at him before curling up on her bed again. Not wanting to disturb her, they waited till 6.30 then decided to wake her in case she did not sleep at night.

"Pippa, pet," said Charles. "You'll need to eat something and if you sleep too much, you might not sleep tonight."

Her tousled head appeared from under the cover and she sat up.

"OK, Dad. Fiona, is it OK to have a shower?"

"Of course love, a shower or a bath ...then a clean pad," she added as Charles turned his back and pretended not to listen to them.

It was a quiet meal. Charles found both his womenfolk a bit distracted and was actually pleased when he was accosted by Mrs Grant who looked very worried. They were sitting at the Penang Bar when he saw her coming through the grounds towards their table.

"Sorry to disturb your evening meal, Charles," were her first words.

"No problem Jean. Let's move over to an empty table."

They did this and sat down.

"I'm sorry I haven't any news for you yet," said Charles. "Mr Soames has moved house and my sergeant hasn't been there yet. The other couple, Mr and Mrs Elliott, are away on holiday with friends. I don't know where they went."

"I didn't know that Phil had moved. Naturally, we lost touch. What I wanted to see you about now is that DCI Hussain has been in touch to ask me to come to the local station tomorrow morning. Should I get a lawyer to go with me?"

"I had hoped that it wouldn't come to this but yes, I think you need a lawyer now, an English-speaking one if possible. I take it you haven't tried to find one since our last conversation?"

"No. I hoped I wouldn't have to."

Charles got to his feet.

"Come on. Let's go to reception and ask if Sean Grafton is still on the premises or if not if we can contact him at home."

He went back to his own table and apologised to Fiona and Pippa for deserting them.

"Just carry on, girls. I'll finish my meal when I get back."

At reception, Anissa rang the manager's office and spoke to his secretary. She put the phone down and told them that Mr Grafton was on the point of going home and would be down to see them right away.

He was true to his word, coming round the corner five minutes later. They sat down in an alcove off the lounge and Charles asked if he knew of any British lawyers who were resident in Penang just now.

"I don't know any myself but as they say in all the best films, 'I know a man who does'," said Grafton.

He used his mobile.

"Declan, Sean here. Look, with regards to the murder at the Rasa, can you get me a good British lawyer?"

He listened then got up and went to reception, coming back with a pen and a piece of notepaper. He spoke, then listened again and wrote on the paper.

"And you'll get in touch first? Thanks, Declan."

"That was the Irish ambassador to Malaysia, Declan Robinson. He's given me someone's name, a friend of his. He's ringing him as we speak. I've to give him ten minutes then call him myself. What's happened to make you need a lawyer, Mrs Grant?"

Jean Grant explained that DCI Hussain wanted to see her at the local police station the next morning and that he had not sounded friendly. Charles looked uncomfortable but said nothing. He caught the manager looking at him quizzically but Mrs Grant did not seem to notice as she sat, nervously pleating her skirt in her fingers.

Sean rang the number he had written down and spoke to someone he called Ewan Johnstone. He explained the situation about the murder of Jean Grant's husband at The Rasa Sayang Hotel and about the local DCI wanting her to report to the local Batu Feringgi station in the morning.

"You will, Mr Johnstone? Thank you. What time?"

He put his hand over his mobile.

"Mr Johnstone wants to know what time you've to be there."

"9.30."

Sean repeated this into his mobile, listened again, then switched it off.

"Mr Johnstone, Ewan Johnstone, will meet you here in the foyer at 8.30am to get more information from you. He'll go with you to the station at 9.30."

Jean Grant was profuse in her gratitude. She looked pale and ill. Charles asked if she wanted to come back to the Penang Bar with him but she declined, saying that she had no appetite that day.

"Please let me know what happens tomorrow," he said. "I'll let reception know where I'll be during the day and they'll page me when you get back. Better give me your room number in case I need to get in touch with you at any time."

"*If* I get back. If I'm not locked up," she replied, her voice quavering. "It's 2348"

Sean and Charles tried to reassure her but their assurances sounded weak even to their own ears. Mrs Grant went off, back to her room and Sean, asking Charles to let him know what transpired if he did find out, left for home. Charles went back to the Penang Bar. Fiona had finished her meal though Pippa was still waiting for a dessert to be brought.

"Fiona. I know it's a lot to ask but do you think you could go and spend some time with Jean Grant in her room. It's above us, room 2348. She looked really ill. Pour her a brandy from the minibar."

"Did you tell her about the blood being found?" Pippa looked up, all agog.

"Try not to listen, pet. Here's your dessert coming."

Fiona got to her feet and Charles took her to one side.

"Sorry, Charles I forgot about little ears," said Fiona apologetically.

"It doesn't matter. No, I felt in all fairness to the police force that I couldn't forewarn her about the blood, so don't mention it."

Fiona went off.

CHAPTER 21

Luckily, Pippa slept right through the night and she was more like her usual self throughout the morning. Fiona on the other hand was rather subdued. She had spent some time the night before trying to reassure Jean Grant but told Charles when she came back to their room later, that it was quite hard, given that she knew that the police had found incriminating spots of blood on Jean's skirt.

"I'd have liked to have told her that forensic experts would be able to prove that the blood had got there when she found the body but of course I couldn't without telling her that we knew about the blood. Why do you feel that you owe some loyalty to the police here after the way they treated you?"

It was unlike Fiona to sound disgruntled. She had been so full of fun throughout the holiday and she always supported him.

"I thought you understood why I'd kept quiet. If she is indeed guilty, then we'd have given her time to concoct a reason for the blood," Charles explained.

"Do you think she's guilty now?"

Her tone was sharp, almost critical.

"No I don't, love. What's the matter? You sound almost like Pippa yesterday. Is *your* period due too," he risked a joke.

Her shoulders relaxed and she apologised.

"As a matter of fact, it is," she said.

After breakfast at the Spice Market which was quite quiet, Pippa and Charles went off to join Rory and Nancy at putting, Charles having left word at reception earlier that he could be found at the golf course after 11am should Mrs Grant wish to speak to him. Only Rory did well this time, coming second to Wilma who must, Charles said to Rory, know every blade of grass on the course, playing as she did five days a week for six months.

Pippa went off with Nancy, saying as she went, "Guess what's happened to me...."

Charles called out to her to come over to them in time for lunch at midday.

"Dad, we haven't had room service yet," were her first words on arriving at their loungers. "Nancy and her Mum and Dad had room service this morning. Can we do that tomorrow? We've only got a week left."

Charles said that they would indeed do that the next day and, satisfied, his daughter went off for lunch, telling Sunny Tan, "Salamat pagi" then correcting herself with "Salamt tengah hari", as she must have remembered that it was after midday. She asked Sunny if he had any children and he said he had a son, not long born, whom they had named Sean after the manager. Pippa and indeed Fiona and Charles, were intrigued to learn that the baby would remain in a state nursery until he was about two years old, his mother and father visiting him there and only taking him home on occasion.

Pippa seemed to have rediscovered yesterday's lost appetite and it was Fiona who picked at her satay sticks, eventually leaving three of her six for Charles.

It was not until 2.45 that word came from reception, via Jill, that Mrs Grant had returned and gone to her room. Fiona offered to go to their room to await a possible phone call from Salma, so Charles went across to the Whites and asked if they would supervise Pippa till one of them got back to the loungers. He took that young lady with him and was not surprised when she was indignant about this, declaring that she was grown up now and did not need to be supervised.

"Just humour your old Dad," he cajoled her, at which she smiled and accepted the restriction with good grace.

In her room on the third floor, Jean Grant was agitated and flushed. She told Charles that blood had been found on her skirt but her lawyer had said that more proof was needed than that in the event that she had discovered her husband's body and the blood could have got onto the skirt then. He had mentioned wanting to see the forensic report when it arrived. Jean had been asked to name anyone who might have wanted to kill her husband and she had told them about the people at home of whom he had made enemies.

"Did you mention your son?" Charles asked her gently.

"No," said Jean, sounding defensive.

"DCI Hussain was sarcastic when I told him about Alan's possible business enemies. He said it was a long way to come to commit murder. I said so why did he think I'd come all this way to do it and he looked furious. I don't think people are supposed to disagree with him, especially women."

Charles grimaced. He had seen Hussain in action too.

"He asked what kind of relationship I'd had with Alan. I said it was OK. He'd been hard to live with at times. I didn't go into details, Charles. Was that wrong of me?"

"I don't suppose your lawyer would have been pleased if you'd handed the police a reason for murdering Alan," said Charles.

"Mr Johnstone said if that was all they had to go on, he insisted that they let me go. They did and here I am."

Her doorbell rang. It was Fiona with more news.

"Salma got the address of Phil Soames and went there. No one was at home. She went to his neighbour who said she hadn't seen him for a few days but that it wasn't unusual for him to be away for a few days at a time."

"Phil has or had a small boat. He and his wife, Ellen, used to spend most weekends at Rhu. Even if he wasn't able to afford to keep his own boat, he probably still has friends with boats there or somewhere else. Loch Lomond, maybe," volunteered Jean.

"Salma said she'd go back in a couple of days' time, if you wanted her to, Charles. She wanted to know if she could question the Elliotts or Mr Soames if they returned."

"I'll speak to her tomorrow. She can't really interrogate them. She has no official standing in this case but it's interesting that the three of them were away from home over the crucial time," mused Charles.

"I mentioned Ethel Kelman and Salma said that one of the other secretaries at Grant's firm had heard that she was going abroad on holiday before looking for another position. That was all I got from home, Charles."

Something in her tone made Charles look closely at her. He excused himself, telling Jean that he was glad that she had not been retained and he and Fiona went out into the corridor.

"There was more, wasn't there?" he asked once the door was closed.

"Yes. Salma found Mrs Grant's son at home in the flat he shares with his sister but her daughter was away. Leonard Brown seems to have been a mine of information and he gave Salma the address. He said he had helped the two on their moving day as he has a large van. The son, Peter, accepted Salma's story that she was looking for Denise to take part in a health survey. He said she'd been away for a while but would be back soon and Salma said it would be too late by then. Quick thinker, our Salma," said Fiona in admiration.

"Though it wouldn't matter if they found out she was police as Jean Grant did ask us to investigate, I suppose," said Charles.

"I know but I didn't think she wanted her children looked into, did she? In fact, did she not say that she didn't want the Elliots and Phil Soames checked up on either because they'd already gone through a lot? I felt that I could mention them but I didn't think you'd want her to know that we were checking up on her family too."

"You did right, love."

Charles was glad to see Fiona looking interested and more like her normal self. "Don't worry. She mentioned the Elliotts and Mr Soames to Hussain today. Although she didn't want to incriminate any of these people, she must have realised that if we're to investigate for her, we have to check up on them," he added. "She told the police here for the same reason, I guess but they obviously aren't going to check them over!"

He looked thoughtful for a few moments, pulling on his left ear lobe as he did when concentrating at work,

"Was this Leonard Brown not curious about why Salma was asking questions?" he asked, finally.

"I asked her that but she said he seemed to accept that Glasgow police were helping the Malaysian police. Should she maybe question Soames and the Elliotts and hope that they think the same?" asked Fiona.

"I don't know, love. I really can't put Salma in danger of being disciplined for unauthorised questioning. At least she's found out that Phil Soames, the Elliotts and Grant's daughter, Denise could have been here. We have to take it from there, I think. If we could get pictures of them..."

"How? Only Jean would be able to give you a picture of Denise and I doubt she will and as for the others..."

Fiona also tailed off, thinking hard.

"Would the firm have pictures on their files?" she said eventually.

"Of Soames and Bill Elliott, possibly and of Ethel Kelman too perhaps but not of Louise Elliott," replied Charles. "As this Leonard Brown is accepting Salma, maybe she could ask him for photographs. I'll ask Salma to ask him but only if she thinks he is still incurious about her role in this investigation. We just have to hope that if the Penang police do reach Glasgow with their questions, they don't get onto Brown or if they do, he doesn't think to mention Salma."

Still ruminating, they went down in the lift to their own floor. It was too late to go for afternoon tea so they went back down to the gardens where they found Pippa still with the Whites who had decided not to go for afternoon tea either as they were planning to go to the Feringgi Grill that night.

"Could we go again too, Dad?" asked Pippa, eagerly. "You said that we'd go again to take photos of the tomato soup being done at the table, remember?"

Laughing, Charles agreed, looking to Fiona for confirmation. She nodded and then Rory White suggested that they get a table for six. This suggestion delighted the girls and they started talking excitedly about what they would wear.

Back in their room again, Pippa went to have a bath and Charles and Fiona went over what they had learned from Salma once again. Then Charles remembered that he had promised to inform Sean Grafton about what had happened to Jean Grant at the police station, so he rang him.

He said his piece then was silent for some time, eventually commenting, "So the poor woman wasn't just attention-seeking after all. Where?"

He listened again.

"When?"

Sean answered that.

"I understand."

Charles hung up the phone and, glad that Pippa was still out of earshot, told Fiona that the woman who had gone to the police in hysterics the day before, had been found murdered.

"Where?" asked Fiona.

"Sean heard from the resident manager. The woman was found in the ladies' toilet on the ground floor of the Golden Sands."

"The one next to the shop."

"Oh, do you know it?"

"Yes. I walked over there when you were putting today to see if they had any postcards of Penang as our shop only has views of the hotel and the toilet was next to the shop."

"Here's the interesting part. Her name was... Louise Edwards!"

"So you think they were over here, under an assumed name! When was the body discovered?"

"About an hour ago. Sean was just about to call me when I rang him. The manager of The Golden Sands will come across and talk to us when he's finished with the police who wanted to see him of course. I said we'd be in the Feringgi Grill, after cocktail hour."

The resident manager came up to the Grill while they were finishing their main course. Pictures had been taken of the tomato soup being flamed at the table and they were debating whether or not they had room for dessert when Sean approached them with a tall, muscular, fair-haired young man whom he introduced as Frederick Weiss.

"I am sorry to interfere with your meal, Sir," said the man. Charles rose and shook hands.

"Charles Davenport and this is Fiona Macdonald," he said, introducing her as she too got to her feet. He introduced the Whites too.

"We've been wondering whether or not to have a dessert but you've made up our minds for us," he laughed.

Asking Rory and Hope if they would mind, once again, taking care of his daughter, and receiving an affirmative reply, Charles and Fiona followed Sean and Frederick to a private room off the bar attached to the restaurant. Once seated, the Goldens Sands' manager apologised for the delay but told them that the police had insisted on seeing Mr Edwards, naturally enough, so they had had to wait till the tourist bus returned, Bill Edwards having been into Georgetown.

"Bill and Louise. It must be them!" exclaimed Charles.

"What bus did he go in on?" asked Fiona.

"The ten o'clock one," replied Weiss, "and he returned on the one which leaves Traders' Hotel at four o'clock."

"I suppose that leaves him out then," said Sean.

"Possibly," said Charles. "but he could have taken a taxi or bus back, killed his wife and gone back again to catch the bus at four."

"Whoever killed Mrs Edwards had to have blood on them," said Weiss. "There was blood everywhere. She was apparently stabbed in the neck and an artery was sliced open."

The young man's face had lost its colour, the freckles standing out on his pale skin.

"So it would have been difficult for someone clothed to escape unnoticed then," stated Charles.

"That's what the DCI, a man called Hussain, said," agreed Weiss.

"So once again we seem to have a bather with a knife. Same MO Fiona, don't you think?" Charles brought her into the conversation.

"Yes, he or she could have cleaned themselves at the wash basins if it was only skin that was bloodied," she contributed.

"Surely there was the danger of someone coming in at the wrong time?" queried Sean.

"The murderer had covered that. There was a, "Toilets Being Cleaned", sign hung on the door. It was a guest complaining about the length of time the toilets had been out of action that alerted my staff to the fact that something was wrong, Sean," Weiss told his boss.

"Did the police let Mr ...Edwards go?"

"Yes but he was told to stay in his room till the morning and not to leave the hotel without permission. The poor man was overcome with guilt. He said his wife had been prone to taking hysterics at the hint of trouble, recently, so he had ignored her statement that she would be killed next. They knew a man had been killed at the Rasa, you see," explained Weiss. "Mr Edwards told me he had sneaked onto the bus to get away from her for a while."

"When did you talk to him?" asked Charles.

"I went to his room before coming here."

Charles asked Sean if he would try to find out subtly if Mr Edwards would be willing to speak to him, in the presence of Mrs Grant tomorrow.

"Ask him if he'd talk to Jean Grant in the presence of a Scottish policeman and if he appears to be unwilling, drop it."

Sean agreed, telling Charles that they could use the same room as before. Weiss was sure that Mr Edwards would agree as he had been fuming at his treatment by the Penang police sergeant. The man had apparently almost bundled him into the room where the DCI was waiting.

Weiss left.

"I saw the look that passed between you at the mention of the names Louise and Bill," said Sean. Is this Edwards the same as the Elliott I looked for in the guest registers?"

"I think the first names are too much of a coincidence," said Charles.

"Wonder if he'll agree to see us. Seems unlikely," said Fiona.

"I'll phone you about 9am," said Sean. "No wonder I was told that there were no Elliotts in either hotel. Someone must have let them away without showing their passports in the Golden Sands."

"Not your fault, Sean," Charles said.

"I can't see what else I can do, love," Charles explained to Fiona as they made their way back into the restaurant.

"I know. Don't worry. I'm sure the fact that one, or now maybe two, British people wanted your help, will cut ice with Mr Knox should there ever be a complaint from the Penang police."

The others had finished their desserts and were having the little chocolates which came after the meal. Charles and Fiona were offered one each and accepted, smiling. It was after ten o'clock, so they all made their way to their rooms, Pippa talking excitedly about the room service breakfast which they were to have the following day and Nancy suggesting that they have it on their balcony.

The families separated to go to their rooms.

"Breakfast in the room suits us fine now, as it happens," were Charles's words as he opened the room door.

CHAPTER 22

It had been an unusually hot day in Glasgow and there were still sunbathers lying on the few grassy patches remaining in George Square. As she got off the bus there, Salma noticed one young man, shirtless, whose back was already turning red. His girl companion, lying beside him, had earphones on and was singing rather tunelessly along with the music she alone could hear. The bus from the South Side had been crowded and Salma had had to give up her seat to an expectant mother. Well, she had waited two stops for the young man in front of her to do it but when it became obvious that he was not going to, Salma had stifled a sigh and got up. Her feet ached in her regulation, flat, black shoes as she had done quite a lot of walking that afternoon when her shift had ended.

She had gone again to visit Phil Soames, even though her boss had not told her to and found him at home this time. She had thought up what she would say, namely that over in Penang, Mrs

Grant had found herself a lawyer who had wanted some investigations done at this end.

Soames who said he had been living on a friend's boat for the past week, asked why Mrs Grant needed a lawyer, in Malaysia of all places.

On hearing that his previous boss, Alan Grant, had been murdered, he had laughed loudly.

"I look about twenty years older than I did about a year ago," he said. "Thanks to Alan Grant. It couldn't have happened to a nicer man. How can I help Jean? Don't tell me she's been accused of the murder. That mouse of a woman! She wouldn't say no to him let alone kill him."

"That's why her lawyer needs help from over here, Sir," said Salma. "He needs to know if there was anyone who might have wanted Mr Grant dead, enough to fly over there and kill him while he was on holiday."

"Seems a ham-fisted way to go about it when it could have been done here," said Soames.

"Maybe if the person came from here, he or she thought that they wouldn't be suspected over there. It seems to have worked as the local police are sure it was his wife," Salma said.

"Well, I had a motive but I was on the boat as I told you, with two friends, all last week. I just got back last night. Anyone else? Well, Bill Elliott was bought out rather against his will. I never did find out what lever Alan had to force him to sell his stake in the company. And I heard that Alan's last secretary left suddenly but I don't know why. I rather lost touch after Ellen died."

Salma had thanked him and was on the point of leaving when he asked if she wanted the address of his friends to confirm what he had said. Delighted at not having had to ask for this, Salma wrote down the address and thanked him for his help. He had not told her anything new but it would seem that he could be ruled out as a suspect.

She drove back to Glasgow, to where Ethel Kelman lived and found that she was still not at home. This time she managed to speak with an elderly neighbour who said that she had seen her leaving with a suitcase about ten days ago.

"She often goes to Sussex, to stay with her aunt," the woman had added," but I don't have an address for her, I'm afraid. I only know because she leaves her cat with me."

As if on cue, a large, marmalade cat insinuated itself between them, purring loudly.

"This is Alphonse. I do so enjoy having him for company, don't I precious?"

She stooped down and scooped the cat into her arms.

"Apart from that, she keeps herself to herself. She didn't tell me but I wonder if she was made redundant, as she was at home some days before she left."

"For how long?" asked Salma.

The woman thought about that.

"I would say about ten days."

"Do you know of anyone she was friendly with around here?" asked Salma.

"You might try Miss Stevens at number eight. They're about the same age I think and I've seen her get out of Miss Kelman's car a few times. She's a schoolteacher. She'll probably be at home. It's school holiday time and I've seen her in her garden recently."

Salma thanked her.

"Would you like to come in for a cup of tea, dear?" asked the old woman.

"No thanks, Mrs..."

"Mrs George."

"No thanks, Mrs George. Look, you shouldn't ask strangers into your house, you know. It's not safe these days."

"But you're a policewoman, aren't you?" said the woman.

Salma was startled.

"What makes you say that, Mrs George?"

"The shoes you're wearing, dearie, so unflattering. Well, if you won't come in, I'd better get this young man's tea ready."

She shut the door, leaving Salma on the step.

"So much for changing out of my uniform," she mused out loud.

She went on to number eight and Kitty Stevens told her that she thought that Ethel Kelman was away on holiday with her boss. She didn't remember where but it was somewhere exotic.

"I kept the shoes on because I knew I'd be doing some walking before and after I met you," she told Penny when that young woman got off her bus in George Square and they were walking up to the cinema complex.

"Why were you questioning the old woman in the first place?" asked Penny.

"Oh...just a burglary in the area," said Salma.

They reached the cinema and took some time to decide which film to see. It was rare for Salma to have a night to herself as, since her Mum died a few months ago, her eldest sister had moved out, leaving her in sole charge of her brother, Rafiq. Tonight, Shazia had offered to babysit for him.

They had too long to wait for, "Shutter Island", to begin, so chose to see "The Ghost". During the wait for the picture to start, they compared notes on their work. Penny had been seconded to another department where she was at work on an armed robbery case.

"I hate working for DCI Plod," she said fervently.

"DCI Plod? Is he new?" asked Salma innocently.

"DCI Dixon's his real name," whispered Penny, looking round surreptitiously. "But he's a real plodder. Not like Mr Davenport. He dresses in black suits with white shirts. Always looks as if he's going to a funeral and he is so slow when he's speaking, I almost fall asleep."

"Have you heard from Frank?" Salma wanted to know.

Frank too had been seconded, out of the building completely, to the police station in Pollokshaws, next door to Penny's church.

"Yes. I rang him last night to see if he'd like to come with us tonight. I knew you wouldn't mind but he's still seeing Sue and they were going out together tonight. He sends his love."

Salma laughed. Things had come a long way from the time when Frank had hated her for her promotion over him and the fact that she was Muslim.

"How's he liking Pollokshaws?"

"He hates it. Nothing ever happens except people coming in for directions, apparently."

"Never mind, we'll all be back together in about a week," Salma comforted her friend.

They enjoyed the film, both of them declaring that Pierce Brosnan still looked great and that the climax had been unexpected. Salma did not have time to go for something to eat as she had promised that she would be home by ten at the latest. Penny said that she would walk with her to her bus stop and wait till the 44 arrived then she would go for her own bus, the 38 to Shawlands.

At the stop, Salma asked her about Gordon, her boyfriend of some months. Penny's face fell.

"We're not getting on so well at the moment. He's still annoyed with me for getting him entangled in that last murder. I've apologised over and over but he won't let it go."

"Do you still see him?"

"Yes but I won't be seeing him for much longer if he keeps it up," Penny said.

On her bus home, Salma's face was sad. She knew how much Penny felt for Gordon Black, her vet boyfriend and was sorry to think that the relationship might end. She was also mentally castigating herself for nearly giving the game away, telling of the shoe episode.

"I don't like keeping things from Penny," she thought as the bus reached the foot of University Avenue.

She reached home just after ten, relieved Shazia of her babysitting duties, though Rafiq had been asleep for some time, and made herself a very late meal.

It was next morning that she heard on Radio Clyde of the bus crash at Alison Street. A car had jumped the lights and hit the 38 bus which had been pushed into the path of a van coming in the other direction. There were two dead and nine seriously injured.

Feeling sick, Salma rang Penny's flat. She was relieved when the phone was picked up but it was Alec, Penny's flatmate who answered and told her that it had indeed been Penny's bus and she was in the Victoria Infirmary with severe head injuries. Her Mum and her stepfather, Jack, had been at the hospital all night but Penny had not regained consciousness. He told her what little he knew about the circumstances of the accident.

Salma went to work in a very subdued mood. The only person she could share the news with there was Bob who as usual was in charge at the desk. He was a fatherly figure and treated the three younger members of staff like his own children. He had not heard the news on Radio Clyde and was aghast when Salma told him about Penny. He volunteered to ring Pollokshaws' Station to tell Frank, as Salma was now in tears. At midday, he rang the hospital but there was no better news. Mrs Maclean came to the phone and said that Gordon was also there with them and that she would phone Salma when there was any news.

At 3pm. Salma rang Davenport in Penang with the news of Phil Soames return and his alibi for the time of the murder.

"Sorry, Sir if I jumped the gun and sorry to be phoning at a bad time. Should I check that alibi out, Sir? I have the address of the couple whose boat he was on."

She listened to what her boss had to say.

"I also spoke to a friend of Ethel Kelman. She said that Ethel had told her she was going away with her boss."

"A quick worker, this Miss Kelman," said Charles. "She'd only just finished an affair with Grant!"

"The reason I'm phoning now, Sir is to tell you some bad news. Penny's been in a bad accident."

She told her boss the details, ending with the fact that his PC was still unconscious. Feeling distraught about her friend, she did not think to say to her boss that Ethel Kelman had not appeared to have started a new job.

CHAPTER 23

It was no surprise to learn from the manager that Bill Elliott did not want to see either Mrs Grant or Charles.

"Not much we can do at the moment then," conceded Charles and they spent a quiet day in the gardens. They ate in The Spice Market and had coffee, tea and a coke in the lounge then went upstairs. They had seen no sign of the Whites that day.

The phone rang about 10 o'clock.

"Oh no!"

Fiona looked up at the anguish in his voice as did Pippa who had been sitting at the desk, writing yet another postcard to her friend Hazel.

"And you say there's been no change since last night? Please phone again tomorrow, Salma and keep us abreast of what's happening."

He rang off and swivelled in his seat to look at the others.

"It's Penny. She was in an accident yesterday and hasn't regained consciousness."

"Is she going to die?" asked Pippa, sounding scared.

"I don't know, pet. I hope not," Charles answered her.

"What happened, Charles?" Fiona wanted to know.

"She was in a bus that was hit by a car and it swerved across the road and hit a large van. A lot of the passengers were thrown out of their seats. Penny was and a heavily-built man landed on top of her. Salma got the news from Penny's flatmate, Alec, after she heard about the crash on Radio Clyde this morning."

Pippa had started to cry. Fiona put an arm round her and they all sat silent for some time, then Charles spoke.

"We won't help Penny, sitting here moping. Let's go up to the Feringgi Bar and try out some of their cocktails and mocktails. It's too early to go to bed."

Knowing that Charles was trying to take their minds off Penny, Fiona agreed and they spent the next hour listening to the band and sipping drinks. Charles even let Pippa sip some of his alcoholic cocktail. Fiona said she would try one of Pippa's mocktails and claimed that it was better than the real thing. Charles took his daughter up for a dance, or what he called a shuffle round the floor.

It was much later than usual when they got back to their room and Pippa was asleep before the other two had undressed. They sat on the balcony and talked about Penny.

"Maybe they're keeping her in an induced coma," said Fiona. "They sometimes do that after an accident to the brain."

"I hope so," Charles said fervently.

"Well we can't do anything about it except say a prayer for better news tomorrow," Fiona said, rising to her feet.

"We'd better keep busy tomorrow."

Charles got up too.

"Come on, let's have breakfast and go into Georgetown and have a trishaw ride. We forgot to order room service last night again but I think it'd be better when we're more in the mood. Eh, pet?"

"Yes, Dad," agreed Pippa.

"Public transport or taxi, Pippa? Come on, wipe your face and make a decision."

"By bus please, Dad."

She gave him a tremulous smile. She had been crying since she woke up.

"Fiona?"

"Bus suits me. I'll shop in the mall there, Prangin Mall I think it's called. I don't think one poor cyclist could pull the weight of three of us."

On the way through the foyer, Charles stopped at reception to ask Anissa if she would inform the manager that they would be out for most of the day and if Mrs Grant or a Mr Elliott or Edwards asked for him, to give them the same message.

It was extremely hot waiting for the bus. The heat shimmered on the road, making it look as if it was covered in water. Charles pointed it out to Pippa and explained that this was what often made travellers in the desert think they saw water.

"A mirage, it's called," he told her "There's a road in Ayrshire that's a bit of a mirage. When you drive up it feels as if you're going down and the opposite in the other direction. I did it once on a bike and it felt really silly cycling hard to go downhill. I think it's called The Electric Brae."

The bus duly arrived, the new one this time, painted bright red, blue and white. They climbed on board and up some stairs at the back of the bus where most of the seats were.

"A waste of space," commented Fiona, once they were seated. "The lower level has hardly any seats at all."

She and Charles kept up a running commentary, pointing out the various buses they saw, bas sekolah, the school bus, painted orange with black lettering, bas persiarian, in blue and white, the tourist bus, and finally the oldest, in grey which they guessed must be a factory bus. They passed by the landmark Macdonalds and the road that led to the manager's house. Charles had told Pippa about the invitation there, next Sunday, and she was looking forward to seeing the two dogs.

The driver took a route past the jetty and they saw a notice advertising a ferry trip to Langkawi, a neighbouring island.

"Would we have time to go there, Charles?" asked Fiona. "I've heard it's a beautiful island, much less commercialised than Penang. It's got a cable car lift and mangrove swamps...and a duty free shop 'cos it's a duty-free island," she added.

"We've got five days after today. I expect we'll want to just stay round the hotel on the day we leave..."

"We've got the train up Penang Hill to do too," Pippa reminded them.

"Sean suggested a day visit to his house, with our swimming things I would think. That's on Sunday. So what about tomorrow at the hotel, just lazing around, Saturday the train up the hill and Monday for the ferry trip? Does that suit both of you?"

"Yes," they chorused.

The bus was in the outskirts of the city now so they kept a lookout for the Komtar and rang the bell when they reached it. As soon as they got off, a man approached them to ask if they wanted a trishaw ride. Mindful to check the price,

Charles asked him how much for a circular tour of Georgetown.

"60 ringgits for three persons," grinned the man.

"And for two?" queried Charles.

"40 ringgits."

Charles agreed to that price and he and Pippa climbed into the little trishaw which was brightly coloured in paper flowers of all hues and had lights which would be lit up at night.

"We'll meet you inside the hotel, Fiona!" Charles called out.

Fiona waved them off, then turned and went into Traders' hotel. She sat in the foyer and ordered a latte, remaining there deep in thought for some time. Penny was a favourite with everybody and it was hard to think of the bubbly, lively girl in a coma, if indeed that was what it was. Keeping Pippa preoccupied on the bus journey had also taken her own mind off the accident but it flooded back now and Fiona looked downcast as she paid for the coffee and went back out into the heat of Georgetown. She thought of the saying, "Mad dogs and Englishmen go out in the midday sun". Luckily the mall was just round the corner. She had heard from Sylvia Bennett that the day she and Lorna had gone into the mall, the air-condition had stopped working but she was in luck, though even with the aircon, she felt sweaty and a bit sick.

A large notice announced that it was, "No carrier bag day" but she had brought their beach bag. There were lots of little stalls selling the ubiquitous fake watches, pashminas and tee-shirts which were copies of named ones like Tommy Hillfigger and L'Accoste. Fiona bought a few trinkets, then was tempted into a shop which advertised a foot massage for 20 ringgits.

It turned out to be a reflexology massage so she had to listen to all the ailments the woman thought she had, things like tense shoulders and a dry liver. She was told to drink more water, then almost slept as the woman began to massage her legs.

The trishaw ride had Charles gripping the side of his seat. The driver pedalled them down busy streets and he found himself staring at huge wheels as they came alongside large lorries. At one point they were even driven the wrong way up a street and he shut his eyes as he saw three lanes of traffic coming towards them. Pippa was loving it, screaming with delight as the other vehicles drove round them. No drivers honked at them, just made way for the trishaw, lending credence to its status as 'King of the Road'. The man propelling them round the city, kept up a running commentary of places they passed and when Charles got used to their precarious position, he began to enjoy the weird shop names such as Ban Heep which was the name of a car salesroom.

The driver took them right to Fort Cornwallis where Charles and Fiona had already been, then down the famous Campbell Street with its myriad of shops. It was a pedestrian precinct but obviously trishaws were allowed down it. Pippa was fascinated by the cages of exotic birds hanging up in the street. The man pedalling them was thin and wiry and did not seem at all tired. He had a black, shiny pigtail which swung from side to side

The trip took about an hour and he deposited them exactly where they had begun their journey, outside Traders' Hotel where they had arranged to meet Fiona.

"We didn't mention a time, Dad," said Pippa.

"I know. That was a bit silly," her Dad replied.

"Can we have a drink anyway?" she asked.

They went up the steps and a liveried doorman opened the door for them. They sat down on the plush, red velvet seats, Charles relaxing his tense shoulders. They had drinks, tea for Charles and a coke for Pippa but there was still no sign of Fiona.

"What will we do, Dad?"

"Well, if we go into the Mall to look for her, she'll probably come out another door and come here then go looking for us maybe. I think we should just sit here, for another half hour anyway."

Fiona turned up twenty minutes later. She apologised for keeping them.

"I hope you haven't had to wait long. I thought you'd be about two hours going right round the city so I had a foot massage and then had a manicure. We forgot to mention a time, didn't we?"

As it was now nearly one o'clock, they decided to have lunch in Georgetown. Pippa wanted to try somewhere outside but was outvoted by the adults who preferred to eat in the hotel.

"I think it'll be safer, tummy-wise, pet," said her father.

"Oh, Dad, don't be a spoilsport."

"Pippa, my tummy's a bit off today already," said Fiona. "Sorry to be so unadventurous but I want something really plain."

That decided, they went into the ground floor restaurant. Fiona chose an omelette but left half of it unfinished, Pippa having lasagne and chips and Charles, a lamb chop with potatoes and peas. Father and daughter finished off with an ice cream concoction, full of meringue and kiwi and topped with cream. Fiona settled for a cup of tea and sipped it slowly.

The service had been quite slow and it was now nearly 2.15, so they decided to return to the hotel by taxi. There were plenty available outside Traders and the journey took about half an hour.

In the event, Salma did not ring them till nearly five o'clock. She had nothing new to tell them about the case and started to apologise but Charles cut her off. Pippa and Fiona heard him tell her that they only wanted to hear about Penny and they saw his face light up.

"Oh, that's great! "

He listened again then rang off.

"It's the best news. Penny's conscious but she'll be in hospital for some time they think. As well as head wounds, she's got broken ribs."

He chased Pippa to get showered and when the bathroom door had closed, he said, "Salma's going to check out Phil Soames' alibi and after that I don't think there's much she can do from the Glasgow end."

"Except find out where Denise Grant went," Fiona reminded him.

"I forgot about her in the excitement of hearing about Penny," Charles admitted. "I'll ask her to ferret that out when she next calls me. Or I'll call her. Now, where will we eat tonight?"

As Fiona wanted to take the material she had bought while Pippa was away, into the local tailor's shop and had been told that early evening was a good time, they decided to try a place called "Magic" which was on the same side of the road.

They were accosted, in a good-natured way, by waiters from every restaurant along the strip, saying no thanks until they came to the one they wanted. It was quite westernised and Charles chose steak and chips. Fiona opted for crab mornay and Pippa for chicken, exclaiming with delight that fried ice cream was on the dessert menu. Their table mats had jokes and riddles on them with the answers on the back.

"What's the longest word in the dictionary, Dad?" asked Pippa.

"I don't know. What is it?"

"Smiles, because there's a mile between each s."

They had a hilarious time and Pippa had her fried ice cream, declaring that it was disappointing. It was a happier threesome who went to bed that night, secure in the knowledge that Penny was out of danger. Charles even remembered to put their order for room service breakfast outside the door at last!

CHAPTER 24

Salma had driven to Helensburgh in the late afternoon and was given directions to the Colgrain area where she soon found the address she had been given by Phil Soames. A woman in her fifties opened the door and smiled when Salma showed her identification card.

"Phil said you might come. Come in, my dear."

She led Salma down a long, narrow hall and into the lounge, a light, airy room, today filled with sunlight. Gesturing to a cream, leather settee, she herself sat down on a hard-backed chair.

"Back trouble," she explained. "I wrenched it on the boat last week. Should have left the hard work to the two men, I suppose. Dan'll be in shortly. He only popped out for milk."

The sound of the front door opening and closing reached them

"Here he is now, unless the burglar has a key!"

She laughed and Salma smiled back. The lounge door opened and a well-built, rugged man with thick, wavy grey hair came in.

"Hi. You must be Sergeant Din," he said, taking a soft seat across from her.

"Yes, a black woman in police uniform. Hard not to know who I am, I suppose," said Salma, somewhat ruefully and they all laughed.

"So you want to know if Phil was with us on the boat last week?" asked Dan. "I can assure you he was. He nearly finished off my stock of whisky too."

"Phil came here on the Monday night, stayed overnight and then left with us, in our car, on Tuesday morning," offered his wife.

"We were on the boat together all the time till we came home. Ate, slept...and drank there for six days and came home on Sunday evening. Phil stayed overnight again and left on Monday morning," finished off Dan.

Salma thanked them, declined their offer of coffee or tea and got home in time to make a meal for herself and her young brother and sister. She had arranged for Rafiq to go to her Uncle Fariz and Aunt Zenib for the evening to allow her to go and visit Penny. Frank had offered to come for her but it seemed silly to drag him across town so she was driving herself.

Penny's Mum sat on one side of the hospital bed, holding her daughter's hand. On the other side, sat Gordon, her boyfriend of some months. Her stepfather was seated in the corridor outside, there being only two visitors allowed at one time. He looked up from his Glasgow Herald in time to see Frank Selby and Salma Din coming round the corner. Salma was carrying a huge bouquet of flowers and Frank, a basket of fruit. They had met in the hospital shop.

"How is she, Jack?" Salma asked anxiously.

"As well as can be expected...I sound like a nurse on the telephone... but it's true in Penny's case. One of the injuries to her face just missed her right eye and she's lucky not to have brain damage. Apparently, she fell into the aisle when the first car hit them, then the large man sitting beside her must have landed on her head at the second impact with the large van"

"Does Penny remember what happened then?" asked Frank.

"She remembers falling off her seat and then nothing else but the man had to be lifted off her. He was unconscious so she got his full weight. They think he hit his head on a pole while falling."

"It said on Radio Clyde that two people were killed," Salma stated, "and nine injured."

"Yes, two people died, the driver who went through the windscreen and a passenger who had stood up to get off and was hurled right to the back of the bus. I think Penny and her large man are the only injured people who've been kept in."

"Is her Mum in with her?" asked Salma, sitting down beside Jack who moved up on his bench to make room for her between him and another visitor. Frank leant back against the whitewashed wall across from them.

"Yes, she and Gordon are in just now. We all came together. Gordon drove us here. It seemed silly to drive two cars all the way from Shawlands to the Southern General. He'll come out shortly and let me in, then Margaret and I'll come out and let you two in. They're very strict here about only two visitors at a time."

"It's took us both ages to find a car space. We came separately," explained Frank.

There was a silence then Frank started telling them about an amusing incident that day at his quiet station in Pollokshaws. An elderly woman had come in report that her husband was missing. Apparently, according to her, he had run off with the young woman next door. Frank had told her that in that case, he wasn't missing. She had argued that she wanted him found and brought back to her. Eventually Frank had taken her details and when he was relieved by another constable, about two hours later, he had gone to see her in one of the high rise flats.

"The lift of course wasn't working so I climbed up seven floors only to find that her husband was there. He had gone next door to babysit for the young woman who lived there with her toddler. He apologised for his wife and said that she had dementia. I know that's not funny but if you could have seen the man, a wizened little guy, about five feet tall, hardly any teeth..."

He tailed off as the swing doors opened and Gordon Black came through them.

He smiled at Penny's colleagues and told Jack he was to go in.

"You sit down, Frank. I've been sitting down in there."

Salma did not smile back and the look Gordon gave her was puzzled. They sat in silence for a few moments then Frank engaged Gordon in chat about some recent football match. Salma got up and walked over to the corridor window and was joined by Gordon.

"Salma, what's the matter? I know Penny's in some state but she'll be OK."

"Do you care? I mean, really care about her, Gordon?" Salma asked intensely.

"Of course I do. Why are you asking?"

"I went out with Penny the night of the accident and she was really upset about the way you keep going on about the time she made that mistake, you know, tried to smoke out the murderer on her own....well with you."

"Well, it was bloody stupid. You know that!"

"Yes and she knows that and she nearly lost the job she loves because of it. Do you really think she needs you going on about it all the time?"

Gordon looked shame-faced.

"I hadn't realised I was doing it so often, Salma. I'm really fond of Pen and I was so scared that night. Also I was mad at myself for not persuading her that what she planned to do was madness. I went along with it, like a fool because I didn't want her to think I was scared. How daft is that!"

"Very daft, so do you think maybe you're taking it out on her...too much and too often?"

"Is she going off me, Salma? I've thought things were a bit cool recently."

"What do you expect, you dope! If the person you like a lot does nothing but criticise you, you must have doubts about their feelings for you. You're supposed to lift her up, not pull her down."

Salma, in her agitation, was striding back and forward and Gordon was doing the same to keep abreast of her.

"Hey you two, what's up? You're giving me a headache. Sit down or at least, stand still." Frank sounded half annoyed, half amused. At that moment the swing door swung open again and Penny's mother and Jack came through.

"Salma, you and Frank can go in now but don't stay too long. She's getting tired," said Mrs Maclean.

"Can I pop back just for a second, please, before you two go in?"

Without waiting for their reply, Gordon pushed through the door, coming back a few minutes later with a huge grin on his face. He walked up to Salma, planted a big kiss on her cheek and said, "Thanks. You're a good friend. Now, the Maclean taxi awaits."

With a bemused look at Salma, Margaret and Jack let themselves be led away downstairs.

"What was that for?" demanded Frank.

"Tell you later. Come on. We've Penny to visit."

They found Penny lying back in her bed with a smile on her face. Her head was wrapped, turban –style, in bandages from which a stray black curl hung down.

Frank, ever tactless, remarked that he had expected them to have shaved off all her hair to which Penny replied calmly, "They've taken most of it off on onc side so I might ask them to shave it all off. I'll have to wear a wig for a while. Should I go blonde?"

She grinned at them.

"Now don't make me laugh. I've got three broken ribs and they don't like me laughing!"

They sat for a while, hearing her account of the accident, what she could remember of it and telling her what they had been doing at work. Frank told his story of the woman with dementia and Penny's face whitened in pain as she found herself unable to stop laughing. Salma sent him away to ask for a vase for the flowers and Penny, suddenly serious, asked her if she'd spoken to Gordon since their conversation the other night.

"I hope you don't mind, Penny. I could see things going wrong for both of you because you were both feeling ...I don't know...feeling that you couldn't get past your silly mistake."

Penny put out her hand and touched her friend's arm.

"I'm not angry with you. Whatever you said, it cleared the air. Gordon told me tonight when he rushed back in, that I was the most important person in his life and he was really sorry. It was himself he was angry with, not me and he was taking it out on me. I said sorry too and I would never, ever try to involve him in anything underhand again."

Frank came back with the vase, looking bemused.

"I asked for a vase and said a bottle would do and they all creased themselves laughing."

"Frank, a bottle to nurses is what men use to pee in," said Penny, holding herself gingerly and obviously making a supreme effort not to laugh again.

"I see you two are getting a bit fond of each other," he retorted, looking meaningfully at Penny's hand resting on Salma's arm. "Something you want to tell me?"

Just then the visiting bell rang, saving the girls from making caustic remarks. Salma rose to her feet and Penny thanked them both for coming.

"Looks as if I won't be back at work for a few weeks anyway," she said, wistfully. "When do our two bosses come back?"

"Next Thursday," Salma told her.

"We never did have time to talk about them going away at the same time," Frank said with a lascivious look on his thin face. He brushed away the lock of hair that was always falling over his eye.

"Never had time to... Frank Selby! We spent a whole evening on the subject after they left," said Penny. She was teasing but her voice suddenly wavered and she put a hand to her forehead. "And you'd better have a haircut before DS Macdonald sees you," she said weakly.

"Come on, Frank. Penny's exhausted. Sorry, Penny. Take care and we'll come up again soon."

Salma almost dragged her colleague up the ward and through the doors, turning to wave as they closed behind them.

On the way out to the car park, almost at the other end of the hospital grounds, Frank mentioned Davenport and DS Macdonald again.

"D'you really think it's just platonic. If they're together. Her in one room and him, with Pippa, in another?"

"Well they could hardly all share the one room and if they did, Pippa would be a bit in the way wouldn't she?"

"I suppose so...a sort of human contraceptive," he laughed. "Did either of them ever explain it to you?"

"No and you've got me as bad as you, believing that they're together, as a couple, in Malaysia."

Salma was quiet as they walked on. She knew that her two bosses were together because she had spoken to them both on the phone. Both had obviously forgotten that no one knew they were on holiday together and she had nearly given the game away to Frank.

To cover up what she had just said, she explained to Frank why Gordon had kissed her and he did not seem to realise that she had almost conceded that their two bosses were away together..

"Oh well," she told herself, standing in front of her dressing table at home, "It's up to them what they say when they come home."

CHAPTER 25

Charles took another early call from Sean Grafton just after he got up on Friday morning. The manager had spent the last half hour with a member of the Golden Sands' reception team. The woman had been distraught and it had transpired that Bill Elliott had told her when he and Louise arrived that he'd left their passports in the small hotel they had stayed at in Georgetown before coming out to Batu Feringgi. He gave their surname as Edwards.

"He told Veronica that he would go into Georgetown as soon as possible and get the passports but she forgot to ask him for them again and only remembered when Louise had been killed and she saw the husband talking with the police sergeant in the foyer."

"What have you done with this information, Sean?" Charles asked.

"I'm about to go to the police station and tell someone there. Is that the right thing to do?"

"Yes it is and we must hope that they'll at least ask Jean Grant if she knows them. Surely they'll wonder if there's a link between the two murders!"

"Who is this man Edwards-Elliott, anyway?" asked the manager.

" Elliott was bought out of the business by Grant and he lost all the money and they had to downsize their house."

"They had a reason then for murdering him?"

"Yes and it looks suspicious that they tried to get away with an assumed name."

"Do you think he killed his wife?"

"Well either he or the person who killed Grant, if that wasn't him. Though he does seem to have an alibi for his wife's death."

"But as you said, he could have come back, killed her and gone back into town."

"OK, Sean, let me know what happens when you tell Hussain."

Charles replaced the receiver and the doorbell rang.

"Perfect timing!" he said. "I guess you got all that, Fiona?"

"Sean's going to tell the police about Elliott being here under an assumed name."

Charles opened the door to find a waiter standing behind a large trolley on wheels. He opened the door wider and told the man to come in.

"Pippa!" Charles called. "Breakfast's here!"

His daughter erupted out of the bathroom, still in her dressing-gown, her hair wet from the shower. The waiter had taken the trolley out onto the balcony, moving the table which sat there nearer to the large bath. He came inside for the desk chair and arranged it at the trolley which had a vase of flowers on is as well as tureens of food and glasses filled with orange juice.

"Sir, Madam. Who is having the full English breakfast?"

"I am," said Charles and was ushered to one side of the trolley.

"And the scrambled egg?"

"Me," said Pippa and she sat down where she was told to sit. Fiona took the remaining place and the waiter lifted her tureen lid to show her fluffy pancakes and a little jug of maple syrup."

They sat in their white dressing gowns, looking out over the beautiful gardens and ate their breakfasts, even Fiona seeming to have found her appetite again.

After breakfast, Pippa blew her hair dry and the two adults got dressed. Fiona packed the beach bag while Pippa dressed and they were down at their loungers by about 10.30. There was no putting on Fridays and they took a walk along the beach, towards the end where they were told there was an army camp. There was also one stall and Pippa persuaded Charles to buy her a sarong to match her bikini.

"I wish we could swim in the sea," said Fiona as they walked back along the water's edge.

"Not worth the risk, love," said Charles. "Tony told me one morning about guests who got stung by the jellyfish. One man had to go to hospital; the weals right across his chest were so big."

"What's a weal, Dad?" asked Pippa. "Not w.h.e.e.l, I suppose."

She spelled out the word she knew.

"No, it's w.e.a.l and that's like a scar," he explained.

It was the first time Charles and Pippa had walked on the beach. Charles did not like sand in his toes and Pippa preferred the poolside and the chat with her friends but Fiona had walked back from the Golden Sands on the beach so when she saw two men approaching them, she knew what would come.

"Oh, ho, beach bums selling something," she warned Charles.

"Parasailing, Sir. Only 50 ringitts each," said the swarthy young man who reached them first

"You like to see cobra?" asked the older man who was carrying a wicker basket with a lid.

Fiona took a step back but the man was not going to lift the lid unless someone paid him and Charles had seen enough snakes at the Snake

Temple to last him a lifetime. Pippa was too busy trying to persuade her father to let her try the parasailing.

"You're a bit young for that, Pippa," he said.

"You can both go up together, Sir. Same price," said the young man, sensing a sale.

Charles agreed and he and Pippa were put into harnesses, Pippa clipped on to Charles who was in front. The boat took off, pulling the ropes taut and taking them sailing off into the blue sky. Fiona went back to the loungers and got the camera. They were by now just dots in the sky but she waited until they came back towards the beach and managed a couple of pictures of them and their very colourful sail, in bright yellow and black.

"Pull! Pull!" shouted the young man and Charles pulled hard on one of the ropes and they landed on the beach, running along the sand till the sail collapsed behind them. Charles fell over and Pippa, still attached to him, fell too. Giggling, she got to her feet and helped her Dad up.

As they reached their loungers, Fiona said, "And now I'll tell you the stories I heard about parasailing accidents!"

She proceeded to tell them what Tony had told her one day, namely that one woman had landed in a tree, another's rope had broken and he'd landed across the main road in some tennis courts and what was worst to her, one rope had slackened and a young boy had come down in the deep sea and the sail had flattened out over him.

"I know you would just need to swim in one direction and you'd come out from underneath it but I'd panic and keep changing direction," she laughed.

They decided for lunch just to have a Hagaan Das ice cream from the trolley that was wheeled through the grounds every day and then they sat and read. Pippa was totally engrossed in her book but Charles looked up to see Fiona staring into the distance.

"Penny for them, love?" he said and she focused on him and laughed.

"Just thinking I might go along to the shops. I need some toiletries."

"Unlike a woman not to bring enough with her," remarked Charles.

"Well it's conditioner. I don't use that at home but I could do with some here," she told him.

"Want me to come with you?" he asked.

"Oh no," she said hurriedly. "No point in two of us getting all hot and sticky."

She went up through the Rasa Wing foyer and Yous offered to drive her to the Golden Sands in the wee buggy that sat outside. She thanked him and took him up on his offer as it was just after midday and the heat was scorching. He offered to wait for her while she crossed the road and did her shopping and she accepted gratefully.

As they were pulling up outside the hotel, a police car was stopping there too and Sergeant Cheng and DCI Hussain got out. Yous opened the door for them.

"How can I get in touch with a guest?" demanded Hussain.

"Reception can ring their room and try the food outlets for you. Who do you want to see?" asked Yous, politely.

"I'm looking for a Mr Davenport, Charles Davenport."

Fiona, on her way past them, stopped.

"He's down in the gardens, Inspector. I can take you to him," she offered.

"Tell him to come up to the lounge," snapped the sergeant.

Fiona bristled.

"Tell him? Don't you mean, ask him?" she said icily.

"In this country, we don't ask," glared Cheng.

Fiona stomped off to the stairs. When she reached Charles, she told him about the summons and warned him to keep his temper.

"I have the feeling they could jail you for nothing out here," she said, anxiously.

Charles put on his tee-shirt over his swim shorts and, reassuring her that he would be patience personified, walked off across the grounds.

The two policemen were standing at the reception desk. Yous sent Charles a warning look and Nancy asked if they wanted a drink.

"Yes, please," said Charles at the same time as the DCI said, "No."

"I'll have a sprite, Nancy," said Charles and walked away to sit down at one of the tables, refusing to be intimidated. The policemen had no option but to follow him but they remained standing.

"Mr Davenport. I've been informed by a guest in the Golden Sands that you asked if he wanted to talk to you. His wife was murdered there the other day. Why would he want to talk to you?"

"Mrs Grant wanted to talk to me because I was familiar with police procedures and she wanted to know if she should hire a lawyer. I told her it would be a wise thing to do. I thought maybe this other man, Mr Edwards, might feel the same."

Even to his own ears it sounded very lame. The sergeant snorted.

"Mr Davenport, you were warned by my superior..."

He gave a servile half bow in the direction of his DCI.

"... not to interfere in the murder of Alan Grant. Do we need to warn you not to interfere in this second murder?"

"Well, they're obviously connected..."

"Oh are they?"

The sergeant's voice dripped sarcasm.

"And how did you work that out...Sir?"

Feeling that he had nearly given things away, wanting them to know as much as possible, yet reluctant to help them either, Charles satisfied himself with the bland comment that surely two murders unconnected was a bit of a coincidence.

Flicking an imaginary speck of dust from his white gloves, DCI Hussain said, coolly,

"I will give you one last warning...Dav...Mr Davenport. If you meddle again in this case...these cases, I will have you jailed. Is that clear?"

"Very clear. In that case, I will wish you well with your investigations."

Charles rose to his feet, picked up his glass and walked off, feeling two sets of eyes boring into his back all the way across the lounge to the stairs leading to the gardens.

When he arrived, fuming, at his lounger, Sean Grafton was sitting on it.

"Bad time with the police, Charles?" he asked.

Glad that Pippa was absent, Charles gave Fiona and Sean an account of his meeting with the police.

"Are you backing out or do you want to hear what was said by Elliott?"

"I want to hear. How do you know?"

"Elliott asked Weiss to wait with him and, surprisingly, there was no complaint about that. Weiss told me."

"So?"

"Elliott told the police that he went into town on the 10.10 bus, met a fellow guest in Traders for lunch at 12. They sat on there till about 2.30 as it turned into a liquid lunch, then he had an hour-long massage - could give the name of the place too, then went into Parkson Grand, tried on some pairs of trousers there, bought a pair and a shirt and got the 5 o'clock bus back here."

"All very convenient," said Fiona. "Almost as if he knew he'd need an alibi."

"My thoughts exactly," said Sean and Charles nodded his agreement.

"I take it he doesn't want to talk to me if he reported me to the police," commented Charles.

"Is that why they wanted to see you?" asked Fiona.

Charles nodded.

"And I'm to be jailed if I get involved again."

"So what will you do?" asked Sean.

"Keep away from Elliott. The fact that he complained about me to the police is the sign of a guilty man, in my opinion. I'll keep up my investigations at home. The innocent won't report me!"

Sean left, saying that he would see them on Sunday, if not before and Pippa came running up to say that Mai Lee had asked her and Nancy to go with her and her parents to see Tony's new Buddhist monastery in a place called Balik Pilau. Behind her came Rory White with the suggestion that the two of them go with him and Hope to the fruit farm, up near the new dam.

"There's a waterfall near there too. We could stop off there if you like. I'll hire a car."

The waterfall had run out of water; the river bed was dry. They shopped at a roadside stall nearby, being shown a ledger of people who had ordered things once home, then went on to the fruit farm which was interesting. After the tour and explanation of how the fruits were grown, they sampled some of the fruits which were unknown to them. They returned to the hotel. Pippa and Nancy came back, talking more about the three dogs they had met at the monastery than about the building itself, though Pippa wondered why the visiting Buddhist nuns had to share a large sleeping room whereas the monks had individual rooms.

"I know she's had her first period but I don't think she's quite ready for the talk on homosexuality yet," laughed Charles, after he had fobbed her off with something about women being scared to sleep alone.

In spite of the police warning and Fiona's attempts to stop him continuing with the investigation, he rang Salma the next morning to ask her to speak to Denise Grant.

"It doesn't matter if she knows that you're police, Salma. Tell her that her mother has asked me to investigate for her. Tell her and the son that the police out here are unfriendly towards their mother and ask her not to mention me if they get in touch. Oh and could you try to get a picture of Ethel Kelman from the factory, maybe from that fellow, Brown?"

Charles listened and rang off.

"Salma spoke to Phil Soames' boating friends and they vouch for him being with them all last week. She and Frank visited Penny last night and thought that though she looked pale and tired, she's doing OK."

They called Pippa in from the balcony where she was sitting reading her book and went to the Grill restaurant for breakfast.

CHAPTER 26

The next day was the one designated for the trip up Penang Hill. After breakfast in the Grill, Amin who was at the door this morning, tried to get Gopal but he was in Georgetown so the man who came for them was a stranger. Charles told him they wanted to go to the Hill and the driver said he would wait for them for only another 10 ringitts, making it 90 ringitts altogether.

"How long will we need to be up there?" Fiona asked him.

"If you want to eat in the restaurant there, you could be a couple of hours but if you only want to see the view and enjoy the ride up the hill, then one hour should be enough altogether, Miss," was the reply.

In the taxi, they discussed their plans, deciding that they would simply take the train up, take some photos of the view and come back down.

There was quite a long queue for the funicular train and Pippa pointed out the entrance to the Botanic Gardens which were nearby.

"Don't let's go there," she pleaded. "Apart from getting funny photos, it was boring."

As they neared the front of the queue, they could look up the steep hillside and the lines of the track which seemed almost perpendicular. Charles explained to his daughter that the one going up balanced with the one coming down so they would meet halfway.

"So if that snaky, rope thing broke on the one going up, both trains would crash down!" she said, sounding a bit frightened.

"I expect so but why would that suddenly happen," laughed her father. "That snaky rope thing as you call it, is made of a really heavy material."

Pippa peered upwards again and Fiona nudged Charles and pointed out a sign saying that in a few weeks' time the funicular would be closed for renovation.

"Better not let her see that," she whispered.

As the down train arrived at that moment, Pippa missed the sign and they clambered on board. There were three small carriages and all were crammed with people. Only about four people had seats. Halfway up, they passed the down train and then they stopped at a station called Claremont.

"That's the name of a school in East Kilbride," said Fiona and she took a photograph of it.

At the next stop, they had to disembark and wait for another train for the next leg. This time they could see very ornate houses built on the side of the hill and a winding path but not wide enough for cars to use.

"I wouldn't want to live in one of those," commented Fiona.

"Tony told us when we went to Balik Pilau that there was a monastery on the side of Penang Hill. One of his friends, who used to work in the hotel, went to live there once and he had to take her food often 'cos they can't make food for themselves while they're there," Pippa informed them.

"Why did she go? Was she still working then?" asked Charles.

"She thought she might become a Buddhist nun. The hotel gave her time off. She decided not to be a nun but she had all her hair shaved off and she wore an orange robe thing. Tony showed us a picture."

"Where is she now?" asked Fiona, as the train moved slowly towards its destination.

"In a cake shop in that Tikus place, the place of the rat," Pippa answered.

"She must be over fifty, then," said Charles. "Jaz told me one day that men retire at fifty-five from hotel jobs unless they're kept on and then it's a one year contract, and women go at fifty."

"I know and there's no old age pension over here either so they have to save hard for their retirement. So Jill said," added Fiona.

The train shuddered to a halt. It was quite scary stepping over a gap onto the platform as through the gap they could see the train lines reaching up steeply. They let everyone else in the carriage go first then Charles jumped off and gave both Pippa and Fiona a helping hand.

The views were spectacular and they could easily make out the high Komtar standing head and shoulders over all the other Georgetown buildings. They were so high that there was a bit of a mist swirling round them and they walked over to two old railway carriages, one first class, obviously the remains of an old funicular, kept here for historic purposes. Pippa got inside and Charles snapped her for posterity then they walked a short way to the building which housed the 'polis' and this time Pippa took charge of the camera and took a picture of her Dad and Fiona outside what must be one of the world's highest police stations.

Having been told by the Whites that there really was nothing to do up Penang Hill except have a meal which was nothing special, they retraced their steps and waited for the train back down. This time their carriage held only two other people, a young, Japanese couple who smiled at them. It was rather off-putting when they folded their hands and seemed to pray the whole way down, then opened their eyes, smiled again and walked off.

Their taxi was waiting for them and their driver, seeing them, came across from the group of taxi-drivers he had been talking to. The journey back took about half an hour and they arrived back at the hotel in time for lunch, this time in The Spice Market as Pippa said she would like lasagne which was not on the Penang Bar menu.

"Though I'm sure they would get it for you, if you asked for it," her father commented as they sat down at a table outside.

"Well, I'm going to test that theory," laughed Fiona. "I was looking at the in-house dining menu last night, the room service part, and I fancy a Monte Christo."

"What's that, Fiona?" asked Pippa.

"It's French toast with cheese and tomato," came the reply.

As Charles had thought, this was no problem, Fiona being asked if she wanted French fries with it.

"No thanks, Prakesh."

"Bring the chips, Prakesh," said Charles. "I'll have them. I just want ice cream apart from that."

They had forgotten that the Spice Market was busy at weekends but the visiting locals seemed to prefer to sit inside and the only inconvenience was that service was slower than usual.

"We're in no hurry," said Fiona.

Lunch over, they made their way to the loungers which, as usual, Tony had made ready with their two towels each. He came across to say hello and they told him where they had been.

"I told Dad and Fiona about your friend who nearly became a nun," said Pippa.

"That is correct. Her name is Janet. She is of Chinese origin like me," Tony informed them. "She was in charge of The Feringgi Grill when she worked here but while the hotel was closed a few years ago, she became fifty so did not come back."

"Gopal left then too," said Fiona.

"Yes. He was asked to come back and did for a while but found out that he preferred running his taxi and left."

" 'Scuse me, Tony. Dad, I'm away to see if Nancy and Mai Lee are in the grounds."

Pippa was keen to be off.

"OK. If you don't come back, we'll know you found one or both of them," said Charles.

Tony left as there were two guests standing by his library hut and Charles and Fiona went up to the room to get changed. They spent some time doing the crossword in the Straits Times and agreed to collaborate after half an hour. With three clues still unsolved, they went for a swim in the Rasa pool, passing the Whites with Pippa and Mai Lee. Pippa got up and asked for the room key, saying that she would swim in the Garden Wing pool with the other two girls.

"I'll go with them," said Rory White.

They did not stay long in the warmth of the pool, taking the fresh towels offered to them by Muru.

"The police came this morning to ask if I'd seen a young woman at the pool, Mr Davenport. That Cheng man asked why I hadn't said and I just told him that nobody had asked," he told them.

They made their way across the grounds to their loungers. Pippa came back with the key just in time for Charles to go up to wait for a possible phone call from Salma. He came back about twenty minutes later.

"Bang on time!" he told Fiona.

"Anything of interest to report?" Fiona asked.

"Salma spoke to Denise Grant on Friday night. Her brother was there, so Salma apologised for lying to him and explained about their mother wanting things found out but that the Penang police were antagonistic towards her and also towards Salma's boss who happened to be at the same hotel."

"And?"

"Denise had been in Singapore with two old school friends. She willingly gave their names and addresses so I told Salma not to bother checking with them."

"So you're sure that Bill Elliott is the murderer, then?" asked Fiona.

"Well, he came to the next door hotel under an assumed name and his wife ends up dead too. Bit of a coincidence, don't you think?" posed Charles.

"What about his alibi?"

Charles was silent. He pulled at his ear lobe. Into Fiona's brain popped the words,

"Right team!" and she giggled.

"What are you finding so funny?" demanded Charles.

"I expected you so say, 'Right team!'" she informed him.

"Am I so predictable?" he asked.

"Well...yes."

"When I get you alone, Miss Macdonald, I'll prove that I'm not!" he said, with a mock leer.

"The alibi, DCI Davenport?"

"Yes. I must admit that is a stumbling block but he could have got someone to kill her for him."

"That suggests an accomplice surely. He couldn't just go up to another guest and say, "Would you murder my wife, please," Fiona contended.

"So you think I should get Salma to check Denise Grant's alibi?"

"Yes, I do. I'm sure Singapore is about the same plane journey to here as it is from KL. Get Salma to check if Denise was on the Penang passenger list at any time."

"OK, will do. I asked her to try to find out where Ethel Kelman went to as well and she said she'll go back to the friend's house. I told her that we'd phone her next time as we're at Sean's tomorrow."

"Good thinking, Batman."

The evening was decided for them by Pippa who came across to say that a nine-some had been suggested, at Sunset Beach.

"Which is where?" asked her father.

"It's along the road and you go down between two of the hotels and sit in seats on the beach and watch the sun going down while you eat. Rory and Hope know a doctor in Penang and he has a girlfriend who took them one year. There's a parrot there and..."

"I know a man who knows a woman who knows a girl with a parrot who..."

"Dad! Stop it. Can we go?"

Pippa glared at him.

"Only if the parrot's going to be there," Charles teased her.

They met up in the foyer after drinks and walked along the road, weaving in and out between the people setting up the stalls. Charles kept Pippa in the inside, as the traffic, especially the motorcycles, came in close to the pavement. They arranged nine seats round two rickety tables and were given a menu each. The girls all chose pizzas and Fiona copied them. The other adults voted for burgers. Cameras came out as the sun went down, Pippa insisting that the parrot be in at least one photograph.

It was a tired but happy group that made its way back to the hotel where the adults had coffees and the girls had lemonade.

CHAPTER 27

"And when were you thinking of giving me this information, Cheng?"

The hectoring voice thundered round the small room and the men in the next room grinned at each other. No one liked Sergeant Cheng who was a bully and fawned over their boss, Inspector Hussain.

"Looks as if the golden boy has blotted his copybook," drawled Les, the only Australian among their number.

"Rav's in there too. He'll tell us what it's all about," said another constable.

"If you shut up, we might just hear for ourselves," piped up the secretary, Lim, the only woman in the station. She was a tiny woman with jet black hair in a neat chignon.

They quietened down and listened. The walls were thin and they knew from their own experiences that when Hussain was angry, he lost his cool demeanour and tended to shout.

Cheng must have answered his superior while they spoke amongst themselves as it was Hussain who spoke once again.

"So there was another person at the Rasa Sayang pool on the day of the murder, a woman on her own. Why, Ravanathan, did you not come straight to me with this information?"

The listeners grimaced in sympathy with Rav. Cheng always insisted that they tell him everything and never went straight to the Inspector. He liked to be the informant and took all the kudos for this service. If Rav said this now, it would add another nail to the coffin of Hussain's displeasure with his sergeant. What would he say?

"Sir, I know you are always very busy so I did not want to disturb you."

"Thoughtful, indeed, yet you told your fellow constables and my secretary who fortunately mentioned it to me, thinking that I would already know."

The men in the next room sent sympathetic glances towards Lim who would certainly hear from Cheng when Hussain was finished with him. However, it was better that it was her who was the culprit as Cheng could not affect her chances of promotion as he could theirs'.

"Yes, Sir. Sorry, Sir," replied Ravanathan.

"Do you think then that someone, apart from Mrs Grant, could have committed the murder on Mr Grant?"

"Well, Sir, this other woman or one of the two couples who were sitting round the pool, could have gone round into the garden behind the jacuzzi part, killed him and come back round without anyone noticing," said Ravanathan, bravely.

"Do you know any reasons for them to have wanted him dead?"

"No, Sir but if they turn out to have come from Britain, then it is possible."

"How did you find out about the woman?"

"One of the pool workers told me the day you sent me back to search the pool area, Sir"

"And now I hear from the Rasa Sayang manager that someone was here from Britain, from Scotland, under an assumed name."

"That's interesting, Sir," said Ravanathan.

"So he and his dead wife could have been one of the couples at the pool that day, Cheng?"

"Yes, Sir."

"You are dismissed for now, Constable," barked Hussain.

The men listening at the wall, moved back hurriedly in case Cheng also left the room but it was only Ravanathan who appeared, looking quite pleased with himself.

"Thanks, Lim. It worked well," he said to his co-conspirator.

"So you planned this, Rav!" said Les.

"Well, this other woman and one of the other couples are possible suspects. The Inspector is so sure that the man's wife killed him that I think Cheng did not want to tell him of another possibility. No one has checked up on the two couples who were at the pool and no one seemed to be taking into account the fact that the woman murdered at The Golden Sands was here with her husband under an assumed name!"

The Inspector's door opened once again.

"...to the Golden Sands and bring that man Edwards...Elliott... here. He should be easy to find as he was told to remain in his room until further notice. Even an idiot should have no trouble carrying out that instruction."

Sergeant Cheng almost scuttled out of the room, not glancing at the men assembled in the adjacent room as he grabbed his hat and left the station. Inspector Hussain appeared in the doorway.

"Ravanathan. Go to the Rasa Sayang and ask Mrs Grant to come to see me as soon as possible."

"Yes, Sir."

Bill Elliott arrived quite soon. He looked belligerent and the men, knowing Cheng, guessed that the sergeant had taken his anger at being spoken harshly to out on this man.

"This is ridiculous. I'm being treated like a suspect. There is no way I could have killed my wife. I was due to go home two days ago. I insist on getting a lawyer, an English-speaking one."

Hussain ushered him into his room.

"Now, Mr ...Elliott, perhaps you will tell me why you stayed at the hotel under a different name."

"It'll sound silly."

"I'll be the judge of that."

Hussian was now his usual, cool, brusque self and the men and woman outside had to strain to hear this time.

"My wife, Louise, thought that if I could talk to Alan...Mr Grant while he was relaxing on holiday, he might give me my job back. He bought me out, you see, because we didn't see eye to eye over the running of the company. We thought it would be better to make sure he didn't get to hear our name so we planned to use Louise's maiden name."

"A bit risky, surely? Hotels always ask for passports."

"Yes but I told them that I'd left them at the wee hotel we stayed at in Georgetown and the woman merely asked me to get them as soon as possible. If they'd refused us a room, I'm sure we could have got one in a smaller hotel on the strip."

"Did you go to the Rasa Sayang on the day of the murder? Remember we can bring in the pool attendants to take a look at you."

"Yes, we did. We wanted to find out what his usual holiday procedure was so that we could engineer a meeting."

"And did you talk to him that day?"

"No. We heard the kerfuffle over in the garden part of the pool and thought it wiser to move off as soon as it wouldn't cause suspicion."

"Don't you think it a bit of a coincidence that your wife and Alan Grant were killed within days of each other?"

"Well, it must be as I can't think why Louise should pose a threat to someone who killed Alan unless he or she thought that Louise had witnessed the murder and why would anyone think that?"

"You tell me, Mr Elliott. Could the murderer be someone you all knew from home?"

"Who?"

"Was there someone else who hated Mr Grant? Someone he'd sacked perhaps?"

"The only person sacked was Phil Soames, his accountant, and he'd been fiddling the books so could hardly bear a grudge. Anyway, I spoke to Phil on the phone before we came out and he told me he was off sailing with friends in a few days' time."

"No one else?"

"Not that I can think of."

The listening group moved away from the wall as Ravanathan came in with Mrs Grant.

He knocked on the door.

"Come in!" said Hussain, impatiently.

"Mrs Grant," said Ravanathan, standing aside to usher Jean Grant into the room.

"Bill! Whatever are you doing here?" exclaimed the woman.

She walked into the room and the door was closed once again. Les told Ravanathan what had transpired while he was away.

"Almost worth being called in on Sunday, me old mate," he added.

Leave had been cancelled after the second murder and up till now they had seen no reason for this decision.

Over at The Rasa, Charles had been having an interesting conversation with Mike Jamieson.

"I just remembered where I'd seen the single woman who was at the pool that day."

Mike had approached Charles at breakfast in the Grill restaurant. He sat down in the empty chair at their table.

"Where?"

"On the plane, coming over here. She was in the seat in front of us and she had quite a long chat with one of the stewards. She was a beautiful, young woman, slim and blonde and I remember thinking how her voice spoiled things."

"How, Mike?" asked Fiona.

"Well I expected a beautiful voice and she had a really common Glasgow accent and vocabulary. You know the sort of thing, 'I seen' and 'I done'. And the ubiquitous 'yous'. It makes me cringe! She was quite nasal too, altogether unpleasant. I thought maybe there was some link between the Grant man who was also from Glasgow, though better-spoken for all his other faults. Lorna said to tell you in case it helps at all, though I know you can't tell the police here."

"I managed to get news through to them via one of their nicer constables that there was a single woman at the pool that day so they know that. Would you contact them, Mike? The station is in Batu Feringgi, across from The Golden Sands."

Mike grimaced but said that he would and got up and left. They finished their breakfast and went back to their room to get their bag packed for their day at the manager's house. They were surprised to see Sean in the foyer when they got there.

"I'm having the rest of the day off," he assured them. "I waited to tell you that Jean Grant's been summoned to the police station again. The nice, young constable came for her. He told her not to worry so she rang me and said she would contact me when she came back and that if she didn't come back, to alert Ewan Johnstone. I've given her my mobile number."

"What happened when you told the police that Bill Elliott was here under an assumed name?"

"I spoke to the Inspector himself when I went to the station. He acted as though I was trying to give him more work, then shouted at the sergeant fellow..."

"...Cheng," put in Fiona.

"Yes, Cheng, for not finding this out. Cheng just about grovelled his apology. Ishmael will be here in about ten minutes. I'll get off now and be there to greet you."

CHAPTER 28

Pippa looked eagerly out of the car window, trying to recognise places she had seen before.

"Dad, there's that board with the sign about three-storey bungalows! They don't look very safe, stuck up on the hill like that, do they?"

"No, they don't."

"Fiona, what does reclamation mean again?"

"It means that the land that those new houses on your right are being built on, has been reclaimed, taken back, from the sea."

"So the sea came in..."

"Years and years ago and now they are really pushing it back out again."

"How can you push the sea back?"

"I've no idea. I just know I wouldn't want to live in one of those houses."

"Especially in a place where there's been a tsunami," added Charles. "Ishmael, where were you when the big wave hit Penang?"

Charles was sitting beside Sean's driver who now smiled and replied that he had been lucky to be in the hotel that day and not out on his motorbike.

"The Baywatch guard shouted to people on the beach to get back and they all ran into the hotels. The wave came through the bottom floor and across to the restaurants on the other side of the road. I was in the foyer and saw all the people. I got my feet wet, that was all. Luckily, I live on the other side of the island so my wife was safe."

"What about your children, Ishmael?" asked Fiona.

"They all live in Kuala Lumpur, Miss," was the reply.

"Look there's McDonalds!" said Pippa.

"Well we're nearly there then," her Dad told her.

They were held up at the lights at the busy intersection and by people coming in cars to eat at the local stalls in the road next to Sean's and then they were there and the big gates were opening electronically and Sean and his two dogs were coming to greet them.

"Oh you wee beauty!" exclaimed Pippa, going down on her knees to stroke Lucky. Habibi nuzzled her other arm and she patted him too.

The adults were going into the house so she got to her feet and followed them, the two dogs bringing up the rear.

"Fiona. Can I have the doggy chews we bought, please? Mr Grafton, is it Ok if I give them both a chew?"

"Of course it is. You'll be their friend for life and please call me Sean."

Marianna was in the hallway to greet them and say hello in halting English. The dogs went off with her and Sean took his visitors outside to the pool area, where four loungers with brightly coloured towels were waiting for them.

"Pippa, before you get wet, how would you like to come to the vet with me?" asked Sean.

"Which one is sick?" she asked anxiously.

"It's nothing serious but Lucky has a rash on his tummy and he hates going to the vet. Maybe you can help take his mind off it."

The pair left with a reluctant Lucky who seemed to know what was afoot, maybe because, as Sean told Pippa in the car, the two dogs went everywhere together, except the vet's.

Sean had to pull the dog from the back seat and carry him inside. Once there it was even harder to quieten the little animal.

Sean and Pippa sat down, after informing the receptionist that they were there and Lucky clambered all over them, even going up on Sean's shoulders at one point. There were notices telling customers not to allow their animals onto the chairs but it was impossible to keep Lucky down. All the pats and strokes from Pippa failed to calm him and there was a bit of a panic when he squirmed out of his collar and made a dive for the door which was luckily closed.

Then they were called to the surgery. Sean lifted Lucky onto the table where he stood quivering like a little blonde jelly while the vet inspected his rash.

Sean was given enough pills and cream to last for a week and was told to return with the dog if the rash did not go away. Lucky pulled Sean all the way to the car and leapt in this time.

When they got home, Pippa held the little dog while Sean put one of the pills at the back of his throat then held his mouth shut and rubbed his throat, only letting him go when he gulped and swallowed the tablet. There was no problem with the cream.

"Habibi is more clever. He gulps dramatically and when I let go of his mouth, he spits out the tablet," Sean told Pippa.

Fiona and Charles were sitting at one of the tables when they went outside.

"We didn't want to go in to swim till you were both back," said Charles.

They all stripped off their outer clothing and were soon in the pool. It was large for a private pool and the water was warm. They all had to duck as tiny birds flew across, skimming the water with their blue tummies.

"A beautiful kingfisher-type bird comes at about four o'clock," Sean informed them. "It sits on the ladder over there and when the dogs see it they chase it, yet it keeps coming back. Occasionally, if the dogs don't notice it, it dips into the water."

"Do they chase anything else?" asked Pippa.

"Yes. They chase a black squirrel. I say,'Public enemy number one' and they dash round the pool."

They stayed in the pool for quite a long time, Pippa delighted when Habibi came in too and doggy-paddled his way round.

"I knew there was a stroke called doggy-paddle but I didn't know why till I saw him do it," she said, delightedly.

"Does Lucky never come in?" asked Fiona.

"I took him in once and he tried to get out at the side, not at the steps so I never leave them in this part of the garden alone in case he might drown. No use tempting him in now when I've just put cream on him either."

Pippa was pulling a float through the water with Habibi holding on to it with his teeth. When she let go, he paddled to the steps and climbed up, shaking himself strongly over Marianna who had come out to tell them that lunch was ready.

"Hope you don't mind a kind of lunch cum dinner," Sean said as they got out of the pool and began drying themselves. In the sun, they dried quickly and were soon seated at the outdoor table.

Marianna brought a variety of dishes, some meat, some chicken and some fish. There were about six dishes of vegetables and two of potatoes.

"Dig in and help yourselves," said Sean.

"Do you ever have to bath the dogs?" asked Pippa.

"Marianna does that. She baths them at least once a week. They're so good. They let her hose them down then shampoo them and even add smelly stuff once they're dry. Habibi hates that. He rubs himself along the grass to try to get his natural doggy smell back but Lucky seems OK with it. She brushes their teeth with toothbrush and toothpaste too!"

After the main course, trifle and lemon meringue pie were placed on the table and they tucked in again. Coffee followed and Pippa asked to be excused to go and play with the dogs inside the house.

Conversation turned at once to the two murders.

"At least Hussain now knows about Elliot and about the folk round the pool who were never mentioned before," said Charles.

"What do you think now, Charles?" asked Sean.

"Well, there were three people who must have hated Alan Grant, plus his son and daughter who didn't exactly love him either. Jean Grant appears to me to be innocent but she was treated badly by him too so might have felt murderous towards him. Bill Elliot could have killed Grant and his own wife, though why he should kill his wife, I don't know.

Another man, Phil Soames, was sacked because of embezzlement and his wife died shortly afterwards but he was in Scotland sailing with friends. Grant's daughter was in Singapore and that's not far from here. His son was at home. Salma met him and he couldn't have had time to get home, I don't think, though it's possible, I suppose."

"Take your pick, Sean," laughed Fiona.

"I've asked my sergeant to try to get a picture of another possible suspect, Grant's secretary. Not his current one but the one before that. She left very suddenly. However, a worker at the factory said she was a pretty girl so it wasn't likely that Grant threw her over, more likely the other way round so she would have no motive."

"Let me sum up what you've said and you can correct me if I'm wrong," said Sean.

"Mr Elliot and or his wife could have killed Grant but why would Elliott kill his own wife?"

"She panicked and wanted to confess all?" put in Fiona.

"Mr ...the sailor..." said Sean.

"Soames," said Charles.

"Mr Soames had a motive but has also a clear alibi," said Fiona.

"Miss Grant could have come across from Singapore and murdered her father. Her alibi is still to be checked out," ventured Sean next.

"That's correct," said Charles.

"And Miss X?"

"An Ethel Kelman," said Fiona.

"She wanted Grant dead because?" queried Sean.

"She's pregnant and he won't support her and the baby," volunteered Fiona, grinning.

Shortly after this, Charles thanked Sean for his hospitality and said that they would get a taxi to take them back to the hotel.

"Don't phone Ishmael. I'm sure that Sunday must be his day off, Sean. I have to get back soon as I want to contact Salma, about five o'clock, if possible."

The taxi came in about fifteen minutes and in that time Pippa had organised a doggy photo-shoot and Fiona had collected their wet swimming clothes and put them in the bag she had brought for this purpose.

"I'll keep you up to date, Sean," said Charles. "Will you tell me anything you hear?"

Sean agreed to this as the taxi peeped outside.

They pulled up outside the Rasa Sayang just after five o'clock and went to their room. While

Pippa was having her shower, Salma rang. Charles spoke to her for a long time then hung up.

"Salma had said she would try to ring later, it being Sunday and she's not at work. The Penang police have contacted the factory by phone, according to Leonard Brown who heard from the new secretary. Apparently they just asked to speak to the depute manager. She had no idea what about."

"Whew! No questioning of people like Leonard Brown then?"

"No. I imagine they just asked if Bill Elliott had worked there and why he had left. Even if they asked about a single woman all they would get was the name of Ethel Kelman and no one there suspects anything sinister about why she left, thinking that she threw him over."

"The photograph?"

"Salma has emailed it to the hotel, care of Sean Grafton."

"Denise Grant's alibi?"

"Not so easy, Salma said. She couldn't think of any reason why Jean Grant would ask us to check up on her daughter and I agree with her. We'll just have to take her word for it that she stayed in Singapore, unless it transpires that a young woman killed Grant."

"Any further forward with Miss Kelman?"

"Salma concocted a devious plan to find out if Ethel Kelman had been to Penang."

Charles told Fiona what Salma had done, adding that the woman had indeed been in Penang at some time in her life.

"It was risky enough doing what she did, without asking her when she had been there," Charles concluded.

Pippa came out of the bathroom, her head in a towel. It was Fiona's turn to get washed and ready for the evening meal, so she left them.

All that was left for Charles to do was ring Rav on his mobile to tell him that there would be a picture of Grant's ex secretary arriving shortly and to inform him that Grant's daughter who had no love for her father, had been in Singapore at the time of the murder.

"I've no idea how you can use this information Rav, unless you suggest to Hussain that you check up on his family at home and as for the photo, goodness knows how you can use that even if I give it to you! Oh and one of the guests here told me that he remembered that he had seen the young woman who was at the pool that day, on the plane from KL. She had a Glasgow accent. I told him to contact the police. I hope he did.

He listened and hung up. When Fiona came out of the bedroom, he filled her in from Rav's end.

"Inspector Hussain now knows that there was a single woman at the pool. Rav is going to have to find some way of suggesting that Grant might have a young, female friend or relative and that this person might have wanted rid of him. There's no way he can just suddenly have possession of Ethel Kelman's picture!"

"Oh, Charles! It's getting a bit dicey now, isn't it? I'm almost glad that Salma couldn't ask for a photo of Denise Grant. You're getting too involved as it is. You don't want to lose your job."

Pippa came in from the balcony in time to hear this pronouncement.

"Why would you lose your job, Dad?" she asked.

"Fiona was just joking, pet."

Charles took his turn of the bathroom then they went downstairs for their pre-dinner drinks.

CHAPTER 29

Salma had spent a long night lying awake, wondering how she could find out if Denise Grant had stayed in Singapore all the time and also how to find out where Ethel Kelman had gone. As the first signs of dawn were streaking the summer sky, she had reached a conclusion about Alan Grant's ex-secretary.

As it was Sunday, Salma had no work to go to. She had promised her young brother a day out if the weather was good and it was, so after breakfast she told him to put on his trainers.

"We're going to be doing some detective work," she told Rafiq who was just young enough to be excited at this prospect. They got into her car and she made her way across the city to the South Side.

"Where are we?" asked Rafiq who had never been far from the West End and Bridgeton. "We've crossed the river so are we somewhere near where Uncle Fariz and Aunt Zenib live?"

"You'd make a good policeman, Rafiq. Yes, we're on the South Side of Glasgow now. They live in Pollokshields but we're not in Pollokshields, Rafiq. We're going to a place called Shawlands.

"That's where Penny, your friend, lives, isn't it?" said Rafiq. "Are we going to visit her?"

"No. I'm afraid Penny's in hospital. Do you not remember me asking Shazia to stay with you while I went to visit her the other night?"

"Yes and I'm old enough to stay in on my own."

"No. Not till you're at least sixteen."

Salma stopped the car at the side of the road, between bus stops in Victoria Road. It was quiet, being Sunday.

"Now listen carefully. I'm going to visit a lady. I need to find out where she's been on holiday. I'm going to pretend I'm doing a survey..."

"What's that. Salma?" asked Rafiq.

"It's what people do to find out how many people do something...say I wanted to know how many people ate cheese and onion crisps, I'd stop and ask people and count up those who said, yes."

"So what's this pretend survey about, Salma?"

"I'm going to go to the station to pick up a clipboard... that's a piece of cardboard you put a piece of paper on," she said, pre-empting the next question. "Once I've got that, I'll tell you what questions I'll be asking."

It only took minutes to go into her room at the station, pick up a clipboard and some A4 paper. Feeling like a thief, she went into DS Macdonald's room and picked up the brochure for Far East Holidays that she had seen lying around some weeks ago. Back in the car, she explained things to her brother.

"I'm going to be asking this lady if she's ever been in Thailand or Malaysia. I'm going to tell her that there's a prize for someone who can describe a beach resort hotel in one of those places, in a hundred words."

Seeing the look of bewilderment on Rafiq's face, she said, "I'm hoping that seeing you with me, will make her trust me. All I want you to do is tell her that your Mum is poor and needs the money from this survey"

"This is fun," said Rafiq. "I'm good at acting in drama, in school. I've to pretend that you're my Mum and I'm helping you with a survey. Yes?"

"Yes."

Salma drove to Shawlands, to Dinmont Road. They got out of the car outside number four. The woman who answered the door had gardening gloves on both hands and was carrying a hoe. She looked impatient when she saw the clipboard.

"I won't take long, Miss..." Salma looked down at her board.

"...Mrs Lawson."

"Mrs Lawson. I'm conducting a survey and if you can help me, you stand a chance of winning a thousand pounds."

"I really haven't got time for this," said the woman.

"Oh please, Mrs. Help my Mum. She has to get a hundred people to help her or she won't get paid," said Rafiq, with a soulful look.

"Oh, OK. What is it you want?"

"Is there any chance that you can describe a five star beach resort hotel in the Far East in a hundred words?"

"Far East? No chance. Furthest I've ever been is Minorca!"

Salma thanked her. She was keeping a careful lookout for Kitty Stevens at number eight and Mrs George at number fourteen who had both seen her before.

She went to a few more houses in the street, asking the same question, until she came to the house pointed out to her by Kitty Steven as Ethel Kelman's, number sixteen. She rang the bell and mentally crossed her fingers.

The young woman who stood on the threshold was a beauty. Tall, slim and with shining blonde hair, she was fashionably dressed in cut-off denims with an off-the-shoulder top in peacock blue. Salma said her piece, adding that one of her neighbours had said she might be able to answer her question.

"I've been down the street without any luck," she said, wryly.

"Wha' is it? "

The voice was grating coming from the lovely, cupid -shaped lips.

"I wondered if you'd ever been to the Far East," said Salma.

"Oh Mum, I hope so," sighed Rafiq. "My feet are aching."

"Aye. A've bin to Phuket and Penang," said the woman.

Salma felt her heart give a leap. Surely it could not be that easy.

"Well, if you can describe a five star beach resort hotel in either Phuket or Penang...are they both in Thailand?" asked Salma.

"Phuket is in Thailand and Penang's in Malaysia. Is therr a prize for this?"

"Yes, you stand to win a thousand pounds. Would you like two tries? You could describe both hotels."

The woman seemed to consider this. Her eyes narrowed.

"Dae ah have to name the hotels?" she asked.

"No. That's not necessary."

As soon as she said that Salma thought that she had made a mistake. Surely a survey would want the hotels' names. However either Ethel Kelman's thoughts were on the prize or she was relieved not to have to name the hotels, for she agreed to describe both.

Salma wrote diligently.

"Thank you, Mrs," said Rafiq, his big brown eyes wide. "My Mum has to get a hundred people to do this before she gets paid."

"...has a large pool and three restaurants and is on a golden beach," finished the woman.

Salma thanked her profusely and told her that she would hear in about a month if she had been lucky. They went to the next three houses on the street then got back in the car.

During the wakeful night, Salma had been unable to come up with any ploy to find out whether Denise Grant had remained in Singapore but she felt that she had succeeded with at least one of the women her boss wanted to find out about. If Davenport recognised the hotel described by Ethel Kelman then she had indeed been in Penang at some time in her life but whether a few weeks ago or years ago remained to be seen.

"You were brilliant, Raf and you looked so sad. Thank you. Now for your reward. What about a meal in McDonald's?"

"Yes please!" said Rafiq.

They went to McDonald's on Pollokshaws Road, through from Victoria Road and Salma treated her fellow detective to a Big Mac and fries, followed by an ice cream and toffee dessert. Rafiq asked if they could go to Silverburn shopping centre after that and she bought him a brightly-coloured tee-shirt.

They arrived home, tired but delighted with their expedition.

Salma waited for Davenport's call. He had said he would be out of the hotel till about five o'clock.

"So you can't think of any way I can find out about Denise Grant?" she asked him when he did call and was relieved to hear him say that there was no way Denise would believe that her mother wanted her questioned about her time in Singapore. She told him about the Penang police only contacting the deputy manager and that she had sent on a picture of Ethel Kelman by email.

It was not till she had hung up the phone, had a shower and mediated between the two children over what DVD they should watch, that Salma wondered why Mrs Grant had not known that her daughter was in the Far East or if she had known, why she had kept quiet about it.

Across the world, the same thought had just struck Charles. They were sitting outside at The Spice Market, having decided that all they wanted after drinks, was a dessert, being still full from their lunch at Sean's. Pippa was inside helping herself to ice cream and all the trimmings.

"Fiona. Why did Jean Grant not tell us that her daughter was in Singapore?"

"Maybe she didn't know, Charles."

"Well, if she didn't know, then that makes me suspicious of Denise. Why keep your holiday destination a secret from your mother?"

"And if she did know, then she must be suspicious of Denise to have kept it from you."

"I'll need to ask her tomorrow, unless we see her tonight."

Pippa returned, their ordered desserts arrived and they ate in silence, Pippa's mouth being too full for chat.

Anissa called to them as they entered the Rasa Wing lounge, to tell them that Mr Grafton wanted Charles to phone him. She got the number and handed Charles the phone. When he rang off, Charles joined Fiona who, with Pippa, had sat down at one of their favourite tables and told her that Jean Grant's interview with the Inspector had gone reasonably well.

"She seems to think that Hussain has transferred his suspicions to Bill Elliott."

"Billy Elliott, Dad? We saw a film about him, didn't we?" said Pippa.

"Not the same one, pet. This is Bill, not Billy."

"It will be a big relief for her if, indeed, she suspects her daughter," replied Fiona.

"It's only just after 8.30. I think I'll get Anissa to ring Jean Grant for me."

Suiting the action to the word, Charles went back to reception. Jean was not in bed and offered to come down to the lounge. Charles stayed at reception and steered the woman into one of the little recesses in the lounge. He let her tell him about her interview with Inspector Hussain that morning although he knew all about it from Sean.

"You've not been completely honest with me, Mrs Grant."

She looked startled.

"You didn't tell me that your daughter was in Singapore when your husband was killed."

Jean Grant flushed.

"I'm sorry. I thought it might make you suspect her."

"Well, I would have been more suspicious if she hadn't told you she was going there."

"I see that now. I'm sorry. It was wrong to hide things from you, especially when you were being so helpful to me."

"When did she decide to go to Singapore? Be honest now, please. I can get my sergeant at home to go and question her you know and we can interview the travel agent she uses or check flight lists."

"She had decided months before Alan decided to come out again, Charles. She and her two friends plan their holidays months in advance. I know she hated her father but not enough to kill him."

"Thanks, Jean."

Charles's softened voice and his return to her Christian name, brought tears to the woman's eyes.

"Come on. Fiona and Pippa are across the lounge. Join us for a pre- bedtime drink."

She put her hand on his arm.

"This is such a mess, Charles. Do you think that Bill Elliott and his wife murdered Alan? But why would he murder Louise?"

"He has an alibi for the time of his wife's murder," Charles told her.

"So someone killed Alan, then Louise. What on earth's the connection?" Jean Grant sounded bewildered.

"Come on. Let's have that drink and leave the puzzling to the police."

They crossed the lounge to where Fiona and Pippa were sitting. They had been joined by the Whites who were leaving the next evening. Pippa and Nancy had exchanged snail mail and email addresses on Saturday and were a bit tearful at perhaps never ever seeing each other again. Maz came up for their drinks' order and talk turned to their visit to Sean Grafton's house, Pippa regaling them all with Habibi's antics in the pool and her trip to the vet.

CHAPTER 30

Sean Grafton rang the room early, before they left for breakfast on Monday morning, to say that the photo of Ethel Kelman had come through to his secretary, Shirley. He asked where they were having breakfast and promised to bring the picture to them while they were there.

The Feringgi Grill was very quiet this morning, it being only 6.30, so Pippa was able to try out her Bahasa on Safari. She was given another word and took out her Chalet School book to write down on the inside cover, 'isnin' which Safari pronounced as 'eastnin'. He spelt it out for Pippa alongside its meaning which was 'Monday'. They were just tucking into their toast when Sean came in and showed them the picture of a lovely young woman with blonde hair. She was skilfully made up, her blue eyes topped with long, curling lashes.

"What will you do with this, Charles?" Sean asked him.

"I'm going to show it to Mr Jamieson, Mike Jamieson. I don't think I told you but he came to me the other day to say that he'd just remembered that a Glasgow woman was on their plane from KL. He said she was lovely but had a common Glaswegian accent. He had realised that she was the woman he had seen on her own at the pool on the day of the murder."

"Do the police know?"

"I asked Mike to go to the station and inform them and I also told the young constable but there is no way I can take this picture to the police."

As luck would have it, the Jamiesons came in for breakfast just before they left.

"I thought we'd be the only early birds. We're going to the mainland today," laughed Lorna. Charles apologised for interrupting them at breakfast, then showed them the photo which they both looked at with interest.

"I remember her too, now," said Lorna. "A very pretty woman with a harsh, grating voice."

Mike agreed that this was indeed the woman he had mentioned and told Charles that he had gone to the station.

"I got no thanks, of course. In fact I was reprimanded for having forgotten! That sergeant has no social graces."

"Neither has his boss," commented Fiona.

On their way back to their room to collect their bag for the day, they met Jean Grant. She looked frail and elderly.

"Jean. It appears that Ethel Kelman..."

"...Alan's last secretary?"

"Yes. It seems that she was here in Penang and at the pool the day your husband was murdered."

Jean Grant had gone pale.

"Do the police know?"

"Yes."

"What reason could she possibly have for killing Alan?"

"Well the affair...sorry..."

"It's OK, Charles. I knew he had affairs and welcomed them as it took the heat off me, as I think I said to you."

"As you also guessed from his renewed attentions to you, he had stopped seeing her, so I can only guess that contrary to what we thought at first, it was he who ended things, not her."

"So she killed out of pique? Not a very strong motive surely."

"There's also Bill Elliott. Maybe the two banded together to kill him. There were a number of stab wounds, remember."

"Yes, I wondered about that. Do you think someone stabbed Alan a few times to make sure?"

"Or more than one person stabbed him," said Fiona, quietly.

Pippa had wandered off down the corridor but might still be within hearing distance.

"It's such a mess, Charles," said Jean. "I'm surprised that they let Annabelle go home when they did. I thought that was a hopeful sign that they didn't suspect me anymore. The way they spoke to her earlier, I think they thought she was my accomplice. She didn't need to rearrange her flights which was fortunate."

"When do you leave, Jean?"

"I should be leaving tomorrow but I don't imagine that I'll be allowed to go until they get this sewn up," she said.

"We go tomorrow," said Charles. "But I imagine they'll be delighted to see us go.

Why don't you get Sean to ring the station and ask what you should do about leaving? He can say that your room is being taken by someone else which it probably is."

Jean smiled at them, a weak smile but some colour had returned to her thin face.

"Maybe we could meet up for drinks later this evening and I'll tell you if I'm joining you on the plane home."

"That'll be fine," said Fiona, patting her on the arm, "but it might be later than cocktail hour as we're going across to Langkawi today. Sorry we have to run but the ferry leaves at 8.30 and we've still to get to the terminal."

They hurried off to the room, picked up the bag that Fiona had packed the night before and were in the taxi by 7.50. They told the driver that they were in a hurry and he wove in and out of the traffic in a way that made the two police people cringe. Arriving at the terminal, with five minutes to spare, they dashed to the ticket office. The ferry pulled away from the dock as soon as they climbed on board. They had to go down steep stairs to the lower deck where the seats were in aeroplane formation, one row behind the other though with six seats to each row on either side. They found an empty row near the back and collapsed into their seats.

"Gosh, Dad. We're going really fast," said Pippa, from her seat at the window.

"Yes. It's a hovercraft type of ferry," her Dad told her. "I wonder if we'll be allowed to go upstairs and outside. It's a two hour journey and I don't fancy being cooped up in here all the time."

They were indeed allowed to get some fresh air but had to hang on tightly to the boat rail as their hair was swept back from their faces and they felt their breath almost being taken from them. Fiona attempted a few photos and they came out surprisingly well. They watched Penang fade in the distance before going back down to their seats. They had all brought books so read for most of the rest of the trip, only looking out of Pippa's window as they saw land approaching.

They docked at Langkawi and Charles walked quickly up a steep slope to where he saw some taxis, Fiona and Pippa coming more slowly behind him.

Fiona's right foot caught in a small hole in the pavement and she went flying, letting go of the camera which shot along the tarmac. Pippa ran after it, picked it up and came back to help Fiona up as Charles came running back to help.

Limping a bit, but assuring them that nothing was broken, she asked if the camera was OK and Pippa pressed the 'on' button and assured her that it seemed alright. The taxi man came to help her up the slope and asked if she needed a doctor but she declared herself able to do without medical help.

They had been given a leaflet on Langkawi, at the hotel, and Charles asked the driver who said his name was Ramez, to take them to see the Langkawi eagle.

"How much would you charge to stay with us for the day?" he asked the young man.

"We want to see Kuah town..." began Fiona.

"...the duty-free shop?" asked the man.

Charles laughed.

"Yes, please and also any other interesting shops for the girls."

"Where else, Sir?"

"We were told to visit the mangrove swamps. Someone who had been, said we could get lunch there."

Rory White had said that the swamps were quite scary but that the restaurant at the end of the boardwalk provided local food which was worth trying..

"Will you want to go up in the new cable car too?"

"If we have time. We want to catch the ferry that leaves Langkawi at 7pm."

"You should be able to do all those things. Do you want to eat again, on the island?"

"No. We'll wait till we get back home. I've heard that there are two fabulous hotels here called the Datai and the Andaman but they're at the other end of the island, aren't they?"

"The traffic is light on Langkawi; only two sets of traffic lights so we could get there and you would have time to eat if we got there by 5pm."

"Would they let us eat there though we aren't guests?" asked Fiona.

"Of course," Ramez said, looking surprised at the question.

He told them the price which seemed very reasonable for the whole day's sightseeing and they set off, Ramez saying that he would leave the eagle till last.

They drove first to the mangrove swamps and walked out on the boardwalk which had been erected through them. Everything was silent and rather eerie and Ramez explained that the water rose quietly too. He left them then. Pippa held tightly to her Dad's hand and looked relieved when they reached the restaurant which was raised above the swamp. It was quite quiet inside and they chose a table away from the windows. The menu was interesting and, feeling adventurous, they all chose snacks they had not eaten before, Pippa opting for little lamb parcels and Charles and Fiona choosing fish.

"I hope this doesn't upset my tummy," said Fiona. "It's been a bit fragile for the last few days."

"You never said," remarked Charles.

"Oh, it wasn't bad. Probably the heat."

The meal, when it arrived, was quite spicy and Fiona left about half of her fish though she finished the rice which accompanied it. She got up to go to the toilet and when she came back, she pointed out a huge tree which appeared to be growing in the centre of the restaurant, its trunk disappearing through a hole in the roof. They enjoyed a cold drink each, then left, thanking the owner for the meal.

"Very cheap," commented Charles.

They walked back along the boardwalk, Fiona reciting, "This is the forest primeval, the murmuring pines and the hemlock," in a spooky voice.

"Fiona, don't," squealed Pippa.

She almost ran the last few yards to the waiting taxi.

The cable car was more fun. They sat, Charles and Pippa on one seat and Fiona on the one facing them, in a little, glass capsule which swayed out into the void. This time it was Fiona who looked scared. She kept her back to the way they were going. They got off at the first station and Pippa was intrigued when a group of Buddhist monks came out of the next car. They were all in orange robes and had shaved heads and Charles had to nudge his daughter to stop her staring at them as they past.

"That's what Tony's friend, Janet, would have looked like, Dad," she whispered.

They took photographs of the view then got into another car to get to the top. Charles recounted a bit from his favourite film, 'Where Eagles Dare', where two of the characters were riding on the roof of a similar cable car. Fiona shuddered and shut her eyes.

At the top, they were almost in the clouds as they had been on Penang Hill so they did not stay long and after buying some postcards in the shop at the bottom, they went back to Ramez and the taxi.

"Now you were very quick both times so would you like to have a short climb to see a waterfall?" he asked them. They said they would and, after a short drive, they reached a lay-by with about three cars in it. Ramez came with them and they climbed till they reached a rope bridge. Fiona declined to cross it but Charles went with Pippa and then they came back and continued their climb. The waterfall was cascading into a pool in which were two European men, being watched from the side by about eight Japanese tourists, with cameras. Fiona surreptitiously took a photo of the swimmers and the Japanese watchers and another one of Charles and Pippa and the waterfall, then they made the descent.

"Now we should get to one of the hotels in time for something to eat. Which one do you want to go to? We won't manage both, even though they are quite close together and share the same beach."

"The nearest one," said Charles.

"That's the Andaman," said Ramaz and put the car into gear.

The entrance to the hotel was very impressive, with two pools in which were lily pads, flanking the path. Pippa went over to one. She looked down at the lilies, then gave a little cry of delight.

"Dad, Fiona, come over and look at this! There's a wee frog on the lily. Look."

There was indeed a tiny little frog sunning itself on a leaf but by the time Fiona had taken the

camera from its case, it had gone into the water.
Ramez had told them to just go to reception and
ask about a meal. They did this and were shown
into an open-air restaurant with water running
through little channels among the tables. Pippa
was fascinated and had to be told to come and
sit down, as the waiter whose name tag read, 'U
Shuren', had come immediately with menus for
them. None of them was very hungry so he advised
them to forego the buffet and choose from the
menu.

"Maybe madam would like to just have a
dessert," he said, handing Pippa her menu.

She giggled as she took the menu and Charles
frowned at her.

"Sorry, Mr Shuren," she said in her forthright
way. "I've never been called madam before."

He smiled at her and suggested that maybe the
two adults would like a starter only. He left them
to choose, coming back to take an order for an
Andaman soufflé for Pippa, six satay sticks for
Fiona and lamb cutlets for Charles who said he was
quite hungry again and would also like a soufflé.

The meal over and paid for, they asked the way
to the beach and on the way passed the shallow
end of the swimming pool which could be stepped
into and had a sign saying, "Monitor Swimming".

"What's a monitor?" asked Pippa.

"It's a large lizard," answered Fiona.

Pippa looked round with interest but there was no sign of the lizard. The beach was deserted, it being time for people to get ready for their evening meal and they were lucky to catch sight of an enormous lizard making its way towards the shady end of the long beach. Fiona went down to the water's edge and called back that the water here was clear and she could see small fish.

"That's the only thing disappointing about Penang," she said when they joined her. "Jellyfish and cloudy sea."

"Yes, but there are a lot of rocks if you go in over there." Charles pointed to the furthest end of the beach. "Come on. If we want to see the Langkawi eagle and do some shopping, we'd better get back to the taxi."

On their way to the capital, Kuah, Ramez asked them if they had seen the rocks at the Andaman beach.

"Yes, we did. Why?" asked Fiona.

"They were never there until after the tsunami and there used to be a little island with monkeys on it but it's got joined to the beach now. It's as if the land moved."

"Did anyone get killed in the tsunami?" asked Fiona.

"Just one old lady. She was in a wheelchair and no one remembered her," said Ramez, sadly.

He stopped in a large square and they got out to go and stand under the huge marble eagle which was the symbol of Langkawi, then he took them to the duty free shop where they bought two litre bottles of whisky, four hundred cigarettes for friends and four huge bars of Cadbury's chocolate, all for about the equivalent of twenty-four pounds.

There was no time for any other shopping as they only had ten minutes to catch the ferry. Charles paid Ramez and thanked him for all his help and advice. Pippa asked Fiona to take a photo of herself with the driver then they boarded the boat.

It was three very tired people who made the journey back to Penang. No going on deck this time and Pippa was sound asleep with her head on Charles's shoulder when they docked at Penang. Knowing that she would be indignant if he tried to carry her as he had done when she was little, he woke her up.

It was nearly ten o'clock when they reached their hotel and Charles went along to the room with his daughter and saw her into bed before returning to the lounge where he found Fiona seated with Jean Grant.

"I'd almost given you up," she laughed. "I sat with Mr and Mrs White earlier. They got off OK and said to say cheerio, again. I had room service then came back about an hour ago and Leong Ping's been plying me with coffees. I'll probably not sleep tonight."

"You sound very happy, Jean," said Charles. "Does that mean that you're being allowed to go home tomorrow?"

"Yes. The Inspector cheerfully informed me that if they found out that I was guilty, I could be extradited from the UK!"

"I wonder if he's detained Bill Elliott and if Ethel Kelman has already gone home," mused Fiona.

"I don't imagine we'll ever find that out unless I meet Rav again," said Charles ruefully.

"I think I'll get off to my bed now, if you don't mind," Jean said. "I imagine you'll be tired too after your day away. You can tell me all about it tomorrow. We'll probably meet in the airport though I'm travelling back business class. We couldn't get it coming out but there were plenty of seats going back for some reason."

Back in their room, Charles rang Salma while Fiona got ready in the bathroom but Salma's mobile went on to answer mode. Fiona came out, yawning deeply.

"Never mind, I'll get her tomorrow before we leave," he said quietly, though Pippa looked deeply asleep. He put his arms round Fiona.

"Thank you for a marvellous holiday, my love."

She gave him a light kiss on the forehead and got quickly into bed. As she turned away from him, he looked puzzled.

CHAPTER 31

O n their last morning, Pippa and Charles
played their last game of putting and Pippa
was delighted that in the absence of Rory White,
her dad won. He received his free drinks' vouchers
and they said goodbye to the people they had met
during their few games there. The Welsh people,
in particular, had been very friendly. They were all
to be there for another two weeks.

"Will you go back to the loungers by yourself,
pet" he said when they reached the fork in the
path, one arm of which led to The Rasa and the
other to The Golden Sands. "I've got someone to
see at The Golden Sands,"

Pippa skipped off happily and told Fiona
that her Dad would not be long. They read in
companionable silence for a while then Pippa
closed her book.

"None of your's and Dad's murders have ever
been as exciting as that one," she said.

"True. I remember seeing the film of your
book. It was the first time that David Suchet played

Poirot. He's so good that I picture him every time I think of Hercule Poirot, just as I see Joan Hickson when I think of Miss Marple. I must show you the videos I have of..."

"...videos, Fiona! How old-fashioned," Pippa teased her.

"I know. I must buy a new TV and DVD."

When Charles arrived, it was from the direction of their room. He was whistling happily. Fiona looked at him and sighed.

"Ready to go for lunch, girls?" he asked, missing the sigh.

"Loose end to tie up?" Fiona enquired.

"Yes," was his monosyllabic reply.

Thinking that it might be something unsuitable for Pippa's ears, Fiona did not ask again.

After lunch and after saying goodbye to Goona and Sunny Tan, they lay for a while then had their last swim in the cooler of the two pools. Fiona got out of the water first and sat at the edge waiting for the others. Charles coming out next, found her silent and a bit sad-looking.

"What's up love? Sad that the holiday's over?" he asked her gently.

A tear trickled down her cheek and she brushed it away impatiently before replying, enigmatically, he thought, "More than you can guess, Charles."

As Pippa joined them, no more was said. They read, Pippa having gone up to the room to get her latest Chalet school book, "Three Go to the Chalet School". Charles surprised Fiona by saying that he had booked them both for a massage on the beach with Mr Foo and his son, for about an hour. Pippa promised to stay where she was, unless she saw Mai Lee, in which case she would chat to her for the last time and be sure to return to their loungers in about an hour.

Charles enjoyed his massage from Tommy Foo who kneaded his muscles quite firmly. As they walked back to their loungers, Fiona thanked him and said that the only drawback to Mr Foo was that he sniffed incessantly though she had enjoyed what he had told her when doing reflexology on her feet. Pippa was waiting for them. She had spoken to Mai Lee and got her email address.

They went to the lounge for their final afternoon tea. Fiona took the beach bag with them this last time as they would be going straight to their room after tea. Once again they had goodbyes to say, to Leong Ping and little Maz. Charles had mentioned tipping their favourite people but Fiona had pointed out that there was a 10% service charge on everything that they paid for and their room rate, so he had decided not to.

"There are so many nice staff, Charles," she had added. "You'd be lobbing out a fortune!"

They said cheerio to the Bennetts and the Jamiesons who left the following day.

"It was nice meeting you all," said Sylvia Bennett.

"Just a pity you weren't allowed to help solve our murder," said her husband, Jack, "I thought at one point that they might arrest that wee woman. Did she get off safely, yesterday?"

"It's today she's leaving. She'll be on the same plane as us and we can chat to her in the airports."

"Have you any idea what will happen to the guilty person, once he or she is found?" asked Mike Jamieson.

"I'm not sure. They might be sent back to Britain or they might be kept here or vice versa if they've gone home already. That'll depend on the skill of the lawyer, I imagine," said Charles.

"Thanks for keeping us clued in," said Lorna.

"Well, Mike at least deserved information as it was he who gave us the clue to the single woman being Glaswegian!" laughed Charles.

Charles, Fiona and Pippa went back to their room, Pippa chanting, "Selamat tinggal" which she'd been saying a lot since last night.

"Goodbye, see you again," she reminded Charles when he asked her. She had been writing all the phrases down in the inside of her Agatha Christie book cover.

"I hope we *will* all come back here again," said Charles, as he opened the room door and looked disappointed when Fiona did not add her agreement.

They still had the clothes they were wearing to pack and their swimming things to put into a plastic bag before putting that on the top of the things already packed. Fiona showered and washed her hair, then Charles did the same. Pippa insisted that her swim had cleaned her and simply changed into her travelling clothes.

In the Rasa Wing foyer, they had a cold drink each, courtesy of Sean who had been waiting for them.

"I have your home email address," he said to Charles. "Can I keep in touch about the murder?"

"Of course. If anything happens in Glasgow, I'll let you know and you can do the same for me if anything happens here."

"Yes, if I ever get to hear anything! I hope to see you all back here again sometime before Shangri-la moves me on."

He kissed Pippa and Fiona and shook hands with Charles.

"Oh, Mrs Grant's gone to the airport already. I'm so glad that they let her go home," Sean said.

Gopal picked them up before 6.30 and he gave Pippa a little doll wearing a sarong and long trousers. The journey took about forty-five minutes and this time they recognised lots of landmarks. Gopal stopped the taxi outside the airport and went off to get them a trolley for their cases. Pippa gave him a big hug and he looked pleased, as he did with the 50 ringgit tip which Charles gave him.

They had to put their cases through a screening process before going up to the desk and getting their boarding passes. The smiling girl gave them their boarding passes to KL but told them that they would have to get the others there, at any transfer desk. Charles lifted the huge case that was his and Pippa's and was horrified to see it come apart at the zip.

"Don't worry, Sir," said the girl. She pointed across the departure hall.

"There is a case-wrapping service here."

Charles heaved the offending case back onto the trolley and, red-faced, went across and had his case cling-filmed. He went back to the front of the queue, apologising to the waiting passengers. Fiona put up her wrapped-up picture and it too was labelled.

The seats at the departure gate were a bit uncomfortable but they did not have to sit in them for too long. Pippa amused herself by looking in the shops and bought two more postcards for her own collection.

Their flight to KL took under an hour but they went wrong there, going to the wrong immigration desk and ending up at the luggage carousels. When Charles asked what to do, he was told he would have to exit the airport and come back in. They did this, feeling silly.

Safely back on track, Charles stopped them and told Fiona and Pippa that he had a surprise for them.

"I've upgraded us to business class in case we never get the chance to do that again."

Pippa squealed in delight and was thrilled with the business class lounge in KL. She wanted to have a shower there but her Dad persuaded her to wait to do that in Dubai when they had more time to spare.

They all slept on the flight to Dubai, Pippa for almost the whole time. Their seats were much wider and they couldn't reach the seats in front unless they took their seat belts off. The cutlery which came with their meal was stainless steel and the napkins were snowy white. Jean had an empty seat next to her and Fiona moved back to sit with her for an hour, to give her some company.

The lounge in Dubai was huge and they had to walk some distance to find four vacant seats together. Charles took Pippa off to the room which housed the computers and she emailed Nancy who had given her her email address, before leaving the day before. Pippa had spent the holiday bemoaning the fact that she had not thought to take Hazel's email address with her and had not made the same mistake with Nancy. Charles rang Salma to check once again that no one had found out her part in the murder investigation. She reassured him.

"Salma went to talk to the old lady neighbour of Ethel Kelman. She came for Alphonse about a week ago, apparently," Charles reported to Fiona.

They had free drinks and snacks then Pippa had her shower. After that they all sat and read till their plane was called. There was a very long walk to the departure gate and then a bus trip round the outskirts of the airport buildings to get to their Boeing 777.

"We'll be home by bus at this rate," said Charles, irritably.

"This happened to the Glasgow passengers last time we came out," Jean told him. "It wouldn't be so bad if we all had seats but there are only about four at each end of the bus as you can see. You can imagine how Alan reacted!"

There had been lots of economy passengers still waiting at the gate. Charles had handed their business class boarding passes and been told to 'just push to the front.'

"In a Glasgow plane queue!" he had said to Fiona. "I'd get a few Glasgow kisses!"

Although they were still tired, they all watched one film at the beginning of the flight but they dozed off after that.

There was a man wearing a kilt at Glasgow to meet the Emirates' Business Class passengers and when he had shepherded them all together, they were taken outside to their cars. It was raining but warm when they stepped outside the airport and their driver stowed their cases quickly and drove them off in a luxurious BMW, asking them if they had had a good time. Charles had made sure that Jean had found her driver and promised to ring her if he found out anything, though he felt sure that she would be informed first. Pippa chatted all the way home to Fiona's flat.

As usual, there was no parking space outside her close, so the driver merely stopped outside and as he was blocking the street, Fiona got out quickly, going round to the boot for her case and carry-on bag.

Charles opened his window and she told him that she would see him in two days' time at work and went hurriedly to her close door.

"What's wrong with Fiona?" asked Pippa with a puzzled frown.

"I don't know, pet. Maybe just sad that the holiday's over or jet-lag."

"What's jet lag?"

"I don't know why we didn't have it when we went. It's feeling tired because of the time difference. Remember that it's seven hours later in Penang so we'll feel like going to bed at about 3pm in the afternoon."

"Will we...go to bed at 3?"

"Better not to because then we'll be wide awake far too early."

About twenty minutes later, the car pulled up outside their house in Newton Mearns. Pippa's Aunt Linda came to the door to welcome them back. Charles had asked her to get them bread and milk for coming home.

"But I didn't expect you to wait for us arriving back," he said now.

He took their suitcases upstairs, dumped them in the appropriate bedrooms, took a small package from his carry-on bag and went back down to find that Linda had made them a cup of tea. He and Pippa sat down wearily at the kitchen table, even Pippa a bit monosyllabic now, as Linda questioned them about the holiday.

"Look, Charles, I can see that you're both knackered. I'll get off home and you can tell me all about it another time."

"Linda, would you mind waiting with Pippa for about an hour."

"Don't tell me - you're going into the station!" she said, laughing exasperatedly.

"Am I so predictable?" he laughed too. "Pippa, will you come out with me to the car?"

Looking puzzled, his daughter followed him into the garage.

"What is it Dad?"

"Pippa, do you like Fiona?"

"Of course I do, Dad. Why?"

Her small face lit up.

"Are you going to marry her, Dad? Can I be a bridesmaid? Nancy was a bridesmaid last year for her cousin and Hazel's been..."

"Pippa! Whoa!" Charles stopped the flow of words.

"Sorry, Dad but is that what you wanted to ask me about?"

"Well...yes though I haven't mentioned it to Fiona yet. I wanted to see how you felt first"

Her face fell.

"Can I still see Mum?"

"Of course, pet. She's still your Mum."

"What would I call Fiona then?"

"I imagine just Fiona but you'd need to ask her. That is, if she says she'll marry me."

"I thought you got on really well. She was so happy...well till the last week," Pippa's voice faltered.

"I noticed that too."

Charles sounded uncertain and a bit nervous.

"Is that where you're going now, to Fiona's?"

"Yes. Wish me luck and don't let on to Auntie Linda. Not just yet. If it goes well, you can be the first to tell her. I promise."

Charles backed his silver-grey Audi out of the garage and, waving to his daughter, drove off down the street.

He felt that it was a good omen when he found a parking space in Grantley Street but was still nervous when he pressed the buzzer for Fiona's flat.

"Who is it?"

"It's me, love. Charles."

There was short silence.

"Come up."

The door buzzed open and he took the stairs two at a time, arriving breathless at her top flat. She smiled a bit wanly at him and he thought he could see traces of tears on her cheeks.

"Fiona. What's the matter? Is it just tiredness or what? You've been quiet and unlike yourself for the last week."

"Sit down, Charles. I have something to tell you. I should have told you on holiday but I didn't want to spoil things there."

"What is it? Have you gone off me?"

His voice sounded hollow.

"Oh no...but... you might go off me when I tell you..."

"Go off you! Never, Fiona. What is it? You're scaring me."

She sat down, nervously plucking at her trouser leg. He sat down beside her and took both of her hands in his.

"Come on, my love..."

At the word 'love', any composure she had, left her and she burst out sobbing.

"Are you ill?"

"I'm pregnant!"

The word hung in the air in the silence that followed.

"Well. That makes what I came to say a lot easier. At least I hope it does."

Now it was Charles's turn to sound nervous.

"What do you mean?" she hiccuped.

Charles got off his seat and knelt down in front of her. He took a small box from his pocket.

"Fiona Macdonald. Will you marry me?"

He opened the box to reveal a solitaire diamond engagement ring, nestling in purple silk.

This time the silence stretched even longer.

Charles looked worried.

"You want to marry me? Even if I'm pregnant... and I won't have an abortion, Charles," Fiona said tearfully.

"I wanted to marry you before I knew. I want to marry you now that I know and you certainly are not aborting my baby!" he said, sternly. "It just means that the wedding will have to be sooner than I'd thought. Just as well that I bought a matching wedding ring, isn't it?"

"When did you buy the ring... the rings,?" she corrected herself.

"The day we left. I'd ordered it from the jeweller's in The Golden Sands. I pinched one of your dress rings to get the size right. Come on, try it on."

The ring fitted perfectly and he told her he would show her the matching wedding ring which was still in his flight bag at another time.

"Oh, Charles! I've been so worried since I began to suspect that I was pregnant."

"When did you?"

"It was when I told Pippa that my period came every month on the dot. I realised that I was about a week late. I got a pregnancy kit from the local chemist. We were so careful except..."

"Except for the first time, when you came to look after me when I had a bad migraine," finished Charles.

He got up from the floor and she rose from her seat and they went into each other's arms.

"Pippa...," started Fiona.

"...Pippa is delighted and I'm sure she'll be thrilled about the baby. Even if she isn't, she'll just have to get used to the idea. Will we tell anyone yet?"

"Maybe wait till after three months, just in case anything goes wrong," said Fiona, her eyes shining.

"Now, as a complete anti-climax, I must get home. Linda's waiting with Pippa till I get back. Is it OK if she knows...Linda, I mean...about the engagement, not about the baby. I promised Pippa that she could tell her aunt if you said yes."

"Did you think I would say no?"

"Well you've been so unlike yourself over the last week that Pippa and I both thought you'd gone off me."

"I'm sorry."

"No need to be. You had a lot on your mind as it turns out. I wish you'd told me right away and saved yourself so much angst. Am I such an ogre?"

"Anything but, Charles, but we're not youngsters and how was I to know that you'd be pleased at the thought of a baby. I didn't even suspect that you wanted to marry me!"

They hugged again and then Charles left. When he got back to the house, Pippa was sound asleep in her bed even though it was only late afternoon. No doubt, being a child, she would sleep right through the night. He said nothing to Linda, honouring his promise to his daughter, letting her think that he had indeed gone into the station. She left soon afterwards and he sat down with a cup of coffee, this time hoping that it would keep him awake, only to open his eyes at nine o'clock at night in time to go off to bed.

CHAPTER 32

After a night of weird dreams and cramp in one calf muscle, Charles did not wake until around nine o'clock. He looked in on Pippa but she was sound asleep so he showered and dressed then made his way downstairs and got breakfast.

"You are not a Feringgi Grill breakfast," he told his plate of Special K and mug of tea.

"Talking to yourself, Dad," said Pippa from the kitchen doorway.

"It's the first sign of madness. Yes, I know."

"Did you ask Fiona? Did she say yes and can I be a bridesmaid?"

"She said yes and was worried that you would mind and I'm sure she'll let you be a bridesmaid. We didn't get around to that."

He looked at her standing framed in the doorway and thought that she seemed to have grown over the holiday.

"We'll need to get you some clothes and uniform for starting school, young lady."

"Yes, my tops are getting a bit tight."

She blushed and disappeared back up the stairs.

Charles rang Fiona who sounded sleepy.

"Sorry, my love. Did I wake you?"

"I slept really badly. Woke up every two hours or so then slept in, of course. Just as well I didn't have to be at work today."

"I'm just up myself. Look, the reason I'm phoning is to see if you would come shopping with Pippa and me at Marks and Spencer's in Newton Mearns, later. We could have lunch there. She needs a new school uniform and I think that she might be ready for a bra."

"Gosh, bras and periods! I feel like a Mum already."

"Talking of which, Mum-to-be, how are you feeling? Are you getting morning sickness?"

"I felt a bit off-colour once or twice in Penang but I feel fine today."

"Pippa's Mum was dreadfully sick for about six weeks."

"Great! Look, if M&S don't have much, as it's only a small clothes' outlet up there, you'll probably get school clothes in Asda's George. What about a tie and blazer?"

"They were handed out ties before they left at the end of June and she says that she doesn't want a blazer. They're not compulsory."

They spoke for a bit longer, arranging to meet at midday and then Charles hung up. They met at the cafe in the centre and had lunch. Pippa demanded to see the engagement ring and asked again about being a bridesmaid.

"Of course you will be. Who else would I choose? said Fiona.

They then went to Marks and Spencer's where Charles bought two school skirts and four white blouses. There was no children's underwear so they walked to Asda at the other end of the mall and Charles declared that he would get some groceries. Fiona picked out two, small, white bras and handed them to Pippa who went into a cubicle.

Minutes later there was a grumpy, "I can't get this thing done up," from her and Fiona went in to help. The 28 A was too small, so she swapped it for a 30 which fitted OK but Pippa did not fill it out so once again she exchanged it, this time for one with some padding. Pippa was delighted with this one so Fiona told her to get changed then come out and choose another one the same size. She chose one in pale pink this time and Fiona bought her two pairs of pants to go with the bras. Charles was waiting for them at the entrance to the store.

"I nearly bought whisky," he said. "Then I remembered that I'd brought home the two bottles from Langkawi's duty-free shop."

They strolled out to the car park, both having parked at the M&S end.

"I'm taking Pippa down to Newlands to see Hazel," Charles told Fiona. "Do you want to come with me and we could go to your house and make some plans."

Fiona was happy to do this. They drove to Hazel's house and Charles went up to the door with his daughter. It was Sally Ewing who opened the door. She smiled at Charles and he thought how well she looked. He hoped that she was now free of anxiety attacks. Pippa ran past her, calling out, "Hazel, where are you? Dad and Fiona are getting married and I'm to be a bridesmaid!" A shout came from above them and they heard feet pounding up the stairs as Pippa joined her friend.

"So much for my surprise news," said Charles, ruefully.

"Did you ask Fiona on a beautiful beach in Malaysia?" asked Sally, smiling in delight.

"No, in her flat in Shawlands, last night," he replied.

"That's the trouble with men. No romance. You'll have to come down for a meal one evening soon and tell us all about the holiday and your wedding plans."

"That would be nice. We're going to go to Fiona's and make the plans now," Charles said. "When do you want me to pick up my daughter?"

"Why don't I give her her evening meal to give you some time on your own? I guess you wouldn't get much of that while you were away," said Sally sympathetically. "Come for her around ten o'clock. I know she'll be tired but they'll have a lot to talk about."

Charles thanked her profusely then he and Fiona drove to Grantley Street. There was no space for either of them to park but they found two spaces on the hill at Tassie Street and they walked back to her flat where he rang "Richards" and managed to get a table for 6 o'clock, on the understanding that they would leave at eight so that another couple could get their table then.

They drank coffee and started discussing the wedding, then suddenly she was in his arms and minutes later they were in her bedroom.

"Do you feel up to this, my love?" Charles asked her gently.

"More to the point, are *you* up to it," she said wickedly.

Charles made love to her tenderly and they fell asleep and woke about two hours later. There was just time to shower and dress before they had to leave for Newton Mearns.

Over the starter, they discussed the wedding.

"Registry office or church?" Charles asked.

"Church, if that's OK with you. I know I don't get to church very often but I always used to go before I started work and I went to Sunday school in Holmwood Parish in Pollokshaws and joined there. Penny goes there too when she can, I think, though we've never met there."

"Thank goodness it's not Robert Gentle who's the minister now," said Charles referring to the minister who had been murdered a few years ago.

"Yes. It's a very pleasant woman minister now."

"Will it not be hard to get fitted in at such short notice?" he asked.

"At Holmwood! I think she's inundated with funerals but not weddings," laughed Fiona.

"It won't be so easy to get a hotel, will it? How many guests do you want to invite?" he asked.

The waiter took away their starter dishes and brought their main courses while Fiona pondered on this question.

"John and Jean, Jill who's my oldest friend, though you haven't met her yet and a cousin from Tarbert who might not come as we haven't been in touch for ages and if you don't mind, Caroline Gibson, sorry, Whittaker. She got married a few months ago."

"Did you tell me that? I don't remember anything about a wedding."

"Typical man. Can't multi-task. You were probably doing something else at the time!"

"Just like women can't read maps without turning them upside down," came the rejoinder.

"So that's six," he added quickly, seeing the light of battle in her eyes.

"What about you? Will you ask your ex-wife? I can't keep calling her that. What's her name, Charles? I know you must have mentioned it at some time but I've forgotten."

"Anita. I won't ask her unless Pippa wants her to come but I will ask her mother, Pippa's grandma Rachel who lives in Aberfoyle. Her husband Len is permanently in care so he won't be able to come. I used to get on really well with Rachel and I know that Pippa will want her gran to see her all dressed up. I'll ask George to be my best man."

Fiona grimaced.

"I know you don't like him..."

"He's such a bore. Always droning on about his last golf game and as for his jokes....OK Charles but let's not have any speeches apart from the one where you say, "On behalf of my wife and myself.""

"My wife and I...that sounds great and you're right. Why put the guests through lots of speeches?"

"Who else?"

"Linda and her husband, Joe."

"Yes."

"Well our team will have to come, with their partners of course and what about Solomon and Martin Jamieson with their wives and Ben Goodwin?"

"Not Grant Knox?" asked Fiona, grinning.

"That would be hypocritical. I can't stand the man, as you know."

"So with your twelve that makes eighteen. We don't need anywhere big then."

"That's true."

"I'd like to ask the Ewings. Pippa would be mad if her friend couldn't see her on the big day!"

"So that makes twenty-three, twenty-six including us and Pippa. What would you say about having the reception in the golf club? It can't get as booked up as hotels do, surely."

"Good idea. Jill would do the flowers I'm sure. She used to work in a florist's as a Saturday job when we were at school."

"Cars?"

"No contacts there, I'm afraid. You?"

"No. We'll just have to look them up in the yellow pages."

They looked through Fiona's diary, coming up with the first Saturday in September as a good date. It would give them enough time to plan and Fiona's pregnancy would not be showing.

"What will you wear?"

Charles was curious.

"That's for me to know and you to see on the day," his fiancée told him.

They finished off the dessert which had been placed before them during the last part of their discussion and as it was a few minutes to eight, declined coffee. Charles paid and they left, arriving back at Fiona's at eight fifteen.

"Is it too late to phone your minister, Fiona?" Charles asked as they sat down in her living room.

"I shouldn't think so."

She rang the manse and spoke to her minister. Charles could tell, from the side of conversation he could hear, that it was going well and Fiona confirmed this when she rang off.

"Margaret can manage that. I can give her a time later, once we've sorted out the golf club."

"What time do you think?"

"Not too late in the day for me to get the jitters but not too early either or no one will be hungry enough for a meal."

"What about the afternoon? Say two o'clock at the church and three o'clock at the golf club. Photographs and drinks, then the meal at five."

"Perfect. What will you wear. Kilt? Suit? Dinner jacket?"

"Why should I tell you if you won't tell me?"

Charles rang the secretary at the golf club and confirmed that the clubhouse was indeed available on the date required and that the female who ran the catering side would be only too happy to provide the meal.

"He said she was used to providing meals for far larger numbers than twenty-six," he informed

Fiona. "I've to see her myself and tell her what we want. What do we want?"

"Probably chicken. Most people like that. Do we have any vegetarians coming?"

They mentally ran through their guest list, coming up with the happy fact that nobody was vegetarian.

"Prawn cocktail as a starter and what to finish?" asked Fiona.

"She makes a fabulous pavlova. I had it at the men's dinner last year."

"That's the menu settled then."

"Don't we want to have a choice of courses?" Charles wanted to know.

"See what she says. If she offers to do more than one course, say... fine."

They sat back on the settee and Charles grinned.

"That must be a record time for planning a wedding, my love."

"Well, we have no mothers to get up tight about old Aunt Mary not being asked and having to ask someone because they were at your brother's wedding," said Fiona.

It was time to go and collect Pippa. Fiona said she would come too as she wanted to show off her engagement ring. They were invited in and Ralph opened a bottle of champagne which he said he always kept for special occasions. Pippa and Hazel were allowed a small glass each. Sally admired the ring and asked if they had made any wedding arrangements.

"Any? We've done it all, except for the cars," said Charles proudly.

"And invitations. We forgot that," Fiona realised.

"Debenhams do a selection of invitations," said Sally. "And wedding present lists if you want them."

Charles looked bemused.

"Wedding present lists. What are they?"

"Don't worry about that, love. We'll be happy to accept whatever anybody wants to give us, Sally. I'd rather risk duplicates than hand out lists."

Fiona was adamant on this issue.

"I've even heard of couples asking for money towards the honeymoon," she said indignantly.

"Honeymoon! We never discussed that either," said Charles.

"We had that before the wedding. Nothing could be as perfect as the holiday we've just had and anyway we'd be massively unpopular at work if we went off again so soon."

"How many cars do you want?" asked Ralph.

"Just one for me and Pippa. The same car can take the three of us to the reception," said Fiona.

"Well how about me asking Colin? You remember him from that awful party? He has a beautiful black Mercedes. He bought it right after

Aimee walked out on him. I'm sure he would drive you on the day. If you fancy that, I'll ask him at work tomorrow," Ralph offered.

"Would you Ralph? That would be great. I think that was the only thing we thought might be a problem with the date so soon," said Fiona, her eyes sparkling with delight that their special day seemed to hold no problem now.

"What is the date?" asked Ralph.

"The first Saturday in September, September the 3rd," said Charles.

"That's what...ten weeks on Saturday," said Sally who had been using her fingers to count. "Will you get something to wear in that time, Fiona?"

"I hope so," said Fiona. "But if I can't get something in that time, I'll just wear something I already have. The dress doesn't matter; it's marrying Charles that matters."

"But I want a beautiful dress," piped in a small voice.

"Don't worry, pet. I'm sure there will be no problem about your dress," Fiona reassured a tired Pippa.

"You're all invited of course," put in Charles and Hazel gave a squeal of delight.

"Home now," said Charles firmly and he put his arm round his sleepy daughter and steered her towards the door. She looked back and murmured a quiet, 'thank you' to Sally. Fiona followed them and Sally walked with her.

"I'll go with you if you want someone to help with finding a dress, unless you're having a bridesmaid or matron of honour."

"Oh would you, Sally? I'd be so grateful. My oldest friend, Jill, doesn't live in Glasgow any more so getting together might be awkward and I think I have to move fast."

"Right, Saturday it is, if you're not at work."

"Shouldn't be, unless there's a case on and as the department has been scattered about, that's unlikely. I'll pick you up if you like."

"We're both near the station. Let's just take a train. It'll be less hassle. Will you bring Pippa or not this first time?"

"Not this time, I think. I want to be very selfish over this. Thanks, Sally. Say eleven o'clock on the platform?"

"That's fine."

Charles dropped Fiona off in Grantley Street, saying that he would see her at work the next day and reminding her to set her alarm and bring the presents they had bought for the team.

CHAPTER 33

"Good to see you back, Sir. Nice holiday?"
Bob, at his usual place at the desk, looked genuinely delighted and Davenport realised that much as he had enjoyed the time away, it was also quite good to be back.

"Thanks, Bob. I had a great time. Come along to the Incident Room at 10.30. Tea and buns and some good news for you."

"Will do, Sir. Thanks."

Davenport was whistling as he walked along the corridor to his own room. He had rung Fiona this morning to make sure that she had not slept in and also to suggest that they tell the staff their good news that day. She had been thinking along the same lines and came out of her room now to greet him.

"Beat you...Sir," she said perkily.

"I didn't see any of the team as I passed their room. I know Penny won't be here but surely Frank should be back from his secondment to.... where was it?"

"Pollokshaws, Salma told us on the phone," Fiona reminded him.

"And Salma's always early."

"I asked her to get us some cakes to celebrate our news. She'll be back shortly," said Fiona.

"Good thinking. I was going to go out myself but you're beaten me to it. Did you tell her what we were celebrating?"

"No I did not. I didn't want to steal your thunder. She probably thinks it's my birthday."

"I thought you stopped having birthdays after the big 4 0. I forgot, I'm officially now your toy boy!"

"Charles Davenport! One month younger does not qualify for that rank. When I want one of those, I'll be looking for someone about twenty years younger than you!"

"Don't you dare!"

As there was no one around he kissed her then continued to his room which looked quite bare with no case folders and other paraphernalia on his desk.

Salma arrived back with the cakes. As she passed Bob, he said he hoped that she'd bought one for him as he had been invited too.

"Wonder what the good news is, sergeant," he remarked.

"Good news? The DS didn't mention good news. I presumed it must be her birthday. Frank, the boss has some good news for us. DS Macdonald must know what it is as she sent me out for these cakes."

Frank, a few minutes late, looked out of breath. He leaned against the desk front.

"I meant to be on time but the alarm didn't go off and Mum forgot the time and didn't wake me till 8.15. I've got some good news too, Salma. I rang Penny's Mum last night and she's getting out today, this afternoon."

"She's surely not able to look after herself yet!" Salma exclaimed.

"No she isn't but her Mum told the hospital that Penny would be coming to stay with her and they said in that case she could be discharged."

"Ah, the late PC Selby. Not picked up any good habits at Pollokshaws then?"

Davenport grinned as he spoke from further up the corridor and, looking relieved, Frank retorted that the only habit he had learned at the Pollokshaws station was how to keep awake through boredom.

"I don't know why they put me there, Sir. It was all old ladies and missing dogs or cats up trees."

"They had a young lad murdered there a few years ago, I believe," said Fiona, coming out of her room and hearing this part of the conversation.

The time dragged as this being their first day back as a team, there was nothing on the agenda.

Davenport called Salma in to thank her for all the work she had done for them while they were away.

"I might go along and see the old neighbour for myself. You said she was a nosy old buddy. She might remember seeing a man visiting Ethel Kelman. If she did indeed murder Alan Grant and she and Bill Elliott were in cahoots, then he would probably have been at her house."

"Is he someone she might remember, Sir?" asked Salma.

"Well, he's very tall, probably about 6 feet 3 and thin. Nothing else remarkable, such as a hunch back or a wooden leg. Wish I had a photo of him."

Salma laughed. She asked what stage the enquiries were at and he told her that apart from Bill Elliott, all the other people involved had been allowed home and for all he knew, Elliott would be arriving back shortly as the police seemed to have no evidence to keep him there.

"I'm surmising of course. I wasn't exactly in their confidence," he said ruefully. He glanced at his watch.

"Think I'll pop over there right now. It'll only take me about fifteen minutes to get to Shawlands. What did you tell the old lady was the reason for asking questions, Salma?"

"I didn't tell her I was police but she knew because of my shoes. She's an observant old thing, but she didn't question why I was there, fortunately. Her name's Mrs George."

Anxious for some time alone with his new fiancée, Charles took Fiona with him. The old lady was slow coming to the door but what she lacked in mobility, she more than made up for in acuity.

"Oh ho, two more police. What is it this time eh?"

Charles and Fiona laughed and looked down at their shoes but she told them it was the fact that police usually came in twos as did Mormons but they were always two men.

"Though that young, black girl was alone which was odd," she mused. "Well, spit it out. What do you want to know? Has Alphonse's mum being raiding the till at work? Wouldn't surprise me, the clothes she wears and away on holiday again."

Charles and Fiona looked a bit bemused.

"Who's Alphonse? My colleague didn't mention a man staying with her."

The old lady cackled with laughter.

"Alphonse is her cat, though she's had a few men sniffing round her. One big fat chap came around for quite a while. Must have had money for he was certainly no looker but he stopped and she's been seeing another man recently."

Fiona piped in here as it was the dream opening.

"This new chap, was he fat too?"

"No just the opposite, a big skinnymalink."

"Taller than me?" asked Charles.

She looked him up and down.

"You're tall, lad but yes, I would say taller than you."

Fiona stifled a giggle at the 'lad', then recovered quickly to ask if Miss Kelman had many other visitors.

"No...well apart from her auntie. Tall too and a good looker with black hair piled up on her head and an hourglass figure. I didn't see any women her own age, except the girl along the road. Guess she was more of a man's woman, if you know what I mean."

Back in his car, Charles was frowning and Fiona asked what the matter was.

"Statuesque was how I would have described her but tall with an hourglass figure would fit the bill just as well."

"Who, Charles? Don't be annoying."

"You saw Annabelle Kilbride didn't you?"

"Yes...oh I see what you're getting at. That would describe her very well. Could she be Ethel Kelman's aunt? I seem to remember Salma telling us about an aunt."

"Do you have any photos of her?"

Fiona thought for a few seconds then said that she was sure she had as she had taken quite a few of various groups they'd been in company with and Annabelle had been with them one evening.

They drove to Grantley Street and Charles waited, parked in the middle of the road while Fiona dashed upstairs to get her digital camera. She flung herself into the passenger seat just as a car came up behind them and she scanned her pictures while Charles drove off.

"Yes. I do have one of her and she's standing beside you and she's almost as tall as you."

They drove back to Dinmont Road and showed the old lady the photograph.

"Yes, that's her," she said. "Nothing wrong with my eyesight," she added proudly.

As they drove back to the station, they pondered the connection here.

"So if Ethel Kelman murdered Alan Grant, it's too much of a coincidence that her aunt just happened to be there at the same time, surely," said Fiona at last.

"And just happened to take Mrs Grant away at the crucial time," added Charles.

"Where does Bill Elliott fit in then and his murdered wife?" asked Fiona, sounding baffled.

"Let's leave it just now, love. I'm going to stop and buy a bottle of champagne to go with the cakes."

They had arrived at the station by this time and as it was nearly 10.30, they called out to the others to join them in the Incident Room. Salma had put out the cream cakes and Charles went to his own room where he kept some glasses, wishing that he had had the foresight to bring some champagne flutes from home.

Frank whistled when he saw the bottle.

"Is it a very special birthday, then, Sir. Your's or DS Macdonald's?"

"All will be revealed shortly, Selby. Come on everyone, get a glass of this and choose your cake."

Once they were all seated with glasses and cake, Charles raised his glass.

"I want you all to raise your glasses to Fiona... who's done me the honour of saying that she'll marry me."

There was a stunned silence then Frank blurted out, "I knew it...Salma...didn't I say..."

He tailed off.

"Cheers, Sir," said Bob with a grin.

"Yes, Sir. Good luck to you both," said Salma with a beaming smile.

Charles turned to Frank.

"Well, Selby? Cat got your tongue?"

"Sorry, Sir. No Sir. I mean, well done, Sir."

"I think it's me you should be congratulating, Frank," said Fiona, her eyes shining as she linked her arm through Charles's. Salma asked to see her ring and said how much she liked it.

They left their team to discuss the bombshell and went back to Fiona's room where they enjoyed their drink. Left to themselves after Bob went back to the unattended desk, Frank and Salma were silent then Frank reminded her of all the times he had whistled "Over the Sea to Skye" in recognition of his bosses' names - Charles and Fiona Macdonald, unfortunately not Flora but near enough.

"You'll be taking all the credit for their engagement, Frank Selby," Salma teased him.

"I wonder when the wedding will be."

"Don't imagine they'll wait too long at their age," said Frank.

"No or we'll be in our wheelchairs," said a dry voice.

Frank spun round, going a fiery red. Davenport had come back in.

"I meant to ask how Penny was. Fiona and I were thinking of going to the hospital to see her tonight."

"Oh Sir, she's getting home today, to her mum's," said Salma, seeing that Frank was still too embarrassed to speak.

"Can you give me her mum's number? I'll phone later and see if she's up to visitors with startling news and can I ask you both not to phone her. I'd like to tell her myself. The wedding, all being well, will be the first Saturday in September and you're both invited, with partners... if you've got one at present, Frank."

He went back to Fiona and recounted Frank's remark and his subsequent embarrassment at being overheard. He told her that Penny was leaving hospital that day and told her that they'd left Bob and his wife out of their wedding numbers.

"I'll phone Penny's mum before we leave for home and see if she's fit for seeing us. I'd like to tell her our news before she hears if from the others.

They went on to discuss the murder again, knowing that they were in no position to do any sleuthing really, yet itching to know the truth.

CHAPTER 34

Penny sat up in bed. The roses had returned to her cheeks and she grinned at her two bosses.

"It's early for you to have left work! Does Mr Knox know?"

"Cheeky! You must be feeling better, young lady. We left at three o'clock as there was no work for us today and we didn't want to come later when you'd be tired," replied Charles.

"Well, how were your holidays. Sir, you went to Thailand...."

"Malaysia."

"Sorry, Malaysia. Was it fantastic? Just as well I hadn't planned to go anywhere! Salma and I were going to go away but with her Mum dying and her being in charge of the wee ones, we'd postponed it. And you, Ma'am, where did you go?"

"Penny, be quiet and let your guests get a chance to speak," remonstrated her Mum who had brought in her visitors.

"It's OK, Mrs Maclean. We're delighted to hear her sounding just like her old self."

"I'll go and make us all a cup of tea, unless you'd prefer something stronger?"

"No thanks. Tea would be great."

Mrs Maclean left the room.

"What a fright we got when Salma told us..." began Fiona.

"....how could Salma tell you? Did she have your phone number? Why did...US? Were you away together?"

Charles and Fiona burst out laughing and Penny lay back on her pillows looking at them, wide-eyed.

"No flies on you, young Penny," said Charles. "Yes, we went away with Pippa and now that we're back, the news is that we're getting married at the beginning of September and we hope you'll be well enough to come ...with Gordon if he hasn't got fed up with you by now."

Penny's shriek brought her Mum scurrying in from the kitchen, looking alarmed.

"Sorry, Mum. I didn't mean so scare you but Mr Davenport and Miss Macdonald are getting married...in September."

"Congratulations," said Mrs Maclean and, looking relieved, went back to get the tea.

They stayed for a while longer, enjoying the tea and finding out how Penny was progressing. She forgot in her excitement to repeat her question about how Salma had been able to get in touch with them in Malaysia.

"I was glad about that. Might tell her later, once the case is all wrapped up but not yet in case word gets to the powers-that-be," said Charles, as they got back into his car. "Can I come back to your place for a wee while, love? I want to ring Rav with the new information about Ethel Kelman, Annabelle Kilbride and Bill Elliott being, shall we say...acquainted. It's only 11.30pm over there. I'll risk waking him."

"Of course, Charles. I take it that Pippa is catered for this evening?"

"I invited Linda over. I told her that Pippa had news for her. Pippa knew that we planned to go and see Penny in the hospital and I told her we would eat somewhere down here so Linda will share her dinner, a casserole made by my own fair hands. Joe's away on a course right now."

Safely ensconced in an armchair, in Fiona's cosy sitting room, he called Rav who answered almost right away.

"Rav, it's Charles Davenport. Hope I didn't wake you...Good. Any progress on the murder that you can tell me about now that I'm safely out of the way?"

He listened.

"That's possible. Good thinking. Have you suggested that to Cheng or Inspector Hussain?"

He listened again and shook his head for Fiona's benefit. Rav had not told his superiors whatever it was that was possible.

"Well, there's been a development over here. Remember I told you that my sergeant had been doing some investigating at this end, well she discovered that Ethel Kelman, the single woman at the pool that day, knows Annabelle Kilbride... yes that's right, the woman who was with Mrs Grant when the murder took place. She also knows someone who fits the description of Bill Elliott. I don't know how you want to handle this, son. Oh, one more thing, did anyone count the stab wounds? I just know there were a few"

He listened again and rang off.

Fiona had been sitting on the floor at his feet. He pulled her up to sit on his lap and kissed her tenderly.

"Rav says that there were no fingerprints on the knife which was one from the Golden Sands and he couldn't see someone wearing gloves round the swimming pool so wondered if the condom he found could have been put over the handle. He sounded a bit embarrassed at telling me that the condom wasn't sticky. These young ones think we're all naive!"

"That was clever thinking. I take it that when you shook your head it was because he hasn't yet volunteered this to his sergeant or inspector?"

"That's correct. He also told me that Ethel Kelman had been staying in a small two star hotel in Georgetown."

"What do we do now, Charles?"

"Don't think there's anything we can do, except surmise. The three of them, maybe four with Louise Elliott, planned the murder. There were five stab wounds..."

"That's only four people."

"I know. Probably one person stabbed him twice."

"So Louise Elliott panicked and they thought she might confess, so she was killed too?"

"Probably."

"Will we ever know?"

"Not unless they unravel things in Penang, in which case I think Rav will find a way to tell us."

Charles looked at his watch.

"Now, will you make me some dinner, wench? I'm starving. I take it that you can cook. I've only ever had snacks up here. Come to think of it, the wedding might be off if you fail to deliver tonight."

Fiona punched him lightly in the stomach.

"You could live off your fat, Charles Davenport. And the marriage is off if you think I'm going to do all the housework and cooking."

They went together into the kitchen where Fiona prepared macaroni and cheese with tomatoes. While it cooked for half an hour, they discussed their wedding and the coming baby. Fiona wanted to go back to work but wondered if she would be allowed to stay at the same station. Charles thought not but said that he would ask Solomon Fairchild, once her pregnancy was common news. They talked about names for their baby, going into fits of laughter when the other came up with something ridiculous such as Fiona's idea of Chafi, using both of their names, for a girl or Macdav for a boy and Charles countering that with Euphemia or Cecil. When the meal was ready, they ate it at the table in her living room cum kitchen, washing it down with glasses of milk as Charles had to drive home and Fiona had declared herself a 'drink-free zone' from now on.

Charles arrived home about 7pm, to be welcomed by his sister who was absolutely delighted with his news and said she would of course come to the wedding with her husband, Joe.

"When will you tell Anita?" she asked.

"Oh, Mum knows," said Pippa, insouciantly.

"What!" Charles was flabbergasted.

"Well, it's not a secret is it and she has her own new man, doesn't she?" retorted Pippa. "I rang her when I got back from school, on my mobile, while Aunt Linda was in the kitchen heating up our dinner."

"*Aunt* Linda?" questioned her aunt. "I was always Auntie Linda."

"I'm too old to call you that anymore," came the reply and Pippa waltzed out of the room, only to be called back by her father who wanted to know what her Mum had said.

"I take it she's still Mum and I'm still Dad, unless it's to be mother and father now?" he asked jokingly.

"Don't be silly, Dad. Mum was fine. She asked about the holiday and I said we'd all gone together. You hadn't told her that. I told her that the wedding was in September and that I'm to be a bridesmaid. She said she'd call you later tonight."

Charles let her go off then. He explained to his sister that Pippa had had her first period while in Penang which explained the 'too old for auntie' bit. He told her his daughter was half woman, half child these days which was quite disconcerting and that he usually judged things wrongly, expecting an adult reaction and getting a child's one, then vice versa.

"For example when I asked if I was to get her a blazer, she said it was a wasted expense...her words...yet when I said that I thought she was old enough now to get her own breakfast, she said she was only 11."

"That'll happen for some years, Charles but I remember when I was in my teens getting fed up being told I was old enough to do things I didn't want to do but not old enough when it came to something I wanted to do, so be patient with her."

On that note, Linda put on her light jacket and left. Charles went upstairs to remind his daughter that she was going off on holiday with Hazel and her parents the following week and would need to tell him what she wanted to take with her. Being in one of her adult phases, she told him quite indignantly that she would pack for herself in plenty of time

"OK, but just remember that Arran in summer will be a lot different to Penang," he told her and went off downstairs to watch some television. Anita rang him just before ten o'clock and she sounded pleased for him though told him that she would rather have heard it from him than as a bombshell from their daughter.

"Not my fault. I was going to ring you tonight but she got in first. You should know our daughter. Did she tell you she'd started her periods?"

It turned out that she had told her mother, informing her that she wanted a new duvet cover in her bedroom down South where she would be going the two weeks before school started.

"Apparently the Lion King is childish, Charles."

They laughed and he told her that he had already had to change her duvet at home.

"How is she feeling about the new school?" his ex-wife asked.

"She's saying very little about it. Maybe she'll say more to you. The friend she made on holiday was a year older and I think she told Pippa a few things to expect. The only thing worrying me is that she's assuming that she'll be in the same class as Hazel and I wondered if I could phone the school the week before and ask if that's possible."

His wife did not think that that was wise. Their daughter would have to learn that she could not always have what she wanted, she told him and he agreed though he said he would continue to hope that both girls would end up in the same class. They discussed Pippa's requirements for the following year, Charles saying that he had bought all her uniform and Anita saying that she would buy her new, casual, winter, clothes.

"Anita. You're very welcome to come to the wedding and bring...James, isn't it?"

"I'll discuss it with him, Charles and let you know. What's the format?"

Charles told her that it would be a church wedding and then the reception for a small number would be at the golf club. Anita had hated his golf club. She did not play any sport and had resented the time he spent there when he was away as often from home as it was, with his work. When she had accompanied him there to social events, she had always been bored when the talk turned to golf, as it often did.

"I might have known. How does Fiona feel about that?"

"She's a member there too."

"So she shares your hobby as well as your work. Bet she plays bridge too!"

"Actually, yes she does."

Anita laughed but not unpleasantly, he was glad to hear.

"Well, she sounds a treasure. I wish you both well."

Charles hung up and thought that everything in the garden was looking rosy. His wife and daughter were happy for him and he had a new child on the way. He enjoyed his work, liked his colleagues there and was about to start a new life with the woman he loved. He just wished that the wee niggle he had about not knowing who had committed the murder in Penang would go away and mentally chided himself for being a typical policeman.

"You don't need to know," he remonstrated with himself as he put out the light in the lounge, checked that everything was off in the kitchen and went upstairs. He looked into Pippa's room where she was sitting up in bed reading.

"Lights out soon, pet," he said, going over and giving her a kiss goodnight.

CHAPTER 35

"So you got a wedding dress, my love. I guess I've not to learn anything about it," joked Charles when Fiona came into his room on Monday morning. They had spent the weekend apart as Fiona and Sally had been shopping both days and Charles had wanted to spend the evenings with Pippa, getting things sorted out for her trip to Arran on the Monday. On the Sunday evening, Fiona had rung him to say that she had been successful that day, in town, in the large Debenhams. They had gone on to discuss other things. The guest list had gone up by two with the inclusion of Bob and his wife and they talked over invitations, deciding to simply buy blank cards and do their own.

Now they kissed each other at Fiona's door, risking being seen, especially by Frank who would make fun of them.

"You've less than no chance of hearing anything about it," Fiona laughed.

"The shop had some lovely dresses for someone Pippa's age, in varying colours, so I think I'll take her there when she gets back from her next trip," she added.

There had been a series of break-ins in the local shops, so they were busy during the morning. Salma and Frank went off to interview the shopkeepers, coming back and reporting to their bosses. There were reports to write up as usual and Frank missed Penny who often helped him with his, as although his computing skills were sharp, his grammar and spelling were weak. Salma heard him grumbling.

"Use the spellcheck, stupid," she called across the room.

"It doesn't help with grammar, moron," he countered.

Fiona, coming into the room, heard the exchange, made in camaraderie, and looked pleased to see them getting along so well after the shaky start when Frank had been bitter about Salma getting the promotion he had wanted and been unashamedly racist into the bargain. Fiona had had to threaten him with disciplinary action but had the feeling that it was Salma's refusal to react that had done the trick, that and Penny's annoyance with him. She knew that the three colleagues sometimes socialised now, along with Frank's girlfriend, Sue and Penny's Gordon and just wished that Salma could find a good partner However, being in sole charge of her two younger siblings and the fact that her relatives might insist on an arranged marriage, made things difficult for her.

"I'm getting to be a matchmaker now that I'm paired off," she mentally chided herself.

"Any further forward, folks?" she asked.

"Well, Ma'am, the owner of the newsagent's had to sack one of his workers, a ...Kevin Laing," said Salma, glancing down at her notes.

"He took it really badly, Ma'am," added Frank, the 'ma'am' coming naturally now, Fiona noticed. Frank had resented her as well when she arrived and she was delighted to see that this resentment had vanished.

"In what way, Frank?"

"He threatened the newsagent. Said he'd be sorry."

"Have you paid this man a visit?"

"Not yet, Ma'am. We'll get onto it after lunch," said Salma.

"Go together, in case he gets violent. Oh, I came to tell you that we're being given Fraser Hewitt again to help out while Penny's away."

"He came in before when you were off when your Mum died, Salma. He's a clever clogs. Been at university," said Frank.

"Frank, when do you go off on holiday?" asked Fiona. "I said it was the first two weeks in August but the DCI thought it was the last two weeks."

"You're right ma'am. I'm off to Ibiza with some mates on Saturday."

"What about Sue?" asked Salma.

Frank reddened.

"She's going away with her brother, Pete and her folks, to Corfu."

They heard the phone ringing at the desk and Bob went past them in the direction of the Inspector's room. The constable came back, followed by Davenport who came into the room to tell his team that he had been summoned upstairs to see Solomon Fairchild, the assistant chief constable.

Seeing that Fiona looked anxious and Salma a bit concerned too, he smiled cheerfully.

"No doubt, the station's smoke signals have been going up and he wants to congratulate me on my engagement. Look after things, while I'm away."

He directed this to Fiona who smiled back.

On the way up in the lift, Charles could not help feeling apprehensive as, in spite of his reassuring words downstairs, he thought that Mr Fairchild would probably have sent for both him and Fiona if he had wanted to hand out congratulations. He hoped that a bad report had not come from the Penang constabulary.

He went into Fairchild's outer office and was relieved to see his secretary smiling at him.

"Congratulations, DCI Davenport," she said, holding out her hand to shake his. "I hope you'll both be very happy."

The door to the inner room opened and Solomon Fairchild, his pink, cherubic face smiling, invited Charles in.

"First of all, congratulations to you and Miss Macdonald. I take it that the holiday was a success!"

"Yes, Sir. Thanks. The wedding is the first Saturday in September and you and your wife are both invited. Would it be terribly rude not to ask Mr Knox?"

"Not rude, so much as not wise, Charles, especially if you plan to move on in the force. I know you two don't get on but if you're inviting me, you'd better invite Grant as well. However, that's not the main reason I sent for you. Sit down. I've a visitor arriving shortly, someone who wants to see you."

They chatted about the recent break-ins and then Charles was in the middle of describing his hotel in Penang when Fairchild's secretary rang through.

"Send him in," he told her.

He rose to his feet and Charles automatically did the same, as into the room came Inspector Hussain. They all shook hands, Charles noticing, bemusedly, that the man was actually smiling at him. They all sat down.

"Inspector Hussain, good morning and welcome to Scotland. You told me over the phone earlier this morning that you've come all the way from Penang in Malaysia. Now, as Inspector Davenport has just come back from there, I hope you haven't come to arrest him."

Charles tried to grin but as this was what Hussain had threatened him with over there if he interfered in the murder case, the grin wavered a little.

"Not at all, Sir. I have come all this way to ask for Inspector Davenport's assistance. There was a murder at his hotel while he was there. I am now led to believe that we allowed two possible suspects to return home here, to Glasgow."

"And Charles can help how?"

"Insp...Charles... knows these people and I have reason to believe that he knows where they stay."

Fairchild's look at Charles was quizzical but he obviously decided to delve into this at a later date as he merely said that he hoped that Charles would give all the assistance he could.

"Charles, take Inspector Hussain down to your department and give him all the help you can. I'll see you later. The three of us...make that four and ask Fiona too... will go out for lunch."

In the lift, nothing was said. They walked along the corridor to Charles's domain and, hearing the familiar footsteps, two anxious colleagues came out of their rooms, Salma frowning, Fiona saying, "Is everything OK Charles? I...."

She stopped short on seeing Hussain who smiled and bowed.

"Come into the Incident Room, Fiona, and you as well, Salma and give Frank a shout," Davenport said.

He ushered Hussain in in front of him and they all followed.

"Sit down, everyone. You too, Inspector."

"Fiona, Inspector Hussain wants our help with interviewing two subjects in his murder case. I've asked Sergeant Din here as I think she will have the information you want, Inspector and I've asked Constable Selby too as we work as a team and he will probably be helping you too."

Hussain glanced round at the others.

"You work in a pleasant atmosphere here, Inspector. Even your assistant chief constable is friendly. Maybe I could learn from this as it seems to have been my ...stiff attitude towards my younger staff that prevented one of them from confiding in me till just the other day."

"Rav...Constable Ravanathan?" said Davenport.

"Yes. You had given him some information. He had no idea how he could pass this on without letting me know that you had become involved but he decided, luckily, to risk my anger."

"And he told you that Miss Kelman, the single woman at the pool on the day of the murder, was friendly with both Miss Kilbride who had befriended Mrs Grant, and Mr Elliott who had also been round the pool?"

"Yes. Have you found out the relationship?"

"No. It was difficult to go ahead. We had no authority, something you kept reminding me of over there, though we think that Miss Kilbride is Miss Kelman's aunt."

"I am sorry. My foolish pride, I'm afraid. Well, I am asking for your help now, officially."

"Who do you want to see first?" asked Fiona.

Hussain looked at Charles in astonishment.

"Yes, Inspector. I allow my team to make suggestions and ask questions. I don't believe that it's only me who has good ideas!" said Charles, seeing his disbelief. Fiona, my detective sergeant, also calls me Charles and I call Sergeant Din and Constable Selby, Salma and Frank, so you can do the same."

"Then to you and...Fiona, I am Shahid," said the man graciously.

Frank spluttered and turned it into a cough.

"I went to the factory, to Mrs Grant's son and daughter's flat, to see Mr Soames and..." began Salma.

"Mr Soames? Who is he?" asked Hussain, frowning.

"He was Alan Grant's accountant who embezzled money to pay for his wife's medical expenses, was found out and sacked," Davenport informed him.

"I thought your National Health Service was free."

Hussain looked puzzled.

"It is but it is often a long time before treatment is available so Mr Soames wanted to get quicker help for his wife who incidentally died during the scandal of her husband's removal from the firm, giving him a motive for murder."

"But he has a cast iron alibi," put in Salma. "I also know where Miss Kelman lives."

"Charles, this is your territory. Where should we go first?" asked Hussain.

"I think we should discuss this before we go anywhere," said Charles.

"There were how many stab wounds?" he asked, sending a warning look to Fiona whom he had told Rav's answer to this question,

"Five knife entries."

"Right, we have Bill Elliott, his wife possibly, Ethel Kelman and Annabelle Kilbride. That's four people. Miss Kilbride was with Mrs Grant when they came back and found that Alan Grant had been murdered. Her job was obviously to keep Jean out of the way, so that means maybe two of the others stabbed twice, that is if Mrs Elliot backed out which seems possible."

"I think that might be possible. I have seen cases where a person was stabbed more than once by one person," said Hussain.

"Me too," agreed Charles.

"Have we any evidence to convict these three?" was Hussain's next question.

"I think we'll need to check passenger lists to KL and Penang..."

Davenport was finding it difficult to remember what he had heard from Rav. He didn't want to let Hussain know that the information had been two-way..

"Frank, you get on to that, please."

"Yes, we'll need proof but I discovered that Miss Kelman stayed in Georgetown which is further proof. Can we get a photo of this woman? It's likely that she killed Louise Elliott, if she's guilty of the first crime. Someone may recognise her," was Hussain's next question.

"Salma…"

"I'm onto it, Sir."

Salma and Frank left together, Charles informing them that he and the others were lunching with Mr

Fairchild and would see them back in the room at 2pm.

Lunch was a pleasant affair. Solomon took them to the Western Club where he was a member and over a delicious lunch, he congratulated Fiona on her forthcoming wedding and reiterated what he had said to Charles about inviting the chief constable. Fiona grimaced but said that she saw his point. They explained to Solomon about the murder committed in their hotel, telling him that the murdered man, Alan Grant, came from Glasgow, had a business here and had amassed quite few enemies.

"There was Phil Soames, the accountant who embezzled the firm's money and was sacked. His sick wife died during this scandal. Then there was Bill Elliott, Grant's partner, who was bought out and subsequently lost all his money and had to downsize his house. He would bear a grudge as would his wife, Louise..."

"...who was next to be murdered, after going to the police and telling them that her life was in danger," concluded Fiona.

Inspector Hussain looked a bit sheepish.

"I'm afraid I dismissed her as a hysterical woman," he said.

"Round the pool on the day of the murder, were what turned out to be a couple and a single woman who had not been seen before. The couple were Bill and Louise Elliott and now we think the woman was Ethel Kelman," Charles went on.

"She was the murdered man's secretary and ex-lover, Sir," he explained to Fairchild.

"How did you find out about this woman?" asked Hussain.

"A fellow guest remembered coming over on the plane with a beautiful woman with a harsh, unpleasant voice. A few days after the murder, he remembered that he had seen her at the pool that day and he came to me," said Charles. "I sent him to see you."

"Yes I remember him. I'm afraid I was annoyed with him. He didn't say that you had sent him to me."

"I asked him not to, for obvious reasons," Charles told him.

"Mrs Grant, the murdered man's wife, had been in the lounge having afternoon tea with a recently-acquired friend, an Annabelle Kilbride, who turns out to know Ethel Kelman so we think her job was to keep Mrs Grant away from the poolside that day," Fiona completed the saga.

"So who actually murdered the man?" asked Fairchild.

"There were five stab wounds, " said Hussain, "and I think that a Golden Sands' knife was used both times as that was what was found in the ladies' toilets alongside Mrs Elliott's body. She was stabbed only once. Her husband has a complete alibi this time."

"Any blood?" asked Charles, already knowing the answer but feeling that he should ask it.

"Yes. There was a lot this time. She was stabbed in the neck. One of the wash basins had blood down its sides. The murderer must have had time to wash."

"Fingerprints?" asked Fairchild.

"None. Ravanathan, my young constable found what he thought was a used condom at the murder site. He realised just the other day that it had not been used for its usual purpose and came to me with the suggestion that this had been placed over the handle of the knife which was used to kill Mr Grant. It was when I congratulated him on this piece of good detective work, that he volunteered the connection between the Kelman woman, Mr Elliott and Miss Kilbride and told me he had been in touch with you, Charles."

They finished off their coffees and got back to the station just before two o'clock.

Salma handed Charles the picture of Ethel Kelman which she had got from the factory.

"Frank?" asked Fiona.

"Ethel Kelman flew out to Penang on the 3rd of July," he told them. "I checked the Elliotts too, to save contacting the hotel and they travelled the next day."

"Good thinking, Frank," said Charles and was rewarded by a grin of pleasure from his constable.

"Can I use your fax machine, please?" asked Hussain. "I'll get this picture sent through and get my men to show it around the Golden Sands."

Salma led the Inspector through to the room which held the photocopier and fax machine. They returned in a few minutes.

"So what do we do now?" asked Fiona.

"We have no proof of the guilt of Ethel Kelman, except for the fact that she was in Batu Feringgi at the relevant time and knew Bill Elliott," said Hussain.

"Which she can explain away by saying that they both worked together at one time," reminded Fiona.

"I think we should worry Miss Kelman by turning up at her door with Inspector Hussain. See if we can rattle her into giving something away," suggested Charles.

"I agree," said Hussain. "We can always go back if we find out that someone saw her in the vicinity of the toilets in The Golden Sands."

That decided, Charles and Shahid Hussain drove off to Dinmont Road. They parked the car across from the house and walked over, noticing an elderly woman pottering in her garden a few houses along. She straightened up and looked at them carefully.

"That's Salma's informant," said Charles, pointing her out to Hussain. "She can spot a policeman at forty yards."

Ethel Kelman came to the door. Although it was only mid- afternoon, she was carefully made up and beautifully dressed. Charles showed his warrant card and she stood back to let them in, looking curiously at Inspector Hussain. She led them into her front lounge and they all sat down.

"Whit's wrang?" she asked in a harsh voice.

"I believe that you have just returned from Penang, Miss Kelman," Charles said.

"Yes. So what?"

The woman looked startled and then her expression changed.

"I know what this is about. Bill Elliott told me. I met him in the street in Batu Feringgi one day and he told me that my ex-boss had been murdered. No loss there."

Charles, giving her ten out of ten, mentally, for quick thinking, asked why she had been in Penang."

"A bit of coincidence, Miss Kelman?" added Hussain, sarcastically.

"Not really. Alan...Mr Grant... and I were going to go there together. Well, he wis goin' with his wife but I wis going too. He had booked me into the Golden Sands next door. He said he would get a thrill out of knowing that his wife wis in the hotel next door when we... got together."

"What changed then?" asked Charles.

"I threw him over, if you want to know."

"What? Just before a grand holiday?" Hussain sounded disbelieving.

"Well I intended tae have the holiday anyway, as I did, though he cancelled the hotel and I had to stay in a cheaper one but I already had ma tickets so he couldn't cancel ma flight."

"And Miss Kilbride? You apparently know her. Why was she there?" asked Charles.

Ethel Kelman looked fleetingly disconcerted but replied quite coolly that Annabelle Kilbride was her aunt, her mother's younger sister and that she had agreed to go along in the first instance so that Ethel would have company when Alan Grant had to be with his wife.

"She'd always wanted to go to Malaysia," finished the young woman.

"What a coincidence that she also got friendly with Mrs Grant," ventured Hussain.

"It was Mrs Grant who spoke to her first and she felt sorry for the woman who had to live with that fat slob," she said.

"I believe that you still keep in touch with Bill Elliott," commented Charles.

"Anythin' wrang wi that?" she demanded. "We worked together and we were both treated badly by Alan Grant."

"I thought you said that you ditched him," said Charles quietly.

"Ah did but he treated me badly while I was with him. Some of the things he wanted me to do... well!"

Back in the car, Charles admitted that the girl was smart and had had an answer for everything.

"We'll need more proof to rattle her," he said to Hussain.

"Let's wait, in the hope that I hear from the station about the photograph. Would you be so kind as to run me to my hotel? I left the hotel's phone number with Sergeant Cheng and they might contact me there. Would it be OK if I came back to see you in the morning?"

Charles said that would be fine and he ran him to his hotel near to the Kingston Bridge, then returned to the station to let his team know what had happened.

CHAPTER 36

Shahid Hussain returned the next morning but not until nearly eleven o'clock, by which time Davenport and his team had discussed what to do next. Salma had brought Frank up to date with the case and he had accepted her apologies for not letting him know anything about it.

They were all still sitting in the Incident Room which was bare, with no pictures or lists of people involved in cases, when Bob brought their visitor along.

"I slept in. I'm sorry. I am always awake early at home," he said.

"It's the jetlag, Insp...Shahid," said Fiona. "Charles and I are still not back to our normal sleeping patterns."

Hussain sat down and Charles asked Frank to get him a cup of coffee.

"Get it from my room, not the canteen, Frank. There should still be some hot water from our coffees so it won't take long to boil."

"Have you had any thought on how we should proceed?" asked Hussain.

"Well, I'd like to pay a visit to Mrs Grant. She knows that Ethel Kelman was in Penang and she just might know something that might help us. It's a faint hope, as I'm sure she would have contacted me if she'd thought of anything"

"You, not me, I see," said Hussain, wryly.

"I will come with you if that suits you but I will be nice to her, don't worry," he added, as Charles looked about to protest.

The two DCIs drove to Thornton Hall. There had been no need to find out the address as Hussain had it in his notebook. The door was opened by a young woman. For a split second, Charles thought that it was Ethel Kelman as this girl was also beautiful and well-dressed with her blonde hair in a swept-up style but then she spoke and her soft well-spoken words dispelled that idea.

"Can I help you?" she asked pleasantly,

"Hello," he said." My name's DCI Davenport and this in DCI Hussain. We called to speak to Mrs Grant. Is she in?"

"Mum, two policemen to see you!" she called, inviting them in. Jean Grant came into the hall and took them into a lounge, large and spacious but rather oppressive, the walls being covered with huge paintings and the windows hung with dark green, velvet curtains. They all sat down, Davenport and Hussain on the settee and the two women on chairs.

"Is there news about the murder?" asked Jean Grant.

"Well, we think that Ethel Kelman and Bill Elliott and possibly Louise Elliott were involved and Miss Kilbride who befriended you, is linked in some way to Miss Kelman..."

"Annabelle! But she was so nice to me and she took me for afternoon tea the day before the murder and on the day itself."

"And would probably have continued to do that until the others got a chance to kill Mr Grant," said Hussain.

"So she was getting me out of the way?" Mrs Grant's voice faltered a little and her daughter leaned over and took her hand.

"Mum, don't get upset. At least we know now that the police don't suspect you anymore. So two people stabbed my father, Inspector."

"But there were five stab wounds, Inspector. Does that mean that they stabbed him a number of times each?" asked Jean.

"Mum. I'll make us some tea...or would you gentlemen prefer coffee?"

Denise Grant was on her feet, pulling out two occasional tables.

The two men said that they would have tea and the talk turned to what Mrs Grant would do with the business and this large house.

"Oh, I'll sell the business. Alan meant to change his will but didn't so it's all left to me and the children jointly."

"Was he going to change it, Jean?"

"So he'd been saying over the last few years, after Denise and Pete left home."

"And this house?"

"I'll stay here and use the money from the business to redecorate. This is not my taste."

She waved at the room they were sitting in.

"I think Denise and Pete will move back here so I'll have a tennis court and swimming pool put in for them and their friends," she added.

Denise came in with the tea. As they were drinking it, she told them that she and her brother were possibly moving back home and Mrs Grant smiled in delight at having her thoughts confirmed.

As they were driving away, Charles spoke first. Hussain agreed with him, ending with,

"I think we need to get back and report to the others and make our plans."

They congregated once again in the Incident Room. Fiona had written all the names of people connected with the case on a flip chart.

"Right team...and Shahid," began Charles.

"Team will do, Charles. I am one of your team for the present," interrupted Hussain.

Charles pulled at his left ear lobe and Frank nudged Salma who glared at him. Charles told them about what had transpired during the visit. He continued "Shahid, tell your man over in Penang to let Elliott come home - lack of evidence, tell him. We"ll go to see Miss Kelman again. Say something, such as we've no evidence to go on so it seems as if the case will be closed…"

"But we would not close a case so quickly," Shahid expostulated.

"I know that but she won't know," put in Charles.

"I'll put Salma and Frank on to watching the Grant house and if they meet up again, we'll go in and confront them all together."

"What about the Kelman house? They might meet there, Sir," said Frank.

"True, Selby. We'll put Fraser onto that. Has he arrived yet?"

"No, Sir."

As he spoke, they heard footsteps in the corridor and young Fraser Hewitt came into the room.

"Sorry, Mr Davenport. I had to stay to finish typing up a report. Have I arrived in the middle of a case?" he asked, shyly.

"You have indeed, young man and got yourself a stint of hanging around a house, I'm afraid, son."

"They also serve who only stand and wait, Sir."

"Eh?" queried Frank.

"A quote, Constable," said Fiona smiling at him.

"Told you he was a clever bast....dick, Salma," said Frank in an undertone.

"Right, team. We wait till Elliott gets home. It's up to you to keep us posted on when he leaves and what plane he catches, Shahid."

"Posted? I will still be here so I will not be writing to you, Charles." Husain looked mutinous.

"To keep someone posted is to keep them acquainted with the facts," Charles laughed. "Of course you will be here."

This was on Tuesday, and on Friday morning, Shahid Hussain arrived at the station to tell them that Bill Elliott's plane would be touching down in the early afternoon.

Fraser was sent off to Dinmont Road where he parked across the road from Ethel Kelman's house and Frank to Thornton Hall where he took up a position near the large gates. Davenport knew that neither young man had been seen by the people involved. Salma would only be drafted in to give them some respite if that was needed and to take them some nourishment if the waiting was long.

Fraser rang through to Davenport at 8.15, to say that a man answering to Bill Elliott's' description had gone into Ethel Kelman's house He had brought the woman whom Fraser had been told was dark-haired and statuesque.

Charles, Hussain and Fiona were getting their jackets when Fraser rang again to say that all three had come out and got into the car.

It was just short of nine o'clock when Frank, almost asleep, noticed a car pulling up at the gates. He was surprised when he contacted his DCI, to find out that he and the others were on their way.

The silver-grey Audi pulled up quietly alongside Frank's car and all three got out.

"We'll give them about twenty minutes," said Charles. "Then we move in."

Once again it was Denise Grant who opened the door. Her smile faded when she saw who it was. Not waiting to be invited in this time, the three police officers strode to the lounge.

Jean Grant was seated facing Ethel Kelman and Bill Elliott on one settee. Annabelle Kilbride, also facing her was sitting on another two- seater settee. All had champagne flutes in their hands. Their faces froze.

"Ah, celebrating Bill's return or Alan Grant's death or both?" queried Charles. Denise sat down suddenly next to Annabelle. Looking at the seating arrangement, Fiona was struck by the fact that Jean

Grant looked as if she was sitting surrounded by her courtiers and she knew that their theory was correct.

"DCI Hussain, over to you," said Charles.

"William Elliott, Ethel Kelman, Annabelle Kilbride...Denise Grant and Jean Grant. You are under arrest for the murder of Alan Grant. Anything you now say will be taken down and may be used in evidence against you."

They sat there as if turned to stone. Annabelle recovered her composure first.

"I never killed anyone," she shrilled.

"No but you were an accomplice. You pretended to keep Mrs Grant out of the way so that when we suspected her at first, as we did, the murderer most often being the husband or in this case the wife, we would have to drop our case, as she had an alibi. And you were there when she stabbed him."

"And I was in Singapore," said Denise Grant.

"Yes but your friends went on a trip one day, leaving you free to travel to Penang. It's only an hour's flight and your name was on the passenger list," said Fiona, coldly.

Davenport spoke now.

"I suspect that you, Mrs Grant, along with Miss Kilbride, did come back from afternoon tea. Alan was still asleep. I had gone into the pool. You covered him with a towel then you stabbed him. You beckoned to Miss Kelman and the Elliotts and your daughter and they came round. Miss Kelman stabbed him as did Mr Eliott. Possibly Louise did too but I doubt it. I think she took cold feet. Did you, Miss Kilbride stab him too, I wonder. I suspect that Mrs Grant stabbed him again as the plan was for five stabbings. You gave away the fact that you were responsible, Mrs Grant, when you mentioned the exact number, something you could not have known after a supposed glance across at the body."

"My original plan was for seven, Inspector but my son wimped out and Phil Soames refused to take part as, much as he disliked my husband, he felt his sacking had been quite fair and Ellen, his wife had borne no grudges before she died. He agreed not to tell the police and just made sure that he had a water-tight alibi."

Jean Grant had stood up, her head held regally.

"The queen in front of her court," thought Fiona again.

"And now Inspector...Inspectors, I'm sorry. Are you now going to tell us which stab wound actually killed Alan?

There was silence.

"No, I thought not, as that would be impossible, especially as he didn't actually die till you appeared on the scene, Mr Davenport."

The police cars ordered by Charles had pulled up outside. Hussain led out Bill Elliott and Fiona escorted Ethel Kelman. Charles was left with Denise, her mother and Annabelle Kilbride.

"No one mentioned a second single woman which was puzzling until I saw how much you resembled Ethel Kelman." he said to Denise.

"Yes beautiful as well, but my daughter has class," said Jean Grant proudly.

"Miss Kilbride, why did you take part in this?" asked Charles.

"I was once jilted at the altar. My niece came to me, raging at Alan Grant ending their relationship. I wanted justice for her and all badly treated women. It's that simple."

"When I approached Ethel, when I found out, to my cost, that he no longer had her as a mistress, she was well in favour of revenge," added Jean Grant.

"What made you finally stop accepting what he did to you?" asked Charles gently.

"The night after he had forced me to have sex with him again, he told me that he had dropped his mistress because she wasn't obliging enough. He slapped me on the bottom and said....said... 'You're ugly but docile, you stupid cow'.

He went on to tell me that Ethel had tickets for Penang but that he'd cancelled her hotel room. Denise had had her holiday in Singapore booked, as I told you, for ages. I thought the coincidence that we would or could all be in the Far East together, was a chance not to be missed."

"And who murdered Louise Elliott? Not your daughter as she went back to Singapore that same day," said Charles.

"I don't think you expect me to tell you that, Inspector," she smiled.

"One more thing. Why did you involve me?" Davenport sounded puzzled.

"Well, it seemed as if Inspector Hussain was hell bent on fitting me up for the murder and I thought you might muddy the waters a bit. A bit of double-bluff too, I suppose, with a bit of arrogance thrown in. I didn't expect us to be found out."

Hussain and Fiona had returned. He motioned to Annabelle Kilbride to go with him and Fiona did the same with Denise Grant. Charles put out his arm for Jean Grant to take.

"In the end, Alan made it easy for us. With his boorish manner, he had ostracised anyone who might have befriended us so the garden area was deserted until you turned up on the crucial day," said Jean, taking the proffered arm. "Denise only had that one day and I was concerned until Fiona went away and then you left for a swim.

He led her out and helped her into the back seat of the fifth police car. The five cars set off. Hussain and Charles watched them until they were out of sight. Charles picked up an unopened bottle of champagne.

"The rest is out of our hands," Charles told his team. "Inspector Hussain wants them taken back to Malaysia but it will depend on their lawyers. I'm sorry Salma that you were left out of the action at the end."

She laughed, "But if I hadn't been here, who would have taken the call from Penang, saying that Ethel Kelman's photograph had been recognised?"

"Yes, that tied things up nicely. She was seen arguing with Louise Elliott outside the toilets. The member of staff who recognised her had gone off on a week's leave that evening so wasn't questioned. That was a bit of an oversight on the part of the Penang police."

"So definitely three murderers, maybe four, maybe five but only Ethel Kelman can be convicted because she killed again," said Salma.

"Sounds almost as strange as Pippa's, 'Murder of the Orient Express'," laughed Fiona.

"Yes, that was a multiple stabbing too," agreed Charles.

"What now?" asked Fiona.

"Well, I'm going upstairs to tell Solomon Fairchild the good news and to hand Mr Knox's invitation to his secretary, then I'm going to phone Sean Grafton as it's after midnight here, so it's after seven am in Penang. After that we are going to enjoy the champagne that I stole."

He made his escape, the cries of, "Shame on you, Sir !"', ringing in his ears.

C0060 15586

FRANCES MACARTHUR

BUSMAN'S
HOLIDAY

Copyright © 2014 Mrs Frances Macarthur
All rights reserved.

ISBN: 1505537282
ISBN 13: 9781505537284